THE ICARUS MIXTAPE

Madelyn Watts

to Elise and Ethan, my own version of The Inklings

to Elwynn, my dearest friend and inspiration

and to my dad, who is responsible for my taste in music

CHAPTER 1

Don't You (Forget About Me) - Simple Minds

In an all-but-forgotten corner of America, there was a tiny town called Asphodel. There was a coffee shop there called The Haunt, which served as the common 'cool' hangout for the town's youth and those who wanted to pretend that they didn't live in such a podunk town.

A girl with dark bobbed hair and impossibly knowing brown eyes sat in the one corner booth in the establishment, sipping a hot chocolate even though it was the middle of August. It was clear that she was waiting for someone. The girl stuck out, but it was hard to pinpoint exactly why. If you were to ask strangers to describe her, they would probably use words like "elegant" or "beautiful." They would have been right, but it was more than that. Those who knew Solae best would have told you about her timelessness. One moment, she could be an old Hollywood starlet, the next moment an Ancient Greek poet, and the next just a modern American teenager.

Solae turned her head as the coffee shop door opened and two people walked in. One, a girl with golden red hair that fell to her waist and a lightly freckled face. Her smile radiated pure sunshine, and her hazel eyes were like two golden halos. This was Ariadne, or Ari, as she was known to friends.

The other person was a tall boy with tousled dirty-blond hair and round glasses that framed bright green eyes.

He had a curious, scholarly look about him, while at the same time his tanned skin signaled that he spent a lot of time outside. He had bony, long-fingered hands that were very distinctly masculine. This was Icarus.

"Hey Solae," said Ari, sliding into the booth next to her friend.

"Hello," replied Solae with a serene smile just before she took another sip of her hot chocolate.

"Hot chocolate in this heat?" asked Icarus.

"Hot chocolate is good year-round," Solae insisted. "What did you get?"

"Iced coffee," Icarus said, "Like a normal person would in the middle of summer."

"Ari?"

"Iced chai latte," Ari replied. "Sorry, Sol, I have to side with Icarus this time."

Solae sighed, "Maybe Theseus will back me up."

"Where is Theseus, anyway?" Ari asked, looking around.

"Fashionably late as always, I bet," said Icarus.

As if on cue, a boy walked through the door at that exact moment. He had a mess of dark curly hair and heavy-lidded, icy-grey eyes. This, coupled with his black Nirvana t-shirt and his haphazardly ripped jeans gave him a look that could only be described as 'cool.' He strolled over to their table and sat at the end of the booth next to Icarus.

"Hi, Theseus," said Ari.

"Hey," he replied, "What's on the agenda for today, ladies and gentlemen?"

"First, we need you to settle something," said Icarus. "What's your opinion on hot chocolate in the summer?" he gestured toward Solae's cup.

"Don't like hot chocolate," said Theseus, and was met with a general outcry, but the matter was ultimately left unresolved.

Once that was out of the way, Ari splayed her hands on the table like she was about to make a grand presentation. "It's almost time for school to start," she said, "We need to do something."

By 'something' they all knew she meant something very specific. They had a tradition involving the old lighthouse on Lake Topaz that they'd kept faithfully every summer for the past three years.

"We don't normally have lighthouse party-planning sessions, do we?" asked Theseus.

"No, but this is the last summer before our senior year," said Ari, "It should be special."

"She's right," said Solae, "We should do something a little different this time."

"I was thinking I could make a cake?" Ari said.

"That's a good idea," said Icarus, "I'll handle drinks."

"I can bring some other snacks," said Solae.

They all looked at Theseus expectantly. He shrugged, "I guess I'll bring something too."

"Like what?" asked Ari skeptically.

He waved a hand, "Don't worry about it. I'll think of something."

"You better, we should do it tomorrow."

"Yes ma'am."

Ari rolled her eyes but clearly enjoyed the banter.

They continued to talk, each enjoying their respective drink of choice. Except for Theseus, who didn't order anything. Anyone who walked by their table would be able to tell that there was a special kind of bond between the four of them. Something that could not easily be put into words. Something that, undoubtedly, would last a long time.

CHAPTER 2

Here Comes The Sun - The Beatles

It was Icarus and Ari who first discovered the lighthouse. Of course, everyone in town knew of its nonsensical existence, but they were the first in many years to see it as a possibility rather than an eyesore.

Icarus and Ari did not remember meeting each other. Their parents had been friends since they were babies, so the two naturally became friends as they got older. A landmark in their friendship occurred when they were twelve and tragedy struck Ari's family.

Both of Ari's parents died in a car accident. It was the first time either of them realized what it was like to take a person's existence for granted. Ari had two older sisters, Cal and Persie, who were ten and seven years older than her, respectively. Cal became Ari's legal guardian after their parents' deaths, and all three of the sisters moved into the family home together.

Ari spent a lot of time at Icarus' house during the mourning period. The Easton family had taken her in as their own while Cal and Persie handled all the heartbreakingly tedious tasks that follow death. One afternoon, they were sitting in Icarus' backyard treehouse eating cookies that his mother had made. Icarus had quickly learned that often the best thing he could do for his friend in her time of great distress was just to be present. So, they spent a lot of time in the treehouse just sitting, not talking.

Suddenly, Ari said, "I want to go somewhere."

"What do you mean?" Icarus asked, "Like travel?"

Ari contemplated. "No, I don't want to go that far. I just want to go somewhere different. Without any grown-ups. I can't stand how they look at me."

"We could go check out the antique shops," suggested Icarus, trying to think of what was within reasonable walking distance.

"No," said Ari, "I want to go somewhere… uncharted." She enjoyed using words like that.

"How about…" Icarus scanned their surroundings from their vantage point. Then, he saw it. The tall pillar that had surely once been bright white but had since been weathered and worn to a dirty gray with bits of brick showing through the paint. The lighthouse wasn't too far away, but there wasn't anything else in its general vicinity due to Lake Topaz' rocky shores. Icarus pointed at it, "How about the lighthouse?"

Ari's eyes lit up with a smile. It was small, but it was the most Icarus had seen from her in weeks. "Perfect," she said.

Lake Topaz, in spite of its bejeweled name, was not a particularly attractive lake. There was not any worthwhile fishing to be had, and the water was much too brown and murky for swimming. The absence of activity on the lake only added to the fact that there was no reason for the lighthouse to exist. It had no purpose so far from an actual coast, but then again, that sort of thing fit perfectly with the town's overall mantra.

Asphodel was a weird little town, but not for the typical reasons small towns are considered weird. Sure, all the common elements were there; a halfway ghost-town vibe, being unable to go hardly anywhere without running into someone you know, and a general feeling of things being the same as they always had been. Yet, there was something else about Asphodel that made all of that seem inconsequential. The town seemed to be a beacon for all things strange and unusual.

Nothing particularly alarming ever happened, of course. No UFOs ever kidnapped anyone; no malicious demonic presences ever terrorized the town. Things just *happened* from time to time, and nobody seemed able to offer a logical explanation. People claimed to see things in Asphodel. Ghosts, mythical creatures, and the like. Things that would normally be written off as coincidences happened far too often to be coincidental. And yet, these strange happenings were never considered remotely newsworthy. It had all become just an integral part of the town's local lore, generally dismissed as an endearing quirk. Comparatively speaking, an out-of-place lighthouse could easily be explained away. The vague consensus of locals was that some rich eccentric had built the lighthouse in years gone by, but nobody had known what to do with it after they were gone, so it had presumably remained empty.

Icarus was fascinated by the rumors of strange phenomena ever since he had been old enough to realize the strangeness of it. He had an adventure-seeker heart and something that might have once been called 'insatiable curiosity.'

Ari went along with Icarus' fascination, though her interest was more a romantic dream of the possibility of magic than it was something to seriously research. And to be quite honest, at this time in her life, this whimsical notion was a comfort that she desperately needed. Either way, the lighthouse was the perfect thing for them to explore together.

It was not too far to walk. Icarus' mother had insisted they bring water and more oatmeal chocolate chip cookies, though. The lighthouse seemed much bigger up close, though it was definitely not as big as true lighthouses that guided wayfaring sailors to shore. To Icarus and Ari, however, it could have been a castle. They intended to go inside, but when they walked up to the door, they were met with a shiny silver padlock, obviously a relatively recent addition.

Ari took a half-step back. "Do you think someone lives there?" she whispered.

Icarus scanned the dilapidated structure, "I don't think so," he said, "I doubt it's livable at this point." He cautiously walked around to one of the windows and peered inside. "Yep, it's just storage, come see."

Ari joined Icarus at the window and saw a multitude of boxes scattered across the circular interior and stacked on top of one another.

"I wonder who it belongs to," she mused.

"I don't know, but it looks like they haven't been here in a while. Look at all the dust."

Patches of light from windows exposed a clear layer of dust that coated the boxes and swirled around in the air as if it were fairy dust. The room was not perfectly round as they had imagined, but more of a large octagon. Aside from the boxes, the room contained nothing save for a spiral staircase wrapped around a large column in the center of the room.

"Do you think someone *used* to live here?" asked Ari.

"Probably," said Icarus. "I bet there's several floors. A bedroom, a bathroom, maybe even a kitchen. There's probably a way to get to the balcony at the top to operate the light if it works."

"Being a lighthouse operator would be fun," said Ari, "If it means you get to live in one."

Icarus and Ari circled the lighthouse and found a small dock on the lakeside where they sat on the edge, letting their feet dangle over the water. They talked for hours about what they might do with the lighthouse if it belonged to them, staying on the dock until the sun began to set, turning the sky to gold and the ripples in the lake to diamonds.

It was the most Ari had talked since the death of her parents; she was starting to sound like her old self again. This small adventure, the lighthouse, the lake, seemed to have a healing effect. It would take a long time for her to fully be healed, but it was a start. They returned to the lighthouse whenever they found themselves questioning what they should do. It became 'their spot', and they never really spoke about it to anyone, until a year later, when Solae entered their lives.

CHAPTER 3

This Must Be The Place - Talking Heads

Both Solae and Theseus were adopted into the group in high school.

Ari met Solae on the first day of freshman year. Having been in the same class as Icarus since kindergarten, Ari always had a friend to sit by in class. This year, they were split up into separate classes for the first time.

Ari scanned her new chemistry classroom. Whoever she sat next to would be her lab partner for the rest of the year, so she must choose wisely. When her gaze swept toward the back of the room, she noticed a girl with short, dark brown hair and a disposition that brought the word 'ethereal' to mind.

The girl's clothing was effortless looking, though probably meticulously styled. She wore a tastefully oversized flannel shirt over a black tank top tucked into jeans. She had accessorized the outfit with a wide, silver-buckled belt and a long silver necklace from which hung an artistic sun charm. Her ears were studded with silver earrings. Her expression was pensive, like daydreaming, but without looking like a total space cadet.

Ari couldn't explain it, but she felt drawn to this girl like she was radiating good energy. Luckily, the other seat at the girl's table was still open. With more confidence than she'd had upon entering the classroom, Ari walked over to the girl's table and sat down in the vacant chair.

They barely had time for more than a 'hello' before the teacher began the roll call.

Ari braced herself and let out a resigned "Here" when her full name, Ariadne Darnell, was called.

The girl turned to Ari, "Your name is Ariadne?"

She sighed, "It's a weird name, I know. I just go by Ari."

"I like it."

Ari was flattered, "What's your name?"

Her new partner smiled mischievously, "You'll have to wait and see."

Ari waited patiently, several other girls' names were called, but her partner was silent.

"Solae McClaine?"

"Here," said Ari's partner.

"Aha!" whispered Ari. "Nice to meet you, Solae."

Both girls pulled out their binders to begin taking notes, and Solae noticed that Ari's was decorated with a collage of flowers, stickers, and other odds and ends representative of her interests. The backdrop of the collage was a printed-off page from a book, and Solae recognized the text immediately.

"Is that a page from *Tuck Everlasting*?" she asked.

Ari beamed, "Yes!" she said, ecstatic to have such a personal interest noticed. "It was my favorite book growing up, I still like to reread it sometimes."

"Mine too," said Solae, "I've never met anyone else who's read it."

This small piece of childhood that they had in common planted the seed of friendship deeper than some other interest might have because it was so intimately unique. Even though they had never met before, Ari and Solae suddenly felt as if they must have always known each other on some level via this shared formative experience. They elected to sit next to each other in the rest of their shared classes. Neither girl would have been able to recall exactly what they talked about that day; it was arbitrary. The important thing was their instant chemistry. They recognized each other as kindred spirits, like a sunrise and a sunset.

When Ari started inviting Solae to hang out with her and Icarus, he didn't mind. He liked Solae, but she was primarily Ari's friend, and Solae thought of Icarus the same way. This dynamic changed on a field trip when Ari stayed home sick.

Icarus and Solae sat next to each other on the bus ride. Solae brought a pink MP3 player and offered one of her earbuds to Icarus. Unbeknownst to Icarus, this was a rare moment of opening up for Solae. She had inherited the MP3 player from her mother, who had abandoned Solae and her father when she was very young. The songs on the device, from the likes of David Bowie, Fleetwood Mac, The Smiths, etcetera, had been foundational in shaping

Solae's music taste. She had since added many of her own songs, but they blended seamlessly with her mother's old songs, aside from generally being newer.

Icarus knew many of the songs, he had heard the same artists while listening to the radio in his dad's car. He enjoyed the authenticity of the old sounds and felt that the lyrics spoke to his soul. He was immediately enamored by Solae's collection; they spent the whole bus ride alternating between listening together and talking excitedly about their favorite songs. They even jotted down artists and songs on sticky notes for each other to check out later.

Music can be a powerful force, communicating things beyond words. Creating attachment between people, things, places, memories. That day, it acted as a bonding agent between Icarus and Solae. They no longer saw each other as 'Ari's friend', and the trio became inseparable. Including Solae in their pilgrimages to the lighthouse was only natural at this point. To Icarus and Ari's satisfaction, she quickly grew to love it just as much as they did, even though she hadn't been with them at its discovery.

Theseus joined the group even later. He moved to Asphodel in the middle of their sophomore year.

Icarus, Ari, and Solae were driving in Icarus' new-to-him truck from school to the lighthouse one afternoon when they saw an old black Mustang on the side of the road. The hood of the car was open and a boy in a black t-shirt and ripped jeans leaned over the engine, inspecting it with a furrowed brow.

"Isn't that the new kid?" asked Ari as they approached.

"Yeah," said Icarus, "Let's help him out."

Nobody objected, so Icarus pulled over next to the Mustang. The boy didn't acknowledge them until Icarus walked right up and said, "Hey man, need some help?"

The boy stared at Icarus blankly for a second before saying, "You people are too friendly around here."

"That's a nice way to say thanks," piped up Ari.

The boy's eyes flicked briefly over to Ari and Solae before looking back to Icarus. "My bad, thanks. I think it just needs a jumpstart."

Icarus nodded, unphased by Theseus' first response. "We can do that, I've got cables in my truck. I'm Icarus, by the way." He held his hand out, and after a beat, the other boy shook it.

"Theseus," he said, and the other three remembered hearing the name whispered around the school, as is generally the tendency at small town schools when a new kid shows up.

As they jumped off the Mustang, they tried to make conversation, but Theseus was stoic. He was interested in the lighthouse when they mentioned it, though. This sparked a conversation about the general oddness of Asphodel, much to Icarus' delight. Theseus was from New York, but his stepfather had inexplicably taken a job nearby, uprooting his family and bringing them here. Everything about this tiny town was bizarre to Theseus, even the 'normal stuff.'

After they got the Mustang running again, Theseus bid them another quick 'thanks' and sped away, leaving Icarus, Ari, and Solae in the dust. They didn't think much of it and continued with their afternoon. The next day at lunch, to their surprise, Theseus sat at their table as if he had always done so. After this, he also seamlessly became an essential part of the group.

CHAPTER 4

Everybody Wants To Rule The World - Tears For Fears

On the day of the lighthouse 'party', Ari and Solae picked Icarus up in Ari's baby blue beetle. The car was Ari's pride and joy; she had immediately enlisted Icarus to help her make mixtapes for it when she first bought it. When Icarus climbed into the backseat of the tiny car bearing a small ice chest of drinks, he could feel the happiness radiating from his childhood friend.

"I take it the cake turned out well?" he asked.

"You'll see," chirped Ari.

"What drinks did you bring?" asked Solae, turning around in her seat to look at Icarus.

"A pack of root beer and some pink lemonade," he replied proudly.

The lemonade was specifically for Solae. Though she had an affinity for sweet drinks, she did not like the carbonation of soda.

"Excellent," said Solae with a smile, and the way her eyes sparkled made Icarus shiver.

"What do you guys think Theseus is bringing?" Ari asked. Icarus could tell she was trying to keep her tone casual, but he and Solae had guessed long ago that Ari had a crush on Theseus.

It wasn't surprising; Theseus had quickly become the guy every girl chased after when he arrived in Asphodel, despite his standoffish nature. He was good-looking, sure, but there was something else about him that drew the eyes and hearts of almost every girl he came into contact with. It was something magnetic, and Icarus noticed that it seemed to attract people who simply wanted to be friends with Theseus, in addition to those who wanted to date him. Icarus was never sure if his friend was aware of this seemingly magnetic quality he possessed. He never used it to his advantage, which Icarus supposed only added to the attraction. In fact, after they'd been friends for a while, Icarus realized that Theseus wasn't interested in making many friends at all. He only hung out with Icarus, Ari, and Solae, adopting a much more open persona when they were alone.

Icarus didn't know for sure if Theseus was aware of the fact that Ari had a crush on him. He would seemingly flirt with her from time to time, but it could have just been his magnetic quality at work. Icarus just hoped that Theseus understood that even though Ari was very affectionate by nature, her crush would not be superficial like some girls' might be.

"I don't know," said Icarus in response to Ari's question. "Knowing Theseus, I just hope it's not something illegal."

"Like what?" asked Solae.

"Booze, maybe," said Icarus.

"Theseus wouldn't do that," Ari said reproachfully.

All Icarus knew was that he'd smelled alcohol on Theseus' breath before. That had only been once or twice though, early on in their friendship. Theseus had pretty quickly realized that kind of thing wouldn't fly in this particular group. So, Icarus just shrugged, "You're probably right."

When they pulled up to the lighthouse, they were surprised to see Theseus' black Mustang already there.

"Did we get the time wrong?" asked Solae.

"No," said Icarus, dumbfounded, "He's just early."

They walked around to the back of the lighthouse to see that Theseus had set up a little card table with a projector that he was fiddling with.

"What's this?" asked Ari.

"It's movie night," said Theseus matter-of-factly. "We're watching a classic tonight."

"Which is?" asked Solae, sounding skeptical.

"You'll just have to wait and see," said Theseus, looking very smug because he knew he'd impressed them.

Icarus, for his part, was a bit relieved. He hadn't really expected Theseus to bring something more dubious, but he never could tell with this friend of his.

"Let's see this cake," Theseus said, gesturing at the little white box Ari was carrying.

Solae spread out the large blanket she had brought, and Ari set the box down in the middle. Looking shy, she lifted the lid of the box to reveal a round cake that depicted the lighthouse in frosting as if painted on a canvas.

"Ari, you've outdone yourself!" exclaimed Solae.

"How long did this take you?" asked Icarus, "It looks amazing."

"Just a few hours," said Ari sheepishly, "It took me a bit to nail down the frosting technique."

Icarus chuckled, shaking his head in amazement. Ari was an artist, but her skills were not limited to one medium. She could try her hand at pretty much any creative project, and while she might not be a master, she could always get the hang of whatever it was incredibly fast compared to most people.

"I bet it tastes even better than it looks," said Theseus, brandishing a paper plate.

As they ate the cake (which did indeed taste just as good if not better than it looked), Theseus started up the projector. It turned out that the movie he chose was *The Princess Bride* and everyone applauded this choice.

After the movie, when it was starting to get dark, Theseus produced a paper bag from somewhere. "I brought something else, too," he said.

They were all taken aback, "What got into you?"

He shrugged, "I got the feeling you guys were underestimating me a little too much. I have to keep you on your toes."

"We didn't doubt you," protested Solae, "You're just never this enthusiastic."

"Do you want to see what's in the bag or not?"

"Yes please," said Ari quickly.

Theseus reached into the bag and pulled out a bundle of colorful sparklers.

Ari gasped, "Where did you get those?"

"Bought 'em on the Fourth of July and forgot to use them," said Theseus.

"I love sparklers," said Ari.

"I know. Why do you think I brought them?"

Ari grinned, face going a little pink, and Icarus exchanged a knowing glance with Solae. It occurred briefly to Icarus that he wished he could talk to Solae like that, but he could never seem to figure it out.

As Theseus began handing out the sparklers, the boys began debating over the legality of the sparklers.

"If you got them on the Fourth, I'm not sure you can set them off any other day," said Icarus.

"That's only fireworks," said Theseus, "Sparklers are good year-round. Stop being such a killjoy."

"What if we start a grass fire?"

"What, like grass fires are magically impossible on holidays? Besides, we're right next to the lake," said

Theseus dismissively as he pulled a cigarette lighter out of his pocket and gestured for Ari to hold out her sparkler.

"I hope you don't use that for its intended purpose," murmured Ari, gesturing to the lighter.

"I don't," said Theseus, as he flicked the lighter with practiced ease, causing the little flame to come alive. "Or at least, not anymore."

"Good," said Ari. She knew how she sounded, but she didn't care.

Icarus, meanwhile, had decided that Theseus was probably right about sparklers being okay. He held out one of his own, but it slipped out of his hand almost as soon as Theseus lit it. He frantically began stamping out the flame as Theseus laughed.

"Icarus, you idiot!" he said triumphantly, though not meanly. "Maybe you will start a grass fire."

"Shut up," said Icarus, but he was laughing too.

Solae met Ari's eyes and rolled her eyes good-naturedly, and Ari had to smother a laugh. These two boys were so opposite, Icarus was warm and sunny while Theseus was like the dark side of the moon, and yet they got along so well. Ari thought it was like what Solae said one time; that Ari was the sweet to Solae's salt. Different, but complementary. There was something within all of them that fit beautifully together, like puzzle pieces.

Ari sighed contentedly as she returned her attention to her own sparkler. In moments like this, she never wanted summer to end.

CHAPTER 5

Stuck In The Middle With You - Stealer's Wheel

All senior students at Asphodel High School were required to meet with the school counselor during the first week of school to discuss post-graduation plans. Icarus, Ari, Solae, and Theseus all managed to schedule their meetings early in the week, either from genuine eagerness or, in Theseus' case, because he wanted to get it out of the way.

The counselor, a middle-aged woman named Mrs. Calloway, was nice in an imposing 'has your best interest at heart' kind of way. Theseus usually did not get along very well with that sort of person, primarily because he was certain that other people couldn't possibly know what his 'best interests' were.

Theseus sat in the old wooden chair in an office that looked like it hadn't been updated in several decades. Mrs. Calloway herself looked as though she had probably inhabited the office for that whole time. She smiled at Theseus in a way that he had come to expect from adults. The way they always smiled at 'troubled' kids. This annoyed Theseus because it made him feel like people could *smell* his childhood clinging to him even after all these years. He could never pinpoint what part of him betrayed his past. The years when his father was around were something he'd rather erase from his mind completely, but when people like Mrs. Calloway looked at him like that, it was difficult to forget.

"Theseus, I'm sure you know that your first SAT score isn't going to give you a lot of options, but there's still time for you to take it again this fall if you buckle down."

"Oh, I'm not taking it again," said Theseus, dreading where this conversation would lead.

Mrs. Calloway's sympathetic smile faltered. "Most colleges–" she began but seemed to intuit (correctly) that this strategy would not work on Theseus. Instead, she opted to be more direct. "Can I ask why you're not planning on taking it again?"

"I don't want to go to college," said Theseus simply, mildly appreciative that she hadn't immediately begun lecturing him. "I think it would be a waste of time and money. I'm not interested in any of the programs out there, and I'm not good at school in the first place."

"I see," said Mrs. Calloway, briefly glancing at her bulky desktop computer. Theseus wondered if she had his grades pulled up on the screen and was confirming his last statement. "Well," she said, making a valiant effort to still sound optimistic. "What *are* you good at? I'm sure you have some interest that you can turn into a career."

"I work on cars part-time," said Theseus, knowing he had to give her something if he was going to get out of here any time soon.

Mrs. Calloway looked relieved to have something to work with. "Have you considered trade school? There are some excellent mechanic programs out there."

Theseus shrugged, he had considered this idea before. He did enjoy working on cars, the only problem is that he wasn't sure how quickly that career path could get him far away from Asphodel, which was his only clear objective for the future. He didn't know exactly where he wanted to end up, only that he wanted to *go*, preferably staying traveling for as long as possible.

Mrs. Calloway took Theseus' shrug as an affirmative and pressed several trade school brochures into his hands, gave him a brief overview of each one, and bid him goodbye. She was probably glad to be rid of him, and Theseus didn't mind in the slightest. He stuffed the brochures in his backpack where they would probably never see the light of day again.

✳✳✳

Ari was a diligent student, even in subjects she didn't much care for. This tended to surprise and impress people who knew of her family tragedy; if Ari had been a different sort of person, she might have been too overwhelmed by grief to continue to keep up in school after her parents' deaths. However, after the immediate shock, she found that throwing herself into her schoolwork and hobbies was the only thing that helped her to process her grief. If she had been idle, she was sure it would have consumed her in the early days. Almost six years removed from it all though, she was remarkably well-adjusted.

Ari liked to have things planned out and prepared. So when she walked into Mrs. Calloway's office for her appointment, she knew exactly what she wanted to do.

"I'm going to apply to the community college," said Ari. She was a very practical soul, despite her romantic artist heart. She knew that she could get into a more prestigious school if she wanted to, but there were several reasons that led her to the conclusion that community college was best for her.

Number one was that she could get the same degree for a fraction of the cost of getting it at some big-name university. Number two was that to be quite honest, Ari didn't care for the loud, impersonal atmosphere of a big school. Number three was that Ari did not want to leave Asphodel. She lived in this small town her whole life and had grown very attached to both the people in it and the town itself. When her parents died, her grandparents in Colorado had offered to take Ari in, even though her parents' will dictated for Cal to become Ari's legal guardian. Ari had refused this offer and continued to live with Cal and Persie in their childhood home. This arrangement might not have worked if Cal and Persie had not been particularly gracious older sisters, nor if Ari herself were not such a responsible teen. But they were, and she was, so it worked.

Evidently, Mrs. Calloway could sense how responsible and prepared Ari was and liked her very much for it. She beamed at Ari, "Do you know what major you'd like to pursue?"

"I want to double-major," said Ari confidently, "In art and horticulture."

Ari's primary inspiration as an artist came from nature. She had an impressive backyard garden at home which boasted delicious vegetables and herbs as well as stunning flowers. Ari did not know exactly what she wanted to do with her life yet, but it was her dream to somehow combine her two loves into a career of some kind.

There honestly wasn't much for Mrs. Calloway to cover with Ari, as she had researched most everything on her own already. Mrs. Calloway did not complain, it just made her job easier. She dismissed Ari with the latest flier for the community college.

✳✳✳

Ever since the idea of college became a serious topic of conversation, Icarus had entertained nothing but the prospect of Ivy League schools. He had always achieved everything he ever tried, won every contest he ever entered, and always had top grades. His only academic "rival" at Asphodel High was Solae, who was set to be the class valedictorian, regulating Icarus to salutatorian. This might have caused jealousy in Icarus if he were not so infatuated with Solae, but he was content to be second-best next to her, he knew she deserved it.

He was aware that getting into an Ivy League school was a long shot, but given his history of achievement, Icarus didn't consider it anything to worry about. He figured that if he met the academic requirements and was able to dazzle with his application essays, there would be no reason he couldn't get in. After all, he had grown up hearing how "smart" he was, "gifted", even. Weren't kids like that, who consumed books at a reading level high above their age, who effortlessly took advanced classes, *supposed* to go to top schools? Wouldn't it all be a waste otherwise?

When Mrs. Calloway heard of his plans though, she was more than a little skeptical. "What are your backup schools?" she asked.

"I'm only applying to these three," Icarus replied, indicating his list which showed Harvard, Yale, and Princeton. In his mind, it made no sense to apply to other schools when he needed to put all his efforts into these three.

Mrs. Calloway looked at him sternly over the tops of her glasses. "You may meet the academic requirements, but I would strongly advise you to find backups. These schools value more than just academic achievement."

Icarus was confused; he knew this, which was why he had filled up an ample amount of his time with extracurriculars, something Mrs. Calloway surely was aware of. His resume was perfect, unless she was hinting that he needed something more still.

When he only stared blankly, Mrs. Calloway continued. "Do you happen to have connections to any alumni? Relatives, or family friends perhaps?"

"No," Icarus said, "Why?"

"It can be helpful to have someone who can get your foot in the door."

"Oh," said Icarus, suddenly remembering an old saying he'd heard, *'It's not what you know, it's who you know.'* He despised that phrase. Why should someone who was fully qualified be overlooked because someone else was cozy with the powers that be? He intended to prove that ideology wrong. He would demand to be noticed. It was a matter of honor now. He would apply with his own merits, and he *would* get in, because that's what was right. Icarus was convinced deep down that everyone had to abide by some sense of rightness, a trait that some might call naivety, but he preferred to think of it as *chivalry*.

✳✳✳

When it came to college for Solae, money was no object. It wasn't that her father was particularly wealthy, but rather her grandmother had built up a substantial college fund for Solae before passing away. The only thing Solae's college education depended on was her grades. With Solae's aptitude for academia, this meant that she could practically choose any university she wanted.

This was a privilege that Solae did not take lightly.

"Your test scores and grades are very impressive," said Mrs. Calloway when Solae was sitting in the old wooden chair. "Have you considered applying for Ivy League schools?"

"Um, not really," said Solae, but this was a lie. "I'm not exactly sure what I want to do yet." This was the truth. She had no idea what she wanted to do with her life, other than an urge to do something *great*. It wasn't fame or money she wanted exactly, she simply wanted something more than a mundane life. She was often envious of Icarus with his books, and Ari with her art and gardening. *They* had passions, something that they could devote themselves to and never get tired of it. Solae wanted something like that, but she had yet to find whatever it was.

"Well, I think you should apply to one or two of these," said Mrs. Calloway, passing her brochures for Harvard, Yale, Brown, and Princeton University.

Solae felt a pang at seeing the orange Princeton logo; it was her mother's alma mater. Solae had a complicated relationship with things that reminded her of her mother. There was a constant battle in her heart between missing her and resenting her. She did *not* want to be just like her, in spite of how often her father told her that she was. In spite of the fact that she had great taste in music. In spite of the fact that she was always the most beautiful and interesting person to look at in all the old photographs.

Would going to an Ivy League school help Solae find what she wanted in life? Maybe. Would going to an Ivy League school make Solae more like her mother? Maybe not, but she would have to do some more thinking about it, away from Mrs. Calloway's office.

The rest of the meeting was spent discussing possible majors, though Solae did not feel that she had a better idea of what she wanted to do with her life by the end of it. All she had was that same yearning, wanting feeling in her chest.

CHAPTER 6

In The Air Tonight - Phil Collins

Every small town makes it its business to have an unnecessary abundance of some kind of business or shop, all of which somehow manage to coexist without running each other out of business. Some towns claim coffee shops, pizza joints, or antique shops, but most towns have their own niche.

Asphodel had seemingly chosen bookstores as its mascot. Not big, corporate chain bookstores, though there was one of those in the solitary shopping center. It was small, locally-owned bookstores that took center stage in Asphodel. Some sold new books, some sold used books, a few sold almost exclusively vintage books, and one was infamous for selling nothing but trashy, pulp-fiction romance books. Even that store was inexplicably still in business, despite everyone 'respectable' in town decidedly avoiding it like the plague.

Icarus, an avid reader since early childhood, favored one of these small bookstores. It was one that specialized in vintage books called The Book Loft, aptly named due to its being converted from an old barn. It even had an actual loft in the back of the store that served as a cozy reading nook. The shelves at The Book Loft often contained books that Icarus was sure he'd be hard-pressed to find anywhere else in the world.

Icarus liked to visit The Book Loft whenever he had a free afternoon. The store always seemed to be empty when Icarus visited, aside from the owner, a kind, older, bohemian-looking woman named Clio. She was always happy to see Icarus when he entered the store, and always answered any questions he had most helpfully. He knew it was a fanciful thought, but he liked to imagine she must curate the books in her store like precious artifacts, finding them on adventures in hidden places.

On this particular day, Icarus convinced Ari, Solae, and Theseus to make a stop at The Book Loft on their way to the lighthouse after school. He was supposed to pick up a book that Clio had put on hold for him. A bell rang upon their entry into the shop, and Clio emerged from the small backroom that was divided from the rest of the store by a simple curtain.

"Icarus, dear! Just the person I wanted to see. And you've brought your friends, excellent, excellent."

Icarus grinned, "Do you need a box of books moved, Ms. Clio?" he asked. Occasionally, Clio would ask Icarus to do things like move boxes or reach very high shelves, in a very grandmotherly way.

"It's something much bigger than that, I'm afraid," said Clio. "Here, I've got your book at the counter. Come over here so I can tell you this."

Icarus glanced at his friends, who looked apprehensive and shrugged. They walked up to the counter.

"What's up, Ms. Clio?"

Clio sighed, "Children, I have some sad news. I'm closing The Book Loft."

Icarus, Ari, and Solae gasped. Theseus raised his eyebrows.

"But why?" asked Icarus, completely crestfallen.

"A lot of reasons," said Clio, "But mainly, I'm getting too old to run this place on my own, and I'm moving away to be with my daughter." She gave them a resigned smile. "I won't be closing until next summer, though, so I'll still be around for a little while."

"This is my favorite bookstore," said Icarus, "I can't believe it."

"I don't remember a time when it wasn't here," said Ari.

"It's been thirty-two good, long years. But all things must come to an end."

There was a moment of silence as if they were all mourning the life of The Book Loft.

"Now," said Clio, "Here's where the four of you come in, if you're willing."

Theseus looked like he wasn't necessarily willing, but Icarus said, "What do you need?"

"I need to get all of my books that are in storage and bring them here," said Clio, "So that I can sell as much as possible before the move." She paused, and there was a new twinkle in her eye. "I know that the four of you spend a lot of time at my storage building already, so I was hoping that

I could ask you to help me by moving all of the boxes here for me. For pay, of course."

Icarus, Ari, Solae, and Theseus looked at each other for a moment, confused. When did they spend a lot of time at a storage building?

Then Ari gasped, "The lighthouse is *yours?*"

Clio nodded, "I bought it shortly after I opened this shop. There was talk of tearing it down if nobody did something with it, but it's such a wonderful piece of history for Asphodel, I just bought it to save it."

Icarus thought it was a little strange how she talked about it as if the lighthouse was some important landmark rather than just the abandoned home of an old eccentric. "We didn't know it was yours," he said, "Did it bother you that we were hanging around there? I promise we didn't vandalize it or anything."

Clio laughed, "I know, I know. Don't worry, I don't mind at all. I just happened to see you all one time when I was driving by, and after that, I just kept an eye out. I knew you weren't anything to worry about. I'm glad you were able to find joy in it."

"Well, thank you," said Icarus, in disbelief over how his two favorite spots in town were linked so closely.

"So," Clio continued, "How about it? I'll pay you all of course, and there's no rush. I just need everything moved by the start of next summer."

The four exchanged looks, then shrugs, which turned into nods.

"We'll do it," said Icarus. "When do we start?"

Clio produced a key from under the counter and handed it to Icarus. "If you don't mind, I'll go over there with you now and give you a few pointers. You can bring your first load over and then just go whenever you feel like it as long as it's all clear by next summer."

"Is everyone good with that?" asked Icarus, looking around at his friends.

"I've got no plans this afternoon," said Solae.

"I just need to be home for dinner," Ari said.

They all looked to Theseus. He shrugged, "Whatever. I could use the extra cash."

"Good!" Clio exclaimed, "Thank you all. I'll just meet you over there in my own car."

The four friends all piled into Icarus' truck, though Theseus had come on his own and Ari had given Solae a ride.

"I can't believe that Ms. Clio owns the lighthouse," said Ari as they drove.

"It's quite the coincidence," Icarus noted.

"Almost creepy," Theseus said flatly.

"I was surprised at first, too," Solae said, "But I think it makes perfect sense. Only someone like her would have the sense to preserve it. It is a unique landmark."

"I wonder what's going to happen to it after she moves away," Icarus said. "I'm really going to miss her shop."

"They better not tear the lighthouse down," Ari said. She was thinking of all the imaginative ways she and Icarus had come up with to repurpose the lighthouse when they first started visiting. She personally felt very attached to the lighthouse; it might not have literally served the purpose of a real lighthouse, guiding ships to shore, but for Ari, it had in a way. She had been lost at sea when her parents died, and the lighthouse had been a beacon of comfort and steadiness. Back then, it was a place she could anchor herself while she processed her grief. Now, it was like an old friend.

Clio got to the lighthouse before them, she stood at the door, waiting. As they approached, Clio took out a key and inserted it into the padlock. Ari felt a flutter in her chest, she had always wanted to see the lighthouse from the inside, but she never thought she'd get the chance.

"I'll just point out a few things before I take back a couple boxes myself, then you can load up in your truck and meet me back at the shop."

The inside of the lighthouse was filled wall-to-wall with boxes, some of which were opened with small stacks of books nearby. They helped Clio load a few boxes into her own car, and then she came back and indicated a few boxes that she wanted first.

"And feel free to peruse any books that catch your eye," she said, "But I close The Book Loft at seven, so please try to be back before then."

Once Clio left them, they began loading the boxes she indicated into the back of Icarus' truck. As Icarus went to pick up a box, a glint of gold caught his eye. There, under a loose floorboard, was something glittering and metallic.

Curious, Icarus slipped his fingers under the floorboard and pulled it up, there was hardly any resistance. Underneath was an old wooden chest with a golden latch, like one might find in a pirate movie. Luckily, there was no lock. Heart thumping, Icarus opened the chest, unsure of what he would find inside…

It was another book. Icarus frowned, confused, though not necessarily disappointed.

"Guys, come look at this old book," he said.

Theseus blew out an exasperated breath, "Icarus, this whole lighthouse is full of old books."

"This one is weird, though," Icarus insisted, "I found it in this old treasure chest." He held it up for them to see.

The others' curiosity got the better of them and they joined Icarus to inspect the book.

"Do you think Clio knew it was here?" Solae asked.

Icarus turned the book over and over, it was clearly very old, black leatherbound, with traces of gold embossing that had long since worn away. There remained an impression of a title: *Reflections of Mythology*, but there was no author name anywhere.

"No idea," said Icarus. He opened the book up to the first page to find a hand-written inscription. "*Once begun, this story must be completed, lest the reader slip through the cracks and find themself trapped in their own reflection,*" He read aloud.

"Creepy," said Ari.

"Yeah," Icarus agreed, frowning at the inscription. He had no idea what it might mean, but reading it made him feel something. It was the same feeling he got when he and Ari had first visited the lighthouse, the same feeling whenever he heard about some strange phenomena in Asphodel. Those were always just rumors, stories from a friend of a friend of a cousin's neighbor. Icarus himself had yet to bear witness to anything strange and unusual. Something about this book though… it made him wonder.

"It sounds like a joke," said Theseus, "Something meant to lure in *X-Files* wannabes like you."

Ari laughed at this, and Theseus looked pleased with himself.

Solae did not laugh, though. She leaned in close to Icarus to study the inscription herself. When she was this close, Icarus could smell hints of something like cloves and honey.

"What kind of book do you think it could be?" She asked, looking up at him.

"I-I don't know," Icarus said, struggling not to get lost in those dark, doe-eyes of hers. Why did it always feel like she was staring into his soul? "Let's find out."

He turned back to the book and turned to the next page, where the actual text began, and began to *read.*

CHAPTER 7

Scarborough Fair – Simon & Garfunkel

Icarus wasn't quite sure how it happened, but at some point, it was like time skipped. He did not know when he stopped reading the book or even left the lighthouse. All he knew was that suddenly he was walking alone down a dirt path toward a looming palace, his arms full of spare parts.

Wait… he slowed to a stop, looking at the ancient and foreign-looking parts in his arms. He caught sight of his clothing while he was at it, too. Was he wearing a dress?

Icarus looked around his unfamiliar surroundings, he was pretty sure that was the *sea* he was looking at to the right. Panic began to rise inside of him, and questions hit him rapid fire, but somehow, he was able to answer himself as quickly as the questions came to him.

Where was he? The island of Crete.

Why was he carrying these parts? To bring to his father.

Who was his father? Why did he need spare parts? His father was Daedalus, the two of them were slaves to King Minos, forced to use Daedalus' genius to build things for the king.

Suddenly, the load in his arms felt much heavier. How did he know all of this? Where were Solae, Ari, and Theseus? Was this a dream? If his father was Daedalus…

did that make him *that* Icarus? These questions, however, were not so easily answered.

One thing he did seem to know was that if he did not hurry up and get back to the palace, both the king and his father- no, *Daedalus*- would be angry. And he somehow also knew that angering them was one of the worst things he could possibly do.

Despite not quite knowing what he was walking into, Icarus forced himself to keep moving forward.

✸✸✸

Ariadne ran through the palace. It occurred to her that running through a palace in a fancy dress was definitely a fantasy of hers, and while this… chiton? Wasn't exactly a ballgown, it was certainly silky and flowy enough to fit the bill.

But all that was just a passing thought in the back of her mind. She had just sort of woken up in a bedroom about five minutes ago, *her* bedroom, apparently, and some instinct was telling her that this was *her* palace and that she, Ari, was the *princess*, even though the last thing she remembered was Icarus starting to read that strange book in the lighthouse.

Icarus. That's who she was trying to find. The same strange instinct that told her she was the princess also told her that she would find him in Daedalus' workshop, a place she knew exactly where to find.

She had to go up a creepy spiral staircase lit by torches, but she finally reached a door at the top of the tower that she knew instinctively was the one she had been looking for. Without hesitation, she opened it.

"Icarus!"

There he was, also wearing a chiton, though his was shorter and plainer. He also didn't have his glasses, which caught Ari off guard a little. It made him look less studious. He had been looking at some sort of chart on a desk in a corner of the room. He froze when she said his name, but relief washed over his features when he turned and saw Ari.

"Ari, thank goodness," he began, but the old man who was standing next to him cleared his throat.

"Is that any way to address the princess, son?" This was Daedalus. He was… Icarus' father? Or at least, for all intents and purposes.

Ari frowned in confusion, but Icarus seemed to understand right away.

Winking at Ari, Icarus gave a slight bow. "I mean, Princess Ariadne, it's uh, an *honor*."

Ari had to fight hard to keep a straight face. "I… uh, need to talk to you," said Ari, momentarily shifting her gaze to Daedalus after she said it, wondering if he thought this was odd at all.

Icarus also looked apprehensively at old man, but Daedalus nodded, so Icarus followed Ari out of the workshop.

"What's going on?" Asked Icarus after they closed the door behind them.

"I was hoping you would know," Ari said.

"Well," said Icarus slowly, like he was still thinking about it. "My memory is a little fuzzy, but I'm pretty sure this is the story from that book."

"So, we're living in a Greek myth?" asked Ari, "And… doesn't the Icarus in mythology fall into the sea and drown?"

Icarus flinched, "I was thinking that maybe since we know what's coming, we could avoid any terrible fates like that."

"I hope so," said Ari, "But that still doesn't solve how we get back to Asphodel, or how we find Theseus and Solae."

"You knew how to find me," mused Icarus, "Do you have any idea about the others?"

Ari thought hard for a moment, then it just came to her, like everything else about their situation had.

"My father- King Minos, I mean- sacrifices people to a… Monster, the *Minotaur*, every year. But this year…" Ari's mouth went dry as she said it, "It's Theseus. He's in the dungeons."

Icarus nodded grimly. "Let's go get him."

They walked at a fast pace through the palace, both of them wondering how real this situation was. And if it was real, what should they do about it?

✳✳✳

Theseus wasn't sure how he ended up locked in a dungeon in ancient mythological Crete, but it probably had something to do with that stupid book Icarus found. All he knew for sure was that he was supposed to fight something called the 'Minotaur.' Hazy memories of a middle school classroom and cartoonish illustrations of a half-man, half-bull accompanied the word. It wasn't often that Theseus felt afraid, but he had to admit to himself that the idea of being killed by something that shouldn't even exist made him a bit jittery.

For what was probably the millionth time, Theseus cursed his stepfather for making them move to Asphodel.

Theseus didn't have much time to contemplate his situation because he soon heard footsteps come padding down the appropriately gloomy hallway toward his cell. He stood up, realized for the first time that he was wearing something that resembled a *dress*, and groaned.

The footsteps belonged to Ari and Icarus. Theseus felt a little better when he saw that Icarus was also wearing one of these dress things, but it actually didn't look that bad. Ari certainly didn't look bad in her dress; the flowing lavender gown made her look sort of like a princess. Or… wait, she *was* a princess. Ariadne, Princess of Crete, daughter of King Minos, the man sending Theseus to his death.

"So, you're here too," said Theseus when they stopped in front of his cell. "I thought I was going crazy."

"You're not," said Icarus, "But I'm not sure how that's going to help us."

"Well, you're supposed to be the smart one, so maybe you can think of a way to get us out of here."

Icarus let out a slightly crazed laugh. "Are you kidding?"

"It's going to be okay," Ari cut in. "We'll figure it out together."

"Hey, where's Solae?" asked Theseus, suddenly realizing that she was the only one missing.

Ari and Icarus exchanged glances, "Neither of us had any idea where she would be, we were hoping you might know," said Ari.

"Nope," said Theseus, "And seeing as how she is the only one who doesn't conveniently share a name with one of the characters in this story, I'm guessing that finding her is going to be a lot harder."

"Seriously," said Icarus, shaking his head. "Wait a minute, what if that's the reason we're here? Maybe Solae is still at the lighthouse because her name isn't in the story."

"Maybe…"

But before they could come up with any other ideas for how to find Solae, all three of them began to feel a strange sensation, like they were physically fading away, and just as quickly as they had appeared in this strange world, they found themselves leaving it again.

✳✳✳

When Solae opened her eyes, she had a strange feeling that she should be blinded by the bright light, but it didn't bother her at all.

She was lying in the middle of a white field, with a clear blue sky above her and all around. Everything was so bright that it seemed to gleam like the sun bouncing off water. The effect created flashes of prismatic rainbows that danced across the surface of the field.

"Solae,"

Solae sat bolt upright and looked around, startled by the male voice. Her eyes landed on… well, he looked like a person, but somehow Solae knew that wasn't the right word.

He was tall, and she supposed he was handsome, but that didn't really seem like the correct word either. His skin was marble, *literal* marble, as if he were a statue come to life. His hair was like amber, and it most certainly did not follow the laws of gravity; it floated around his head as if he were starring in a shampoo commercial. His eyes were startlingly blue, maybe even glowing, but Solae couldn't be sure with all the bright light. He was wearing a white chiton with a gold belt and a blue cape that did not obey the laws of gravity either. Solae thought the cape was a little much.

"Who are you?" demanded Solae.

"I am called Phoebus Apollo," replied the man. He walked across the field towards her.

"Apollo…" said Solae in a dazed voice, "Of course you are."

"Of course," agreed Apollo, holding out a hand to help Solae up.

Solae accepted his hand and stood up, but as she did so, she noticed that her skin was, quite literally, *glowing*. She stumbled backward, holding her arms out in front of her, staring at them; she was the color of a sunset. She, like Apollo, was wearing a white chiton and gold belt, and somehow, Solae's glowing skin did not shine through the white fabric.

As she moved, she noticed that the shimmering of the fields danced with her. The blinding light was coming from *Solae*, she was the source of it. And what was more… she looked at the ground, realizing that it wasn't ground at all. Solae had achieved what every little kid dreamed of- she was walking on a cloud. Her feet were bare, and she realized she did not feel anything under them. Yet wherever she placed her feet, she felt supported as if walking on the strongest ground.

"What's happening?" Solae asked, looking at Apollo.

"We have to go," replied Apollo simply, taking Solae's hand and leading her to the opposite edge of the cloud. Solae didn't really have a choice but to follow, she just sort of floated along with him.

At the edge of the cloud was a golden chariot with three golden horses, just floating in midair. When Solae got close, the whole thing sparkled. They stepped into the chariot, and the horses immediately began galloping through the air. Since there was no ground for their hooves to click against, it was completely, eerily silent. Not even the wind whistled in Solae's ears.

She looked over the edge of the chariot with no fear; something told her that she could not fall if she tried, even though the ground was miles below them.

"Where are we going?" She asked.

"Across the sky, as always," said Apollo. "The mortals need the sun to live."

Mortals. The sun. Apollo.

"Are you telling me you're a god?" asked Solae through thinly veiled disbelief.

"Some mortals do make up stories to that effect," he said with a smile, "But we are not gods, we are simply immortal forces of nature."

"Right… so you're the sun?"

"No, Solae, that would be you."

"*Me?*"

"Yes, at least from the perspective of the mortals. But you are still Solae, too."

Solae was getting tired of his cryptic replies. "Well, if you're not the sun, why are you here?"

"Think of me as your driver," he glanced at her with what she could only describe as a mischievous grin, but the emotions behind it felt bigger than that.

"Can the… 'Mortals' see me?" she asked tentatively.

"They see the sun. They do not see Solae."

"How do you know my name?"

"You ask too many questions." said Apollo.

"I–" Solae started to raise her voice in protest but stopped. She felt like she should be getting a headache right about now, but she couldn't feel anything at all.

"You are not from this place, Solae," continued Apollo. "Some force brought you here, but soon you'll go back home, I believe."

For some reason, it took Solae a minute to realize that by home, he meant Asphodel.

"Don't worry though, you'll return here," said Apollo in a reassuring tone.

"What if I don't want to?" retorted Solae.

"Until your stories are complete, I don't think you'll have much choice."

"What?"

This time when Solae looked at Apollo, it was like looking up from below the surface of the water. All his edges were blurred.

"So many questions," he said again, turning to face her. His voice was all echo, reverberating in Solae's head like ripples in a pond. "I have a feeling that if you just wait, the answers you are looking for will come to you."

Then, everything faded away.

CHAPTER 8

Oh! Darling - The Beatles

When Solae opened her eyes again, the clouds were gone. She was in the lighthouse, standing exactly where she had been when Icarus started reading the book. From glancing around at the others, she assumed she wasn't alone in just having experienced something that was surely too fantastical to be true.

Theseus reached over and tugged on a lock of Ari's hair.

"Hey! What was that for?" She demanded.

"Just checking," said Theseus, "I'm not really sure what's real at the moment."

"I think it's safe to say that whatever just happened… happened," said Icarus. Then, he did a double take when his gaze fell on Solae. "Hang on, where were you, Solae?"

"I'm not sure," she said, "Where were you?"

Icarus held up the book, "I guess you could say we were in *here*. We were all in the places of people in the story. I was, well, Icarus, Ari was Princess Ariadne, and Theseus was… Theseus."

"It was annoyingly predictable," added Theseus.

"Except," said Ari, "We had no idea where you were, Solae. I somehow knew exactly how to find Icarus and

Theseus, but none of us had any idea about how to find you."

Solae, who had begun to put the pieces together from the moment Icarus had explained their roles, only half-heard Ari.

The myth of Icarus, she thought, *And I'm the sun.*

The realization horrified her, and she didn't know how to look at Icarus. Would she have to watch him fall to his death because of her? Could she somehow prevent it?

"I think I was in the same place," she said, "Well, sort of."

"What do you mean?" asked Icarus, "Who were you?"

At that moment, Solae realized she had a choice. What if not telling Icarus that she was playing the part of his downfall was the way she could save him? If Solae remembered correctly, most Greek myths ended in tragedy because the heroes tried to avoid a prophecy, thus inadvertently bringing the very thing they tried to avoid upon themselves anyway. How many of them could have escaped their fate if only they had remained in blissful ignorance? So, Solae made her choice.

"I'm not exactly sure where I was," she said, which was not technically a lie. She really had no idea where she had been, location-wise. "I'm sure it was in Greek mythology, though."

"How could you tell?"

"Well, I don't normally wear a chiton," said Solae sarcastically.

A smile flickered across Icarus' face, "Fair enough."

Then Ari said, "What do we do now?"

"Clio might know something about this," said Icarus slowly, "I mean, we found the book here, where she stores all her extra books."

"She has some explaining to do, then," Theseus said darkly. "I didn't sign up for any of this paranormal stuff."

Hope blossomed inside Solae. Theseus was right, if they stopped helping with the books, and never went back to that place, Icarus would not even have the chance to fall.

But Icarus said, "I don't know if we have a choice about finishing the story." He was thinking about the inscription.

"Maybe the inscription is an exaggeration," said Ari, catching onto his train of thought.

"Maybe," said Icarus, but he sounded doubtful.

"Let's go find out right now," said Theseus.

They finished loading up the boxes Clio had indicated into Theseus' truck, though they were careful not to touch any other stray books, and then headed back to The Book Loft. They said almost nothing the whole way there, it was like they were holding a collective breath in anticipation. When they walked into the shop, the bell announced their presence, and Clio smiled at them from the counter.

"Ms. Clio," said Icarus tentatively, "Something… weird happened at the lighthouse."

"Oh?" said Clio with a knowing smile.

Theseus, not one to beat around the bush, interjected, "Lady, one of your books transported us to ancient Greece, what's that about?"

"Crete," Icarus muttered, but Ari elbowed him, and Theseus shot him a dark look.

"Strange things tend to happen here in Asphodel, as I'm sure you know," said Clio.

"Are you saying this is connected to all of that stuff?" asked Icarus.

"Indeed," Clio said, "In fact, it is part of what spurred all of the strange things in the first place."

"Like… magic?" Icarus asked breathlessly.

"Call it what you will."

Icarus felt a little light-headed. He had never met anyone else who seriously entertained the idea that something supernatural might actually reside in Asphodel. He still couldn't quite believe this was all happening.

"Well, I'm not going back," Theseus said, crossing his arms.

"You must," insisted Clio. She produced a piece of paper and a pencil and began to sketch a Venn diagram. She pointed at one of the circles. "This is the plane that we exist on," she said, then pointed to the other circle,

"Legends, folklore, myths, and the like all exist in this plane." She shaded in the place where the two circles intersected. "Sometimes, there is a pocket in between, where the two planes bleed into each other, and usually this is caused by someone *interfering* where they shouldn't."

"Like you?" asked Theseus.

"Like the founders of Asphodel," said Clio coolly. "Children, the reason that so many strange things happen in this town is because the founders of this city believed that they could take some of the magic from this other plane for themselves. They used old rituals to essentially rip a hole in the space between the two planes."

"I'm guessing that's bad," Ari said.

Clio nodded, "Asphodel is in a perpetual state of fading away because it is trapped in a pocket between these two planes of existence. Most people know something is different or strange about it, but they can't tell what. Now your eyes have been opened, and you can see where the two planes meet. This will become more evident as time goes on, you will be able to see this place fray at the edges."

"Oookay," Theseus said, "But that doesn't explain why we have to act out Greek tragedies."

"You are sewing the hole closed," said Clio, "You are the needle, the story is the thread. When you go back and forth, you are literally sewing it shut. Your energies are currently hovering between the two planes as well, and the only way to ground them again is to *finish your stories*."

The way she said 'finish your stories' sounded particularly meaningful, like they all had different stories rather than just one among the four of them.

"What happens if we don't?" asked Solae who had been quiet until now, soaking up the information.

"Asphodel would continue to fade away until even the memory of the place disappears. But more immediately," She said with a glance at Theseus, "Your energies would fade away."

"Why didn't you warn us?" demanded Theseus.

"There was a warning," said Clio, opening the book to show the inscription.

Theseus scoffed and turned away.

"Do we have to finish the story right away?" asked Icarus.

"Clio shook her head. "You can't remain in the other plane for that long. You can space out your visits and just go whenever you go to clean out more books. I expect you'll start to feel it pulling you back when it's time." She rummaged around in her pocket and handed them each a fifty-dollar bill. "Consider this your first installment. Thank you all so much for helping me with the books," she said with a wry smile, "Now if you don't mind, let's move them inside quickly. I do have a shop to close."

They made quick work of moving the boxes of books into the shop, quietly but excitedly talking amongst themselves as they did so.

"I can't believe it's real," said Icarus, "I mean, I knew there was something special about Asphodel, but this…"

"I guess we can't tell anyone," said Ari, "I mean, who would believe it unless they experienced it themselves?"

"Yeah, not looking for anyone to think I'm crazy," said Theseus. "Also, an important question that I think everyone forgot- what happens if we, y'know, *die* in this other plane?"

Solae felt like her heart stopped momentarily. Icarus couldn't die. She watched him, his hands were steady as he finished closing up the truck bed. He knew the myth but didn't seem to be concerned.

"Nobody is going to die," Icarus said calmly.

"Easy for you to say," said Theseus, "You just have to follow one simple instruction. I have to fight a monster."

They were all quiet now. Solae realized she had been so concerned about Icarus that she hadn't even thought about the danger Theseus was in.

"I'm supposed to help you," said Ari. "We'll make sure you're prepared." She sounded worried, but hearing someone else worry seemed to bolster Theseus.

"Maybe you're right, I can take this thing. Especially with your help."

"We should all do some research before we go back to that place," said Icarus.

"As long as we don't find another magic book."

Theseus then bid them all goodbye and drove away in the Mustang. Ari turned to Icarus.

"Can you take Solae home? I told Cal I'd be home for dinner and I'm already late."

"Sure, if Solae doesn't mind," said Icarus, and privately, his heart fluttered at the thought of spending time with Solae, *alone.*

"I'm with you," Solae said simply and walked around to the passenger seat of the truck.

"Alright then," said Ari, "See you later."

It was a fifteen-minute drive to Solae's house from The Book Loft. For the first five minutes, both Icarus and Solae were awkwardly quiet for different reasons, although they were connected.

Solae was quiet because she liked Icarus. Maybe even *like* liked him. This was why she couldn't decide whether or not to tell him that she was the sun in this story they had stumbled into. She didn't want to see him get hurt, and she honestly wasn't sure if her being the sun meant anything. She remembered looking up the meaning of her name when she was younger; it came from the French word, *soleil*, which means 'sun.' At the time, Solae, a rather vain child, had merely thought she was special for having a 'French name.' Now, she thought about how her friends had been placed in the story according to their rather convenient names. Maybe that's all it was. Her name meant 'sun' so of course she would be the sun. It didn't have any bearing on real life. Still… if she did tell Icarus, would he see her differently? Would he take it as a sign to distance himself from her?

Icarus was quiet because he *liked* Solae. He was vitally aware of the fact that this car ride was the perfect opportunity to tell her how he felt, but he didn't want to mess it up. How could he convey the magnitude of feelings that had been building up since that fateful bus ride two years ago? Two years was not very long, but at the same time it *was*. He wanted to tell her, but he had been waiting for the right moment for a long time now. Icarus was the sort of person who waited for all the conditions to be right before doing something. He liked to savor important moments so that the full weight could sink in. Now, the conditions were quite literally magical. The experience of finding out that magic, or something like it, really existed invigorated Icarus. If he didn't say anything now, he probably never would.

But rather than just come out and say it, he decided to work up to it. "I can't say I blame Theseus for being upset about this whole thing," he said, "We'll all have to make sure he comes out alright."

"I'm not really worried about Theseus," said Solae, "He's a fighter."

"That's true," said Icarus, "But still, the Minotaur."

"Theseus doesn't die in the myth," said Solae, and though she didn't say it, they both knew that there was an unspoken, *but Icarus does,* at the end of that sentence.

"I'll be fine," said Icarus quietly.

"How do you know?" Asked Solae, unable to keep her voice completely level.

"Because I know what's coming," said Icarus. "I know what happens if I fly too high." He glanced at her and smiled, "I know these myths backward and forwards."

Solae remembered how over a month ago, Icarus had told them about how he had applied to several Ivy League schools. He'd been so excited when Solae revealed that she had applied to some of the same schools as him.

"Please don't worry about me, Solae," said Icarus as they pulled into her driveway. He looked at her again, and Solae saw a look in his eyes that *meant* something.

Feeling panicked, she hurriedly unbuckled and got out of the truck, "Thanks for the ride," she said.

Now or never, Icarus thought to himself as Solae closed the truck door. He thrust the truck into park, pulled the emergency brake, and threw himself out of the truck. "Solae, wait!" He ran around to meet her. She looked surprised but stopped. "I have to tell you something," he said, taking a deep breath.

Solae didn't say anything, but her eyes widened like she might already know what he was about to say.

"Solae," began Icarus, "You're one of my best friends, but I want to be more-"

"Don't!" said Solae, and suddenly Icarus felt her cool fingertips against his lips, stopping him from speaking. He closed his eyes at the touch, feeling like his heart might just flip-flop out of his chest and splat on the sidewalk. "Please don't finish that sentence," said Solae, "I can't take it."

Now Icarus' heart felt like it would sink down into his stomach to be digested into primordial soup. "I-I'm sorry," he said when Solae took her hand away, unsure what he could possibly say to this.

"No, it's not your fault," said Solae, and he had never seen her so distressed. "It's me," she said with an exasperated sigh, "I have a lot of junk in my past."

"What happened?" He asked because she looked so sad, and he wasn't quite sure how to comfort her when he didn't know the cause.

Solae looked up at the creamsicle sky for a moment before replying. The sky felt more personal to her now. "My mom left when I was little," she said, "My dad has never been the same since." She shuddered as if expelling the bad memories from her system. "I couldn't rely on anyone, so I trained myself not to *need* to." She looked him in the eye for the first time during this conversation. "I don't know how to be there for someone, or let them be there for me, so I don't know how to be... with someone."

Icarus stared at her. Solae had never mentioned this before, to any of them. He knew that her mom wasn't in the picture, but the way Solae had always talked about it, so nonchalantly, he never really thought about the impact it might have on her. It suddenly had him questioning how well he knew her, which hurt because he thought he *knew* her.

"I–I'm so sorry, Sol, I didn't know," said Icarus, wishing he could hug her or do something, anything to take away that pained look on her face.

"I've never told anyone that, not all of it at least," said Solae. "It's something I need to deal with on my own."

"But… you don't have to, you know?" Icarus said a little hesitantly.

Solae shook her head, "Don't say that, because you know what the worst part is?"

"What?" said Icarus, dreading the answer.

"I like you *too*, Icarus!" There was a catch in her voice.

Icarus' heart began to stir again, "So be with me," he said, taking a step forward, "Nobody is going to leave you this time." He looked into her deep, dark eyes and made a promise, "*I* won't leave you."

Solae seemed to falter for a moment, then she whispered, "That's not what I'm afraid of."

"Then what is it?"

"I'm afraid of hurting *you*."

Icarus almost laughed, "Why would you hurt me?"

Solae took a deep breath, "Like I said, my mom left," she said again, "And my dad… Well, he's distant, but when he is present, he always says the same thing." She looked up again, trying not to let her tears escape.

"Which is?" asked Icarus, though he was almost afraid to push any further.

"That I'm just like my mom."

Neither of them spoke for a moment. They just stood there, both looking like the tension between them was pulling one toward the other like an unstoppable force, but the weight of everything Solae just said also stood between them like an immovable object.

Finally, Icarus spoke. "You know, you don't have to be like your mom."

"What if I can't help it?" protested Solae, "What if I'm… I'm… *fated* to be like her?"

"I don't believe in fate," Icarus said promptly.

"You're telling me you don't believe in fate after what just happened to us today?" demanded Solae, "After we were just transported to *Greek mythology?*"

"Just because things outside of our control happen, doesn't mean that we can't control our own choices," said Icarus earnestly. "Do you want to hurt me, Solae?"

Solae blinked, "Of course not."

"Then you don't have to," said Icarus. He took a deep breath, "Of course, you don't have to be with me if you don't want to, either… but I kind of get the feeling you do." He looked at her hopefully.

Solae looked into his eyes, soft and green, and her heart began to melt. "Yes," she said, "But… I need time to think about it first."

Icarus nodded, the hope was beginning to grow, but he knew he should step away now. "Okay, that's fine- good, I mean. Um, goodnight, Solae."

"Goodnight," said Solae, and she watched as he walked back to the truck and drove away before going inside her house.

CHAPTER 9

Stairway to Heaven – Led Zeppelin

Solae's heart didn't stop pounding until she was in her bedroom with the door shut. Part of her wanted to collapse onto her bed, melt into the blankets, and disappear. Another part of her wanted to dance around her room to the sound of soft music with romantic lyrics.

The logical part of her, though- the part of herself she trained to be bigger, *stronger*, than the rest of her- demanded that she follow her normal nighttime routine. The calming rituals would probably help soothe her racing heart and mind. First, Solae donned a pair of lounge pants and her mother's old Princeton University sweatshirt. She then pushed her hair out of her face with a headband and washed her face in the bathroom attached to her bedroom. Her father had not wanted to sleep in the master bedroom anymore after Solae's mother left, so he had switched rooms with Solae.

Just wearing the old orange sweatshirt was already starting to calm Solae's nerves. Sweatshirts in general were her favorite item of clothing; even though they were so casual and cozy, she felt like they could have a certain chicness to them if properly styled. This sweatshirt, though, was a particular comfort as one of the few relics Solae's mother left behind, like the pink MP3 player.

Princeton Unirversity was where Solae's mother, Morgan Flores, had gone to become a historian, which had somehow landed her here, in Asphodel, after graduation. She had met Solae's father, Amos McClaine, fell in love, got married, and gave birth to Solae. Of all the places in the world, this is where she had settled, or at least *seemed* to settle. Solae didn't think she'd ever forgive her mother for abandoning her at seven years old, like that was any kind of age to graduate from a mother's care.

Despite that, wearing her mother's sweatshirt and listening to her old MP3 player still brought Solae a strange sense of comfort. Now, after thoroughly completing her skincare routine, Solae put her headphones on and pushed play on the MP3 player, letting the music envelope her.

She wondered about her own future and how she still had no idea what she wanted to do with it. She had told Icarus that she was like her mother, but she had always wondered how much of that was actually true. She wondered if her mother kept secrets, just like she was keeping her role in Reflections of Mythology a secret from her friends.

✳✳✳

Theseus did not go home right away. He stopped for a fast-food meal and drove to a park where he ate in his car with the windows down. He thought about the mythological excursion he'd just been on with the others while he ate. Contemplating how much he despised being forced into things. Rolling his eyes at Icarus for getting them into this. Thinking about how weird Solae was acting afterward. But his mind kept coming back to land on *Ari*. She had worn a flowing light purple dress, her hair had looked like flames against it. She was a princess. He realized

71

that he was looking forward to seeing her again, even more than usual. He finally drove home when the sun was almost done setting, when the trees began to paint their long shadows over the world.

He parked in the driveway of the house and went in the front door as quietly as he could. He found his mom, Theresa, in the kitchen making herself a cup of tea. She beamed at Theseus when she saw him.

"Hi Mom," he said, scanning the kitchen and living room.

Theresa read his expression, "Mark and Erik are out, they're getting ice cream to celebrate Erik's SAT scores."

This was a pleasant surprise. It wasn't often that Theseus had time alone with his mother without his stepfather and stepbrother. In the old days, though it was nightmarish, Theseus had enjoyed the feeling that it was he and his mom against the world. He loved to remember the time after his father left when it really had just been the two of them. Theseus hadn't needed anyone else. Theresa *did*, though, and Theseus would not begrudge her that.

"How was school?"

"It was fine. I hung out with Icarus, Ari, and Solae after."

"Oh, that's good." Theresa stirred her tea. She had been worried about Theseus and school since Mrs. Calloway had called about Theseus 'not applying himself' after their meeting. Theseus brought up his friends to offset this; she was glad that he was hanging out with a better crowd than in New York. With his old New York friends, Theseus tended to get in a lot more trouble. That had pretty much completely stopped once they moved to Asphodel and Theseus had started spending time with Icarus, Ari, and Solae. Not that there was much trouble to get into in a town like Asphodel anyway. Except trouble of the supernatural kind, apparently.

"Oh, there was something I wanted to tell you," Theresa continued after sipping her tea. "Your Uncle Jack is coming to visit for a while in the spring."

"My Uncle Jack?"

"Jack Bryant, my brother."

Theseus squinted one eye shut. Vague memories of letters to and from a 'Captain Bryant' surfaced in his mind.

"Isn't he in the Navy or something?"

"Not quite, he's the captain of a research vessel," Theresa said proudly. "He doesn't get many opportunities to visit. He did once a long time ago, but you probably don't remember."

Theseus would take her word for it. He didn't like to purposefully remember things from 'a long time ago' anyway.

"Why is he coming?" he asked.

"Oh, he just wanted to see us," said Theresa, "I think you'll like him. You remind me of how he was when we were growing up."

Theseus was struck by this statement. He did not look like his mother with her honey-brown hair and green eyes. He was, to his resentment, the spitting image of his father, Silas Gray. Everything from his dark curls and blazing silver eyes, even the angular shape of his face. It was more than that, though. Theseus' darkest secret was that there was anger inside of him. He wasn't always *angry*, but he never had to reach far for it. This darkest secret was also his greatest fear- that he was just as much like his father on the inside as he was on the outside.

Now though, his mother said that he reminded her of her brother. The way she smiled made him think that maybe Captain Jack Bryant was a good person. Then again, she had thought Silas Gray was a good person when she married him. Theseus had an unexplainable hunch that there was something he was missing here, that there was some factor about this uncle of his that he didn't remember.

The garage door sounded, announcing the arrival of Mark Robbins and his son, Erik. Mark was Theresa's husband. They both came into the house, and Theresa greeted Mark with a kiss.

Theseus, not one to hang around people he didn't like, simply said "Goodnight," and went to his room. He was not surprised when there was a knock on his door only a few minutes later. Mark opened the door, though he remained in the doorway. Theseus did not turn to face him.

"Why weren't you at dinner, Theseus?"

"I got dinner while I was out."

"You worry your mother."

"She doesn't worry as long as I'm not out late."

"She's worried about you at school."

Theseus paused, "I'm figuring it out."

"You're going to end up like your father. You think your mother wants that?"

Theseus felt the anger inside him like a small flame licking at his insides. This was why he did not like his stepfather. Mark had never trusted Theseus, devil-spawn that he apparently was. He treated his mother well, though, so Theseus did his best to keep quiet about it.

He turned to face Mark, who took a step backward at Theseus' expression. Part of Theseus liked that Mark was afraid of him, instead of the other way around. He knew that this would only add fuel to the fire, though, so he schooled his features back to indifference before walking over to the door.

"I'm going to bed," he said flatly and shut the door in Mark's face.

✳✳✳

Ari normally listened to music while driving, but her mind was too full this time. She pondered the afternoon's events in eerie silence the whole way home. She had gone along with Icarus' theories about Asphodel in the past, but she wasn't sure that even *he* actually believed that something supernatural would ever really happen. But here they were.

She did her best to set this train of thought aside when she got home. When Ari walked into the living room, she saw that a feast of homemade pizza, popcorn, and candy was spread out on the coffee table. Friday night was always movie night in the Darnell sisters' house; it had become a beloved tradition, firmly ingrained in their tiny culture.

"Hey," Cal said at Ari's appearance. She and Persie were already sitting in their designated spots, on the vintage green sofa and the whimsically-patterned armchair. "Where have you been?"

"I was hanging out with Solae, Icarus, and Theseus," said Ari as she took her place on the sofa next to Cal. "Sorry, time got away from us."

"Oooh, *Theseus*," said Persie, "How is that going?"

Ari rolled her eyes. She had not exactly told her sisters about her feelings for Theseus, but Persie had a sixth sense about these kinds of things.

"It's not 'going' at all," said Ari, "He's not my boyfriend."

"Yet," said Persie.

"We might not ever get together."

"You'll never know if you don't *do* something about it."

Ari just shrugged, not wanting to dwell on the subject any longer. She turned to Cal, who was not so prone to being interested in her non-existent love life. "What movie are we watching?"

"Meet Me In St. Louis," said Cal, grabbing the TV remote.

Ari and Persie both made sounds of approval at this announcement. The three Darnell sisters were all wildly different from one another, and yet the same. Cal had short, practical hair. Persie's hairstyle changed as frequently as the seasons. Ari preferred to keep her hair long. Yet all three of them had the same particular shade of golden-red hair. Ari had her art and her garden. Persie worked at a salon and hoped to open her own one day. Cal was working on her doctorate in chemistry and was quite the amateur chef. They all expressed it differently, but all three sisters had the touch of creativity.

One thing they were all in complete agreement on, however, was their love for old movies. They rewatched their favorite movies many times over, but never tired of them. Friday movie nights were usually able to lift Ari's spirits, no matter what kind of day she'd had. It was the perfect thing to oust *Reflections of Mythology* from her mind, for now at least.

✳✳✳

Icarus sat in his truck for several minutes before going inside his house. How could he face his parents and act as though everything was normal when possibly the two most monumental things of his life so far had just occurred, one right after the other.

He had discovered that magic was real. *Really* real. He had experienced the impossible, and what was more, his friends had experienced it with him. Somehow, this enhanced the magical quality of it all. It reassured Icarus of the reality of their trip to mythology because they couldn't have all hallucinated the same thing at the same time. Well, except for Solae, who had a slightly different experience.

Solae. She was the other monumental occurrence. Icarus had been flying the whole way home on the knowledge that she liked him back. It completely overshadowed the fact that she hadn't said 'yes' to actually going out with him, until he pulled into his driveway, that is. Then the overwhelming sense that he had ruined everything sent him crashing down. He wouldn't know either way until Solae told him, all he could do was run through their conversation endlessly in his head.

Finally, Icarus knew he had run out of time. If he stayed outside much longer, his parents would come out to check on him, and they certainly wouldn't let the matter rest until they knew exactly what was wrong. Eli and Tyra Easton were not overbearing exactly, but they were always very concerned when they sensed that something was bothering their only child. Icarus, however, did not want to share on this occasion. He was not ready to share about Solae, and as for *Reflections of Mythology*… Well, he didn't think they would believe him if he told them. How could they if they didn't experience it themselves? Icarus shook his head, steeling himself, and went inside.

"Icarus? Is that you?" called his mom when she heard him come through the front door.

"Yeah, Mom," said Icarus as he set his backpack down in the entryway.

The Easton house was a particular brand of upper-middle-class suburban. They lived in one of those cookie-cutter housing developments, and Icarus was sure that the interior decoration was just as cookie-cutter as the rest of the houses on their street. It could have been a model home with its level of just-so-ness.

Luckily, Icarus was not late for dinner. His mom was just finishing up setting the small round table when Icarus walked through the dining room and into the kitchen to wash up. His dad passed him going to sit at the table and gave Icarus a good-natured clap on the shoulder.

"Hey, boy," he said, his customary greeting.

"Hey," Icarus replied as he washed up and joined his parents at the table to eat.

"How was school?" asked Icarus' mom.

"Good."

"Anything exciting happen?"

"Not really. I was out with Ari, Theseus, and Solae afterward."

The conversation shifted to each of Icarus' parents talking about their day, and Icarus did his best to make interested-sounding noises at appropriate intervals, but his mind kept wandering. There was a lull in the conversation, and Icarus saw his parents exchange a look. They were onto him already; he didn't understand how they did it.

"Icarus, is there something wrong?" His dad prompted.

"No," said Icarus, "Everything is fine." And then, because he knew he had to give them *something* or else they wouldn't drop it, "Well, there's this girl I want to ask out."

Icarus' mom gasped. "Who is it?"

"I don't want to say yet, in case it doesn't work out."

His parents exchanged looks again. "Are you worried we wouldn't approve of this girl?"

"No, nothing like that," Icarus said quickly, "I just don't want to get my hopes up too much."

His dad chuckled and reached around the table to thump Icarus on the back again.

"Well, let me see if I can guess who it is," said his mom, "Oh! Is it Ari?"

Icarus laughed in embarrassment, "No, Mom, Ari is just a friend."

Icarus' mom spent another couple minutes guessing names of girls in his class, though Icarus had never even spoken to most of them. His mom was on the PTA, though, so she knew a lot of the other parents. Icarus wondered vaguely why Solae's name didn't come up. Perhaps his mom assumed that she was like Ari, just a friend.

However, in case she did guess correctly, Icarus spoke up. "Mom, please, you're making me nervous."

"Alright, fine," she said, resigned.

"Just let us know if you have any questions," said his dad.

Icarus nodded but knew that a conversation about dating with his parents could prove to be the most excruciatingly awkward thing he'd ever experienced. Mercifully, they dropped the subject for the rest of the evening.

After dessert, Icarus stole upstairs to his room, which was charmingly cluttered compared to the rest of the house. The walls were covered with bookshelves, save for the space over his desk, which housed a corkboard covered with a collage of blurry, cryptid-related photos, newspaper clippings, and sticky-notes that he wrote his own field notes on. Icarus scanned his small library and selected a book on mythology from one of his shelves and began to read, desperately trying to keep his mind off Solae, and instead on the afternoon's strange adventure.

He had always assumed that any sign of supernatural activity that he came across would be something like Mothman or the Loch Ness Monster. Something fuzzy and unclear, completely foreign. But Greek mythology? It didn't make any sense, but it wasn't like Icarus was going to complain. In fact, part of him thought that these mythological excursions might prove to be enjoyable, even though supposedly the entire town's future was riding on them.

CHAPTER 10

1979 - Smashing Pumpkins

The next day was Saturday, a glorious occasion for those in school or with a five-day workweek. Icarus' head was still spinning from the night before. Had it really only been last night when everything earth-shattering occurred? It felt like a lifetime ago. He remembered with sudden clarity how he had gone to his parents with his troubles about Solae. Why, *why* had he done that? Now, it was all they were going to think about when they looked at him. He needed a different perspective, from someone who actually knew Solae. Not Ari, she would undoubtedly tell Solae about it. Icarus had learned long ago that the two of them shared secrets as if confidence with another person automatically included both of them. That left Theseus, and honestly, Icarus didn't know why he hadn't gone to Theseus about this in the first place. Surely, he had more experience in this area.

Icarus knew that Theseus worked the morning shift on Saturdays, so he stopped at a drive-through for breakfast and showed up at the run-down car shop where Theseus worked, donut and coffee in hand. He parked across the street from the shop and walked over to the garage where Theseus' own Mustang was currently parked while he leaned over the open hood. The shop had predictable lulls, during which Theseus worked on his own car.

"Hey," said Icarus as he came to stand next to Theseus. He held up the coffee and donut bag. "I brought you breakfast."

"Hey," said Theseus, pausing his work and wiping his hands on a rag before turning to take the donut and coffee. "Thanks, man." He took a sip of the coffee, "I needed this. Barely slept last night."

"Same here," said Icarus. He took a deep breath, "Theseus, I may have really messed up last night."

Theseus snorted, "I'm guessing you mean other than getting us into a contract with a magic book?"

Icarus winced, "Yes…"

"What happened?"

"I asked Solae to be my girlfriend."

Theseus nearly spit out his coffee from laughter. "Really? I didn't think you had the guts."

Icarus shrugged. "I think that whole thing with *Reflections of Mythology* gave me a boost."

"No kidding. So did she say no?"

"Well… not exactly." Icarus gave Theseus a brief and vague summary of what Solae had said about being afraid to hurt him. He left out most of the stuff about Solae's mom, though. That was hers to tell. "In the end, she said she wanted to be with me, but she had to think about it."

Theseus shook his head in amazement. "Wow, sort of a piece of work, isn't she?"

"Hey."

"What? I'm just saying."

"I thought it sounded promising," said Icarus hopefully.

"Maybe, but she could just be trying to let you down easy."

"Should I tell her to just forget it? I don't want to ruin our friendship."

Theseus held back from rolling his eyes. He sometimes forgot that Icarus was naive enough to think friendships ever really lasted. Theseus knew better.

"It's too late for that now," he said. "Have you ever gone out with a girl before?"

"No," said Icarus, "I've only ever liked Solae. Since freshman year."

"And you waited this long to do something about it?"

"I wasn't sure if she felt the same way, and then I was waiting for the right moment, and–"

Theseus gave him a playful shove, "I'm just messing with you."

"Come on, I'm freaking out a little, here."

"I think it says something about your priorities that you're more freaked about this than you are about *Reflections of Mythology*."

Icarus sighed, "Don't worry, I'm still going to do more research."

"Good," said Theseus as he threw away his empty cup and the donut bag and went back to his car. "I'm not thrilled about the prospect of being gored by a minotaur."

"Hey, that's not going to happen. We'll make sure of it."

"So, Solae," said Theseus after a short pause. "She said she likes you too?"

"Yes," said Icarus.

"I'd give her some time if I were you." said Theseus.

"You think so?"

"Yeah, just let her cool off. You picked a really fantastic time to bring this up, y'know, when both of you were stressed from being transported through time and space."

"You're right," said Icarus, running a hand through his hair. "I'm an idiot."

"Sometimes," agreed Theseus, "But that's sort of an endearing quality with you."

Icarus laughed, "Thanks, I'm actually starting to feel better."

"I am an untapped fountain of wisdom."

There was another lull in the conversation while Theseus dug around under the hood of the Mustang for a bit. Icarus took a seat on a nearby stool.

Then Theseus spoke again. "Can I ask your opinion on something?"

Icarus raised his eyebrows, "You don't usually want other people's opinions."

"Well, I do now."

"Alright, I'm listening."

Theseus paused again, which clued Icarus in that this subject was one that Theseus was hesitant to bring up. Icarus held his breath, Theseus was rarely so open, which sometimes made Icarus worry about him.

"My uncle is coming to visit in the spring," said Theseus, "He's going to stay for a while.

"Is that… bad?" Asked Icarus, because Theseus paused again.

"I don't think so," said Theseus, "But I can't shake the feeling that it's kind of important somehow. Do you have any family like that?"

"I'm not sure," said Icarus, "I mean, I have relatives who only come to town for holidays."

"I don't have a normal family experience," said Theseus carefully, and deliberately. He never, *never* told anyone about his father, not everything at least. Most people knew that his real father wasn't in the picture, even if it was just because both he and Erik made it very clear that they weren't blood-related. He could give Icarus a tiny glimpse, though. He needed to talk to someone about this. "You know, my dad left my mom for someone else when I was ten."

"I knew it was something like that," said Icarus. "I'm sorry, man."

Theseus waved a hand dismissively. "Don't be, that's not the point. What I'm trying to say is that I don't know my extended family very well. We've never lived close to my mom's parents. This uncle, 'Jack' is my mom's older brother. Apparently, he's usually at sea, he's some sort of ship captain. That's why I don't really know him."

Icarus nodded, clearly impressed.

"My mom said that I've met him before, but…" He sighed, "I don't think the circumstances were very good."

When he hadn't been able to sleep last night, Theseus had tried to remember Jack, but all he could picture was the badness of the time when Silas Gray had been around. If meeting Jack had coincided with that cursed time period, it was jumbled in with all the raised voices and dodged punches. It couldn't have been good.

"What did your mom say about it?"

"She said he was good, but she also said that *I* remind her of him."

"Ah," said Icarus, and Theseus appreciated that Icarus knew him well enough to know why that comment might be cause for concern, but didn't think any less of him for it.

"Our parents see us differently from how we actually are," said Icarus. "Their perception might be better or worse than we deserve, but it's because they'll always see us as children."

"Poetic," said Theseus, "Translate."

Icarus chuckled, "Your mom probably sees you differently from how you see yourself. I don't think her saying that is a bad thing."

"Okay," said Theseus, pondering. "I still don't know why he's coming."

"Well, it sounds like you and your mom haven't seen him in years. Maybe it's just time for a reunion."

"Maybe," said Theseus, "I just get the feeling that there's something else, too."

"I guess you'll just have to find out."

"I guess so."

❋❋❋

Ari and Solae, diligent students that they were, made plans for Ari to come over to Solae's house that Saturday so they could study together. When Ari arrived at Solae's house, she knocked on the door, waited for a minute, and was surprised when Solae's father, Amos McClain, answered the door. Normally, it was Solae herself who opened the door. She mentioned something once about not wanting to bother her father. Amos was kind, though Ari always thought he looked a bit tired, or even fragile.

He greeted her with a smile, "Hello, Ariadne, come on in. Solae is in her room. I don't think she's left since coming home last night. Maybe you could check on her?"

Ari nodded politely, "Of course," she said, but privately thought it was odd that Amos hadn't checked on Solae himself.

She ventured down the hallway to Solae's room. The door was closed, so she gently knocked.

"Sol? It's Ari."

"Come in."

Ari opened the door and brushed aside the colorful beaded curtain that hung inside the doorway. Solae's room felt like a sacred space to Ari. Solae was very good at making things aesthetically pleasing, especially her room. She almost never turned on the overhead light, but instead had a few atmospheric lamps, as well as sheer curtains that allowed light to filter in pleasantly when she opened the blinds. The walls were an old-fashioned olive color. All the furniture had a natural wood finish. The bedspread was a muted rust color, and there was a rug full of faded jewel tones spread out on the floor. There were a few plants, most of which were gifts from Ari.

Solae was sitting cross-legged in front of the floor-length mirror she had propped up against the wall, applying a delicate flick of eyeliner, a skill that Ari was slightly envious of.

"Hey," said Ari.

"Hey," said Solae, not looking away from her reflection.

"Um, are you okay? Your dad asked me to check on you, and honestly, *that's* what worries me."

Solae put down the eyeliner and laughed, a little helpless-sounding. "Sorry about that, everything's fine."

Not believing her for a moment, Ari asked. "Is it about yesterday?"

Solae hesitated but turned to face Ari. "Sort of. Something actually happened after the whole magic-book thing." There was a hint of nervousness in her voice.

"What happened?" asked Ari, setting down her bag on the bed and sitting down cross-legged in front of her friend.

"Icarus… wants to date."

Ari tilted her head to one side, "Huh, somehow I did not see that coming."

"Right?" said Solae, "And this is stupid, but it honestly threw me off more than the, uh, other thing." This was only sort of true, Solae realized as she said it. It was all tangled up together; half the reason she was so shaken up about Icarus was the fact that she was playing the part of his downfall in this other, mythological world.

Ari laughed. "He did pick a weird time to bring it up. That's very Icarus-like of him." She paused for a moment in anticipation, then prompted, "So, what did you say?"

"I said I needed to think about it," Solae stood up now and began to pace. "I don't know what to do. I mean, I think I really like him…" Ari's face lit up in excitement, but Solae held up a hand as she continued. "But what if it doesn't work out? I don't want to hurt him."

Ari shrugged, "There's no way of knowing if it'll work out until you try it."

"Maybe it's better if we don't date at all, then," Solae said, biting her lip nervously.

"Or maybe it'll be a what-if that you'll regret forever if you don't give it a try," said Ari. "I mean, you said you like him, right?"

Solae sighed wistfully, "I think so? I feel butterflies when he laughs or looks me in the eye, and he's so thoughtful and beautiful…" she threw up her hands in an exasperated gesture, "He's literally *golden* Ari, what if… what if it doesn't work out and I ruin him?"

Ari stood and walked over to Solae, placing both hands on her shoulders. "You wouldn't ruin him, Sol, he's not fragile. It sounds like you both really like each other, so I think it's worth taking a chance."

Solae held eye-contact with her for a moment, then sighed again, hopelessly. "I just… need to think about it more."

"Fair. But if I were you, I'd just go for it."

"I know *you* would," Solae said with a smile. This was one of their differences- Solae was more inclined to follow her head, while Ari went headlong after her heart. "Let's just forget about it for now, though," she said, "I need to think about something else."

"Okay," said Ari, "But you have to tell me the minute you decide. Well, you should probably tell Icarus first, but I want you to know."

"Well, of course. You will be informed immediately."

"Excellent."

The rest of the day was spent on schoolwork while making conversation about anything other than romantic prospects, though mostly focusing on the miracle of the magic they'd discovered the day before. All the while, though, Ari's mind couldn't help but wish just a tiny bit that it had been her and Theseus who'd had a heart-to-heart conversation the night before. She wouldn't have turned him away with a 'maybe.'

CHAPTER 11

You Might Think - The Cars

Two weeks later, the briskness of autumn began to settle over Asphodel. It was finally chilly enough for jackets, the leaves began to change color on the few trees that weren't evergreens, and pumpkins were staring to appear on front porches.

Reflections of Mythology had somewhat faded into the background for Icarus, Ari, Solae, and Theseus. Apparently, the whole town slipping away was a very subtle thing. Neither Solae nor Icarus had said anything to each other about their conversation on that ride home. Things had been slightly awkward at first, but with Theseus and Ari both helpfully pretending like they knew nothing about it, they were able to mostly ignore it for the time being. Icarus was following Theseus' advice of waiting for the subject to come up naturally but was starting to feel nervous about how long it had been.

Icarus, Theseus, and Solae were all sitting in their usual booth at The Haunt one afternoon. They were waiting for Ari, who worked part-time at the next-door plant nursery, to get off work and join them.

Theseus looked from one of his friends to the other, making eye contact with Icarus for a moment. The guy looked like he needed help, and Theseus felt a bit obliged to give it to him. He thought for a moment, and suddenly a thought crossed his mind. *Perfect solution.*

"I'm going to go over and talk to Ari. She should have gotten off work by now," he announced. He gave Icarus, who looked slightly panicked, a wink. Theseus slid out of the booth and casually strolled over to the next door over. Ari was standing behind the counter, and her eyes widened a little when she saw him. He casually walked over and leaned on the counter.

"Hey, princess."

"Shh!" said Ari, looking around the almost empty store furtively, but fighting a smile. "We can't talk about that here."

"Why would anyone think that me calling you 'princess' means that you're actually a princess in a magic book?" asked Theseus. "For all anyone overhearing us knows, I just think you're pretty." He held her gaze as he said it, hoping to fluster her.

Ari's face flushed light pink, but she didn't look away. "And *do* you?"

Theseus blinked, it was his turn to be taken aback, but he recovered quickly. "Who wouldn't?" he said coolly.

This time Ari did look away, her blush deepening. Then she lifted her gaze to meet his, looking a little fierce. "What do you want, Theseus?" she said, though not in an unkind tone.

Theseus flashed a smile, "Just trying to give Icarus and Solae some time to talk. It was getting pretty unbearable over there."

Ari gasped, "You know about that?"

"Of course. Even if Icarus hadn't told me, it's obvious that something's up with them."

"True," said Ari. She felt excited by their initial flirtatious exchange; she was pretty sure they'd flirted before, but rarely so blatantly. "So, what should *we* talk about while they talk?"

Theseus shrugged, "I mean, while we're on the subject, aren't you supposed to help me out with the Minotaur?"

"Says who?"

"Well, Icarus said that's how the original myth goes."

"And who says I have to follow that?" Of course, Ari did plan to help Theseus however she could; Theseus doubtless knew this, but to her satisfaction, he played along.

"Well then, I guess I'll just have to win your favor."

"If you can."

"That sounds like a challenge."

"Maybe it is."

"Maybe I'll take you up on it."

✳✳✳

Meanwhile, Icarus and Solae discussed the implications of Theseus going to speak with Ari, alone. They had no way of knowing what was being said, but it was still effective in easing the tension between them.

"The prince from a faraway land goes to woo the beautiful princess," said Solae in a staged pretentious voice.

Icarus laughed, but then said, "Do you think he's serious, or just leading her on?"

Solae contemplated, her expression turning back into her careful and musing self. "He wouldn't do that to Ari," she said, "She's too much of an angel."

"Right, but you know Theseus. They're so… different. I just don't want Ari to get hurt."

Solae glanced at Icarus out of the corner of her eye. "Just like I don't want you to get hurt."

Icarus stared at her for a moment, almost wondering if he had misunderstood. Was it finally happening? Was this the moment of truth?

At his sudden, burning attention, Solae felt her heart speed up. Why had she said anything? "Ari can take care of herself," she said quickly.

"So can I," said Icarus.

Solae's pounding heart skipped a beat. That was a point. Maybe she didn't need to protect him.

"Solae," Icarus said gently, "Maybe you're worrying too much about the future."

Solae looked down at her drink. Maybe he was right, maybe Ari was right, but there was no way to know for sure unless they tried. She could let down her guard, just follow her heart for once; and if a heartbeat was any indication of what the heart wanted… she certainly had her answer.

She exhaled slowly and made eye contact with him so that he would know what she meant. "Okay."

Icarus didn't say anything for a few seconds. Solae could practically hear the wheels turning in his brain. He was trying to determine the next best move, like it was a chess game and she had just put his king in check. She loved that about him, how careful he was despite all his talk about not worrying about fate or the future.

"So," said Icarus finally, "Does that mean I can take you on a date?"

She turned to face him. His desperate attempt to stay casual charmed her, making her want to charm him in return. "I daresay you could," she said, grinning at him.

He stared at her for a moment, and then laughed, in both joy and disbelief.

His laugh. Oh, his *laugh*. Solae had to look away. She had already fallen for this golden boy much more than she realized. She would do her very best not to tarnish him.

CHAPTER 12

Should I Stay Or Should I Go - The Clash

Theseus loved driving. It was an escape from everything that annoyed him about life. He could forget about school, forget about his stepfather, forget about the past, forget about *Reflections of Mythology*, forget about Asphodel altogether. The only things that existed in his world right now were the roar of his engine blending with the sound of grunge rock on the radio, and the strip of road he was barreling down.

He saw something coming up- a light blue car pulled over on the side of the road. Recognition brought Theseus back down to earth, and he hit the brakes, slowing down just in time to pull over behind Ari's beetle. Ari herself was sitting on the hood of the car, phone to her ear, but evidently whoever she was trying to call was not picking up. She turned around when she heard Theseus pull up. Her face lit up at the sight of him, sending a jolt of something electric through Theseus.

He got out of his car and strolled over to Ari. "Having trouble?"

Ari slid off the hood of her car. "Flat tire," she said, gesturing at the passenger side front tire. It was indeed flat, *very* flat.

"Do you know how to change it?" asked Theseus.

"No," said Ari, looking a little embarrassed. "I was trying to get ahold of Cal, she's the handy one. My signal is really bad right here, though."

"Do you have a spare?"

"I think so."

"Alright," said Theseus, already turning back to his car to get the necessary tools. "I'm going to teach you how to change it, then we'll get it to the shop."

"Thanks, Theseus," said Ari, beaming at him.

When Theseus returned with a wrench and a jack, Ari had already retrieved the spare tire from the trunk. They sat down together next to the offending tire, and Theseus walked Ari through the process step-by-step both verbally, and sometimes by demonstration.

"I'm honestly a little surprised you don't know how to do this already," said Theseus, "Given you're so resourceful and all."

"Thanks," said Ari, "But I'm just resourceful in an artistic way."

"Hey, who said working on cars isn't artistic?"

Ari quirked an eyebrow, "It's mechanics."

"I'll have you know that it is a *delicate* and *fine* art," Theseus said, pretending to be offended.

Ari laughed, "So does that mean you're an artist too?"

"Precisely."

"My mistake, it's always a pleasure to meet a fellow artist." Ari held out her hand for a mock handshake.

"Likewise," said Theseus, grasping her hand and giving it a firm shake. He noticed a new glint in Ari's eyes.

When the spare tire was successfully attached, Theseus instructed Ari to follow him in her car to the shop. The whole drive, Ari couldn't help but feel like something was about to happen. She rarely had one-on-one interactions with Theseus, and the circumstances felt a bit romantic- he had shown up in her hour of need, chivalrously helping her with the tire, making sure she got to the shop safely… And Ari was sure that it hadn't been strictly necessary for their hands to touch so many times while they changed the tire.

Unfortunately, the shop was already closed for the day when they arrived. "Leave your car here," said Theseus. "I'll take you home and make sure it gets taken care of tomorrow."

Ari sighed, "Sorry, this is ending up being a lot of trouble."

"Nah," said Theseus, "This is just what I do. C'mon, let's get you home."

Just what I do. Ari wondered if Theseus had ever helped other girls whose cars had broken down. She wondered if it mattered that it had been her. *That's not what he meant,* she thought.

She climbed into the passenger seat of the infamous black Mustang, which she had never ridden in before. It was like the stars were aligning perfectly.

"So, are you still against helping me with the labyrinth?" asked Theseus as they drove. "I mean, I am helping you with your car."

Ari had forgotten about that conversation they'd had at the plant nursery a few days ago. "Is that what this is about?" she asked teasingly.

Theseus winked, "I mean, what kind of man would I be to ignore a damsel in distress?"

Ari rolled her eyes, "I wasn't in distress."

"And what if some hooligan had stopped by instead of a gentleman like me?"

"Are you a gentleman? You look like you could be a hooligan."

"I'm only a hooligan on the weekends," said Theseus. "Perfectly upstanding citizen during the week."

"Lucky me," murmured Ari. "Anyway, I *suppose* I can help you with the labyrinth."

"You're too kind."

The conversation did not take a more romantic turn, despite Ari's light attempts at flirtation. She was too nervous to be bolder about it.

"Thanks for the ride," said Ari when Theseus pulled into her driveway, feeling a bit resigned. "See you at school tomorrow."

"I'll be here at 7:30," said Theseus.

Ari turned to face him. "What do you mean?"

"To give you a ride to school," he said matter-of-factly.

"Oh," was all Ari could manage to say. She knew she should come up with another witty response, but the smug way Theseus was grinning at her made her mind go blank. "Um, thank you," was all she managed.

"Goodnight, Ariadne."

"'Night," said Ari as she awkwardly scrambled out of the car. She didn't look back but made her way to the front door as quickly as possible without running. Once inside, she couldn't help herself and let out a shriek of excitement.

Both Cal and Persie called from the kitchen.

"Are you okay?" Cal sounded concerned like she was afraid something was wrong.

"What happened?" Persie sounded excited like she had correctly interpreted Ari's exclamation as positive.

Ari joined them in the kitchen, sitting on a barstool behind the counter. Persie was sitting on the counter, computer in lap. Cal was scooping cookie dough onto a pan. They both stopped what they were doing at Ari's dramatic entrance, looking at her expectantly.

"My car got a flat tire," began Ari happily.

Cal and Persie exchanged confused looks.

"Aaand guess who stopped to help me."

Cal shrugged, but Persie kicked her feet in the air. "Oh! Was it Theseus?"

Ari pointed at her in confirmation. "Yes, but that's not all. He helped me get it to the shop where he works, gave me a ride home, and…" she paused for effect, "He's picking me up for school tomorrow."

Persie held up an electric-blue nailed hand, "Wait, did you ask him to, or did he offer? Big distinction."

"He offered."

Persie nodded approvingly, "This is an *excellent* development."

"I think it's a good sign," Ari agreed.

"Wait, is this the guy you like?" asked Cal.

Ari nodded, feeling her face flush slightly.

"Why doesn't he just ask you out, straight up?"

Ari shrugged, "That's just how Theseus is," she said, though she couldn't deny that the same thought had crossed her mind on multiple occasions.

"It's all part of the game, Cal," said Persie. "You have to work up to it. Maybe if you looked up from your textbooks more often, you'd have an opportunity to experience it yourself."

Cal rolled her eyes, "I've dated before."

Persie made a *pfft* noise, blowing her bangs around. "Not in the last three years."

"I've had other things to focus on," said Cal.

"I will say," said Persie, speaking to Ari now. "There's nothing wrong with getting the ball rolling yourself."

Ari sighed, "Yes, but I never know what to say. I get so…" she fluttered her hands in imitation of a butterfly, "Around him."

"It's simple. If he takes you home again tomorrow, invite him to come inside. I'll be here, so I can be your wing-woman. Or better yet, if he doesn't ask you out by the end of the day, just ask *him* out."

"I'll try," said Ari, but privately, it was hard to imagine being so bold toward Theseus. Maybe she should just try channeling Persie and see what would happen.

✳✳✳

When Theseus got home, everyone was already sitting down to eat dinner.

"You're late again," said Mark as Theseus sat down and began dishing up.

"I was driving Ari home," said Theseus, secretly relishing the opportunity to prove that he was not as depraved as they might assume. "Her car had a flat tire on the side of the road."

Theresa smiled, "That was nice of you, Theseus."

He shrugged, hiding how much his mother's note of approval truly mattered to him.

"Ari Darnell?" Inquired Erik.

Theseus nodded but did not bother looking at his stepbrother. He vaguely wondered why Erik cared, seeing as how they stayed well away from each other and their friends. Erik did not say anything else, though, and the rest of dinner passed in polite conversation, though most of the talking was done by Theresa and Mark.

After dinner, as Theseus made his way to his bedroom, he was aware of Erik following him. He could have just been going to his own room, which was just across the hall, but Theseus had a suspicion that was not his only motive. Sure enough, when Theseus made it to his room and did not immediately close his door, Erik leaned on the doorframe.

"So," he mused, "Ari Darnell."

"What about her?" demanded Theseus coolly, unsure of where this was going, but knowing that neither of them were one to strike up friendly conversations with each other.

"I'm just surprised," Erik said casually, "That someone like her would go for someone like you."

"I don't know what you're talking about."

"Oh, come on. She's not called the 'Angel of Asphodel High' for nothing."

"So, what, you came in here to comment on how she's a good person?" asked Theseus, turning to glower at Erik. "And she doesn't like when people call her that, by the way." People tended to use that epithet behind Ari's back in a mocking way, though privately he thought it was an apt description, in a much more sincere sense.

"Oh yeah? Why's that, because it's all a front?" Erik said, a certain nastiness creeping into his tone. "I bet that's it. I mean, if she's getting involved with you… People will talk."

Theseus took a step toward Erik, that familiar anger rising inside of him. "Don't talk about her," he said, "She's never done anything to you."

"If she were really as good as she pretends to be, she wouldn't get close to you."

Theseus paused, searching Erik's face, which was glaring right back at him. "Wait," he said, smirking as understanding dawned. "You're jealous."

"Shut up," Erik shot back, too quickly.

"You're jealous because Ari likes *me*."

"I said shut up." Erik's face reddened with anger.

"Why? Because I'm right?"

Without warning, Erik's fist shot out and punched Theseus, his fist making solid contact squarely over his cheek.

Theseus reeled back, emotions surging through him. The pain brought memories to the surface, memories of similar bursts of pain brought on by fists. Only then, he had been scared. Now, he felt anger, but also a kind of exhilaration. He had been waiting for this moment without realizing it. Waiting for an excuse to fight Erik.

He threw himself forward, staying low, and landed a punch on Erik's nose. His fist came away bloody, but he thrust another punch into his gut. Erik doubled over, and Theseus' foot shot out, sweeping Erik's legs out from under him, and Erik hit the floor. Theseus looked up briefly, and his stomach dropped, all the fight going out of him at once. Theresa stood at the end of the hallway. She was staring at Theseus, face white, body rigid.

Theseus stepped back from Erik. "Mom," he said, not caring how frantic he sounded. "I'm sorry, it's not what-"

"Go to your room, Theseus," said Theresa in a low voice that he had not heard in a long time. "I will be there in a moment."

It did not occur to Theseus to disobey, simply because it was his *mother*. He went into his room and sat on the bed to wait. Erik had gotten up now. He was fine, other than his bleeding nose.

"Are you okay, Erik?" Theresa asked, though there was no sympathy in her voice.

Erik nodded, looking abashed.

"If I ever catch you fighting again-"

"What happened?" asked Mark, who had just joined Theresa.

"The boys were fighting," said Theresa, "It got physical."

"What?" Mark turned from looking at his son to glare into the room at Theseus.

"I will handle Theseus," said Theresa firmly. "Please take Erik and speak to him and help him clean up that blood."

Mark nodded curtly and motioned for Erik to follow him back toward the kitchen.

Theseus' heart was hammering as Theresa entered his room, closing the door behind her. A sick feeling entered his stomach, extinguishing the burning anger.

"Mom," said Theseus, trying to keep his voice level. "It wasn't what it looked like."

Theresa closed her eyes, "Do you know what it *looked* like, Theseus? Standing over Erik like that, do you know *who* you looked like?"

Theseus felt a tightness in his throat but forced it away. "I know, mom," he said quietly. "I'm sorry, but it wasn't like that, really."

"Oh? How was it any different?"

"He was provoking me," said Theseus desperately. "And he did this before I ever touched him." He pointed at his throbbing cheekbone, which he knew would soon turn into a black eye.

Theresa looked at him, then sighed. "He was wrong too, but you're the one who carried it too far."

"I wasn't thinking."

"I know, and that's the biggest problem." She sighed again, some of the cold rigidity leaking out of her as she came and sat down next to Theseus on his bed.

"Self-control, Theseus," she said. "It's the most important thing you need to learn."

Theseus' face burned with shame. "I'm sorry," he said again.

"Then prove it," said Theresa. "I know you don't get along with Erik, but you need to apologize."

"Okay."

"I don't even want to see another argument between you."

Theseus nodded silently.

"That's it, then," Theresa said. She sounded relieved, but she did not smile as she stood and left the room, or when she returned with an ice pack for Theseus' eye before leaving him alone.

Theseus did not move from his bed for a while. He hated Erik. Hated him for being suggestive about Ari, even though Theseus had taunted him about being jealous. One of the things that drew Theseus to Ari in the first place was the fact that she *didn't* look at him the way everyone else did. As childish as it sounded to him, Ari saw good in Theseus. Maybe it was just because she herself was so good, but it didn't matter, Theseus liked how it felt. Erik had questioned Ari's goodness, and even hinted that he might spread rumors about her at school. Theseus regretted getting carried away with Erik in front of Theresa, but he was not sorry for defending himself and Ari. He would not, no matter what, take a hit without fighting back. He had promised himself that a long time ago. The part he was sorry for was that if his mother hadn't come along, Theseus didn't know if he would have stopped. His mother had been right- without more self-control, he would be well on his way to becoming just like Silas Gray.

CHAPTER 13

Take My Breath Away - Berlin

Icarus pulled up to Solae's house feeling like his heart was in his throat. He took a deep breath and let it out slowly, still in disbelief that this was happening. He got out of the truck, taking the single rose he'd brought with him. It was golden yellow, the petals deepening to red at the tips. They were keeping things casual for this first date, but Icarus was ever the romantic. He would have given Solae all the flowers in the world if he could, but this one rose would do for now.

He rang the doorbell and after a few seconds, Solae opened the door. She was wearing a red corduroy overall dress over a thin black sweater, with tights and Dr. Martens. She looked like herself, but at the same time, more beautiful than Icarus had ever seen her before. Maybe that was partially the excitement.

"Hi," said Solae in a soft voice.

"Hi," said Icarus. He held out the rose, "Um, you look really nice. This is for you, by the way."

"Thank you," said Solae, smiling as she took the rose from him. "Here, come inside for a minute while I put this in some water."

Icarus stepped inside, and while he waited for Solae, it dawned on him that he had never actually been inside

Solae's house. There seemed to be quite a few windows letting the sunlight in, but ironically, the natural light gave a melancholic feeling to the place. It was lonesomely quiet, with the only noise being the faint drone of a TV coming from somewhere. Icarus could hear every step of Solae in the kitchen, every sound of her retrieving a glass vase, filling it with water, and setting it down on the counter. There were few decorative, homey touches to the house, giving it a bare and desolate feel. All this combined with what Solae said about her dad being distant made Icarus wonder if Solae felt lonely living here.

"Okay, I'm ready," said Solae, coming back from the kitchen and grabbing a small, purple drawstring purse from a hook in the entryway.

"Should I… say hi to your dad or something?" asked Icarus. It had dawned on him that he wasn't sure he had ever properly met the man.

Solae shook her head, "It's fine, I told him you were here. He's not really a people-person."

"Got it," said Icarus, still feeling a bit bewildered that he didn't at least want to meet the guy taking his daughter out.

"So," said Solae, "Where are we going?"

"I was thinking we'd do dinner," said Icarus as he opened the truck door for Solae, "You like Pizzaz, right?"

Solae nodded, Pizzaz was a local pizza restaurant. It was her favorite, as Icarus very well knew. There was an awkward quietness as Icarus got into the truck and started it, but he had prepared for this. "Want to listen to music?" he asked.

"Yes," said Solae, grateful for this conduit of relatability to grasp onto. "What do you have in the tape player?" she asked, reaching for the radio.

"Juicebox," said Icarus with a smile.

"Excellent," Solae said, and pushed play.

'Juicebox' was the name that the four of them had given the mixtape they had created together. It was full of all their favorite old songs, that for the most part were probably at the height of their popularity when their parents' generation was in high school. This mixtape was the very essence of what the friendship between all four of them was made of. It was extra meaningful to both Icarus and Solae, though; as the music enthusiasts of the group, they had been responsible for most of the composition of Juicebox. As for the name of the mix, neither of them could remember exactly where it came from, but it had gotten to the point that the name was inseparable from the music.

When Solae pressed play, a dreamy song by the artist Berlin started playing. It was the exact right thing they needed to cut the tension, and Icarus and Solae fell right into easy conversation about music the whole drive to the restaurant. However, when they made it to the restaurant, it was all awkwardness again. Whatever magic the music had brought was gone, and Icarus and Solae fumbled, tripping over each other's words. They split a pepperoni pizza, giving each other nervous grins between taking bites and making timid small talk.

Icarus was starting to panic. He tried to tell himself that first dates were *supposed* to be awkward, that this was all normal, that he wasn't immediately ruining everything.

Then, out of nowhere, Solae said, "Remember what Clio said about magic and Asphodel being like a Venn diagram?"

"Yeah," said Icarus, "What about it?"

"Well, haven't you done a lot of research on um, strange and unusual things that happen in Asphodel?"

Icarus nodded enthusiastically, grateful to have something else to latch onto at last. "Asphodel is a regular gold mine for urban legends and weird sightings."

Solae leaned forward and Icarus noticed that familiar, excited gleam in her eye that gave him a heart palpitation.

"Like what?" she asked.

Icarus began explaining all of Asphodel's local legends, or at least, the ones he had learned about so far. He started slowly at first, aware that not everyone was as interested in these things as he was, but Solae's rapt attention soon put him at ease, and he really began to dive in. Some legends were older than Asphodel itself, belonging to the Native American tribes that had been wiped out centuries ago. Some were from the time of cowboys or the Great Depression, and some were more modern, surfacing only within the last decade or so. One story in particular caught Solae's attention, regarding one of the old cemeteries downtown. The legend was that the cemetery was haunted by the ghosts of every person who had been buried there.

Sightings occurred from time to time, usually around the start of autumn.

"So, hypothetically," Solae began, eyeing Icarus in an almost apprehensive way, "If we were to go to the cemetery now…"

Icarus shrugged, "We'd have a statistically higher chance of experiencing a sighting."

Solae nodded, looking nonchalant, then sat back in her seat. She stared intently at the table, but Icarus could practically hear the hum of excited energy emanating from her being.

"Solae?" she looked up instantly, locking eyes with him. Icarus grinned, "Do you want to check out the cemetery?"

"Yes!" Solae burst out immediately, then paused, looking a bit sheepish. "Some first date that would be though, huh?"

"I think anywhere with you would make a good first date." Icarus knew it was an incredibly cheesy line as soon as he said it, and he half-expected Solae to roll her eyes, but instead, she looked away, face flushed, smiling shyly. Icarus didn't think he'd ever seen her react that way to something he said.

"So, cemetery?" he asked again, and Solae nodded.

Icarus paid the check, and they headed back to the truck, the exhilaration of it all carrying all the awkwardness from before away.

"I'm assuming this sudden interest in strange and unusual phenomena is because of *Reflections of Mythology*?" Icarus asked.

Solae nodded. She had to admit that when she hadn't been thinking about Icarus for the past few weeks, she was thinking about the impossible possibilities of what had happened to them in August. It wasn't a frenzy, but it was always in the back of her mind, turning over and over as she contemplated how this might be a chance to tap into something *more* than just normal life.

"I just… want to know what's possible," she said.

"Anything is possible," said Icarus.

"I guess that's true," said Solae.

They pulled up to the cemetery just as it was starting to get dark. Icarus backed into the parking space near the cemetery and opened the tailgate so they could sit and watch the cemetery. This cemetery had not been used in a very long time. It was so old that there was a historical marker sign outside the gate. In fact, the whole of downtown Asphodel deserved a historical marker sign. There was nothing that came close to resembling a skyscraper, just old shopfronts, a few of which still bore their original names, but most had been converted to antique shops or cafes like The Haunt. Parts of the streets were even still made from rust-red bricks.

"What exactly are we looking for?" Solae asked, excitement coursing through her veins as she sat next to Icarus on the tailgate.

"I'm not exactly sure," confessed Icarus, "I've never seen a ghost myself. The reports just say that they tend to appear after dark, especially during autumn." He turned his head to look at Solae, who was fixated on the gravestones behind the wrought-iron fence. Under the streetlight, she seemed to have an incandescent quality. He scooted slightly closer to her, so that their shoulders brushed against each other.

"I would have offered to take you sleuthing for this stuff sooner if I'd known you'd enjoy it this much," he said.

Solae laughed, "You should have."

"Yeah," said Icarus, her laugh was intoxicating. "I should have." He looked down, Solae's hand was splayed on the tailgate between them, her fingers looked impossibly delicate compared to his own. He took a deep breath, what if he held her hand? Just as he started to reach for it, though, Solae gasped.

"Icarus, look."

Startled, Icarus attempted to follow Solae's gaze into the cemetery, but he didn't see anything unusual. "What do you see?" he whispered.

"I'm not sure, it's- wait, there's another one!" she turned to him, eyes wide and shining, "Do you see them?"

Icarus' eyes scanned back and forth across the cemetery. "No," he said, but Solae sounded so sure, he didn't trust himself. "Where?" he asked.

This time, she took his hand and used it to point at an area of the cemetery that Icarus must have passed over. "Right there," she whispered.

Icarus squinted, what he thought was just mist was now faintly glowing and starting to take on the shape of people. His heart skipped a beat, though he couldn't tell if it was from what he was seeing or from Solae holding his hand. Icarus looked at Solae at the same time that she looked at him. What passed between them was the elusive but elated understanding that they were seeing something few others had seen, and even then, others probably would not have as much understanding of what they were looking at.

Icarus lowered his hand, but Solae did not let go. Their fingers became tentatively intertwined, sending a shiver down both of their spines. They sat and watched the spectral show before them for a while, and it soon became apparent that Solae could see the ghosts much more clearly than Icarus could, and she could see more of them.

"It would make sense if there were different degrees to how well people could see this kind of stuff, don't you think?" Icarus said, with a note of excitement in his voice.

"Maybe," said Solae slowly, "I guess that would explain why there are sightings, but no real evidence."

"Exactly."

"But why is there a difference between us? We both know about magic, we're both involved with *Reflections of Mythology*."

"I'm not sure," said Icarus, "Maybe you're just that special," he gave her hand a little squeeze.

Solae looked down at their clasped hands. She knew her hand was getting sweaty, but Icarus didn't seem to mind. Maybe his hand was sweaty too, she couldn't tell. She looked up again at Icarus. He was no longer staring into the cemetery, but at her. There was meaning in his gaze, and a lot of it. It tugged at her heart… too much, too fast.

"It's getting late," Solae said abruptly.

"Oh, I can take you home now if you want."

"Thank you. I don't want my dad to worry."

"Solae?" Icarus said tentatively, his expression changed to something gentler.

"Yes?" she said.

"Are you okay?"

"Yes," she said automatically. *Tell the truth,* she thought. "I really like this. I'm just scared of moving too fast."

He smiled, "Okay, how about this?"

She looked at him expectantly.

"You set the pace," said Icarus. "I'll follow your lead. I don't want to mess this up because of something that can be easily fixed."

"That's good of you." She was surprised by the amount of relief she felt at this suggestion.

Icarus shrugged, "Does it make you feel better?"

Solae nodded, "A lot better, thank you."

Icarus started to let go of her hand, but Solae held on.

When she got home that night, Solae's emotions were riding high both because of Icarus and because of the ghosts. The feeling of experiencing something nobody else did and the feeling of being with *him* mingled together until she could barely tell the two feelings apart. All she knew was that Icarus had opened her eyes to a new world, whatever that was, and she couldn't wait to experience it again.

CHAPTER 14

Everywhere – Fleetwood Mac

Ari got ready for school the next morning and walked out the door at exactly 7:30 to see Theseus' black Mustang pulled up to the curb. Trying not to smile quite as broadly as she wanted to, Ari got into the car. When she saw Theseus, however, the smile vanished completely.

"What happened to your eye?" she demanded, indicating the purple bruise at the top of his right cheekbone, encircling his eye.

Theseus blew out an exasperated breath as he started driving. "I may have had a slight altercation with Erik last night."

"Erik?" asked Ari in surprise. She knew that Theseus and his stepbrother were not fond of each other, but she thought they generally just avoided each other.

"Yeah," said Theseus, "And before you give me a hard time about it, I was defending your honor."

Ari stifled a laugh, "My honor?"

"He said something about you that he shouldn't have."

Part of Ari wanted to ask what, but she had a feeling that it would only make her feel bad. She already felt a little strange about it. Erik was in several of her classes, and he always seemed polite. Politer than Theseus was to most people, anyway. She watched Theseus as he drove, keeping his eyes on the road. She studied the bruise on his cheek. She had to admit to herself that the thought of someone fighting for her caused a flutter in her chest.

"Theseus?" Ari said.

He glanced at her out of the corner of his eye as they pulled into the school parking lot. "Yeah?"

"Please don't get in fights for me," she said. As Theseus put the car in park, he opened his mouth to protest, but Ari leaned forward and planted a light kiss on his bruised cheek. "I appreciate the gesture, though."

Before he could say anything else, before she started blushing, she popped open her car door and started walking toward Icarus and Solae, who had also ridden together in Icarus' truck. She dared to glance back over her shoulder and was struck to see that Theseus had gotten out of the car but was just leaning on the roof, staring after her. She quickly looked away, just as surprised by her own boldness as he was. Maybe channeling her older sister would actually get her somewhere.

The whole way to their first class, Ari grilled Solae about her date with Icarus. Solae was forthcoming, but not exactly about what Ari had been asking about.

"He took me to the historic cemetery downtown," said Solae excitedly.

"He- what?" Ari frowned. This was strange, even for Icarus.

"There have been a lot of ghost sightings there," said Solae, "We wanted to check it out. And we *saw* them." She smiled, eyes burning brightly.

"Whoa," said Ari, taken aback, unsure what to do with this information. "Like… actual ghosts?"

Solae nodded enthusiastically, "It was incredible."

"Cool…" said Ari. She supposed it was good that her two friends were both into researching this stuff, but one supernatural encounter at a time was good enough for her.

"So, what about Icarus? How did things go with him?"

A somewhat enamored grin came over Solae's face. "He held my hand," she said softly, "It was… magical."

Ari grinned, "More magical than the actual magic?"

Solae laughed, "I don't know, they might be tied."

"What about all that stuff you were feeling before?" Ari asked on a more serious note.

Solae looked thoughtful, "I still feel a little nervous, but I told Icarus, and he said we can take things as slow as I want." She sighed happily, "I really like him, Ari."

Ari grinned, "I better be your maid of honor."

The color drained from Solae's face, and she laughed nervously, "It's a little early to be making predictions like that," she said.

"Maybe," Ari mused teasingly, but she was distracted when she saw Erik, Theseus' stepbrother, enter the room sporting a busted lip. He caught Ari's eye, and a dark look came over him. Ari looked away quickly, a prickle of nausea in her stomach.

As much as they had all forgotten about *Reflections of Mythology* amid everything else, Icarus, Solae, Ari, and Theseus felt the book calling them back to the strange world of mythology that very day.

After school, Ari was retrieving her things from her locker when Erik materialized next to her.

"Ariadne," he said, his voice was conversational, but at the same time, it was as if there was something unpleasant beneath the surface. Ari's guard was immediately up; she and Erik hardly ever spoke. Now he was seeking her out after the fight with Theseus that had apparently started because of something Erik said about *her.*

"Hi, Erik," she said warily, not turning from her locker.

"I noticed Theseus gave you a ride to school today," he said.

Ari turned to look at him, "What about it?" she couldn't quite put her finger on it, but something about the way he said it made her nervous. His tone, body language, even just the fact of him talking to her right now.

"I just wanted to warn you about Theseus," Erik said, he took a step closer to her and Ari felt herself tense up involuntarily.

"Theseus has been my friend for two years now," she said, hoping her voice sounded firm.

"I don't know what he's told you," said Erik, "But he has a bad past," His tone was almost happy, like he was excited to tell her this.

Ari frowned, taking a step back from him. "I don't think you should be telling me this," she said.

"No, listen," he took another step closer. "Theseus is not who you think he is. I don't know what he told you about how he got that black eye-"

"He said he got it from a fight with you," said Ari coldly, "Because of something you said…"

She trailed off, suddenly feeling very strange, but it had nothing to do with how intimidated she felt by this conversation. It was like being light-headed, but the feeling was spread all over her body. She reached for the wall, but her hand met nothing where she expected to feel solid brick. The world was going in and out of focus. She looked at her hands and found that she could see right through them.

Erik did not notice that anything was amiss. He was still talking, though Ari couldn't hear anything but a ringing in her ears. He took *another* step towards her, but when Ari tried to step back, she stumbled, and accidentally backed into something solid. No, *someone* solid. She looked up, the world was right again, everything came back into focus. Theseus was standing directly behind her.

"Are you okay?" Theseus asked quietly.

"I'm not sure," Ari whispered back. In truth, she had no idea what had just happened.

Erik had drawn up short at the sight of Theseus, retreating the steps he had just advanced.

"Are you bothering her?" Theseus asked lightly, though his eyes looked dangerous.

"No," said Erik curtly, but he immediately turned and walked away.

"What happened?" Theseus asked when Erik was gone.

Ari, who was still getting her bearings, had never seen Theseus so serious. "I don't know," she said, a little shakily. "Erik came up to me and started talking, but then I started feeling weird, like I was… fading away."

As she said this, something tugged at the edge of her memory, but before she could decipher it, Theseus' face suddenly became very pale. He, like Ari had done only a few moments ago, swayed on his feet and reached for the wall to support himself. To Ari's horror, his hand seemed to go right through the surface of the wall. She realized that Theseus wasn't just pale, but *transparent.*

"Theseus!" Ari reached out and caught hold of his arm, and just like that, he was solid again.

"What was that?" he muttered, looking shaken, very un-Theseus-like.

"*Reflections of Mythology,*" Ari blurted, her memory clearing. "Clio said we'd feel it when it was time to go back. That must be what's happening."

Theseus groaned, "Right."

"We have to find Icarus and Solae."

"Yeah, and remind me to kill Icarus when we find him."

"We will not be doing that," said Ari with a flickering smile. "But your input is appreciated."

✳✳✳

Icarus was fading in and out of daydreams all day, so he almost didn't notice when the book began to call him back. He leaned his back against his truck, watching for Solae to come out of the school. He hadn't been able to stop thinking about her all day, unable to believe that their date the night before had really happened.

Then he saw her, walking out the doors, starting down the steps to the parking lot. He grinned and stood up straight, but as he did so he suddenly felt strangely light. His vision became blurry, he could no longer feel the solidness of the truck behind him. He met Solae's gaze and saw terror in her eyes and felt his own heart drop. He could see right through her, as if she were one of the ghosts they'd encountered the night before. Her foot went through the next stair she tried to step on, and Icarus threw himself forward even though he couldn't quite feel the ground beneath his own feet. Solae was falling, he had to catch her, even if just to soften the impact.

He made it to her just in time. Icarus reached out for her, and Solae reached for him. He took a wide stance, even though he wasn't sure it would help much in this state. But miraculously, as their hands touched, they both became solid again. Icarus felt Solae's full weight crash into him, but he was now able to stand firm and keep them both from toppling over.

Solae gasped, wrapping her arms around him tightly, "Thank you," she said, "I don't know what happened."

Icarus hugged her briefly before letting go, "I think I know," he said. "I think that was *Reflections of Mythology*."

Solae's eyes lit up, "We get to go back," she said excitedly, but then excitement turned to fear. "Icarus, you have to be careful-"

"You don't have to worry about me," Icarus said, taking her hand as they walked to the truck. "I have a feeling this time won't be when I fly. Besides, we need to find you in the mythology, you may have a terrible fate to avoid too."

Oh, I definitely do, Solae thought. She was still resolved to not tell Icarus about her role in this story, even though they were in a relationship now. She didn't need to burden him or make him feel like she had betrayed him, she just needed to work things out on her side. She did feel excitement alongside her anxiety about returning to the world of myth. She needed that thrill again, the thrill of experiencing magic. And maybe this time, she'd be able to learn more about it since it wouldn't be such a shock. She had been making a list of questions to ask Apollo ever since the last trip, since he seemed to have a special kind of knowledge about it all. She wanted to know how magic worked, she wanted to know *why* it existed, and... why could she apparently see more than Icarus?

"Icarus!" they turned at the sound of Theseus' voice shouting from somewhere behind them. They turned to look and saw Theseus approaching with a glare, Ari following close behind, looking shaken.

"You have got to get us out of this," Theseus demanded once they got close.

"I don't think I can," said Icarus, shocked at this hostility. He had thought Theseus had come to terms with the task they'd been given, but maybe being so jarringly pulled back in after not really having to think about it for such a long time had made him forget. "I'm sorry," Icarus said.

Theseus scoffed, turning away toward his car. "We'll meet you at the lighthouse," he said, "Come on, Ari."

Ari looked apologetic, but at the same time pleased that Theseus wanted her to ride with him.

Icarus and Solae looked at each other, "I guess we should go," Icarus said. He was quiet as they got into the truck and started following Theseus and Ari, one hand on the wheel and one draped over the center console. Following her instincts, Solae tentatively reached out and held his hand.

Icarus glanced at her with a slight smile but sighed. "I really am sorry for getting all of you roped into this."

"I'm not," said Solae. "As weird as it sounds, I'm glad we found this. I want *more*."

"It's a relief to hear you say that," said Icarus, "Because I'm kind of glad too. I guess that'll be our secret."

"Our secret," repeated Solae, feeling the butterflies come to life in her chest. She liked that thought. She wondered where this secret might take them. She pictured more excursions like the night before. The two of them seeking out all the strange phenomena they could find, all over the country, even the world. Untethered, secured only to each other and always moving on to the next adventure. She was surprised at her own line of thought, realizing that this was the first time she had ever pictured what her future might look like. The fears she had expressed when Icarus first asked her to be his girlfriend felt far away.

When they reached the lighthouse, Icarus led the way inside and picked up the unassuming *Reflections of Mythology*. He looked at each of them, taking in Solae's quiet eagerness, Ari's nervous determination, and Theseus' simmering indignation. He made eye contact with Theseus as he said, "Ready?"

Theseus held his gaze for a moment but didn't say a word. Just nodded. Icarus felt a pit in his stomach, as well as a twinge of his own anger. Theseus knew it was not his fault that they were in this situation. Besides, didn't the importance of what they were doing- saving this whole town- outweigh how they felt about it?

"Ready," both Ari and Solae said softly.

Icarus opened the book and began to *read*. Even though they were all expecting it this time, it was still impossible to tell exactly when reality melted away.

CHAPTER 15

Heroes – David Bowie

When Icarus 'woke up', he was already in Daedalus' workshop. He was helping Daedalus put the finishing touches on something large and feathery, and after a moment of getting his bearings, he realized that it must be one of the *wings*. A wooden frame, filled with wax and feathers. Such a contraption would never work in the real world, but here... where nothing made sense... it just might.

Suddenly Daedalus halted his work, frozen in fear. "They're coming," he whispered, and threw a sheet over the wing, just before the door to the workshop flew open and two guards stood in the doorway.

"Boy," said one of the guards, gesturing to Icarus, "Come with us."

Daedalus stepped a little in front of Icarus, "Why?" he demanded.

"King Minos requires an extra servant to attend his party. Do not try and stop us, old man."

Daedalus stepped aside, "Fine. It's not as if we have important work to do here," he grumbled.

Obediently, Icarus followed the guards, not wanting to cause any trouble. This part was not in the myths that he was familiar with, but he also knew that myths and legends were as fluid as water through the years. He took the opportunity to stare at his surroundings as he followed the guards. During the last trip, he had not had time to properly appreciate *where* he was. After all, even if he were to someday visit Greece and Crete, seeing the ruins would not be the same as seeing them in their prime, like this.

The guards took Icarus to the courtyard, a grand space open to the night air, hanging gardens surrounding it. Four long tables laden with food stretched the length of the courtyard, with guests reclining on both sides of all the tables. At the end of the room, a man who had to be King Minos lounged on a throne. He had an impressively long, dark beard and severe eyebrows; he looked nothing like Ari, who stood to the right of his throne, looking a little more done up than the last time, and a lot more nervous. On the other side of King Minos, stood Theseus, looking thoroughly bored.

Someone thrust a water pitcher into Icarus' hands, "Stand with the other servants," said a guard, pointing out a line of people dressed in similarly plain chitons and all holding various trays of food and drink pitchers.

Icarus hurried to get in line, just as King Minos began to speak.

✹✹✹

Ariadne found herself standing next to King Minos' throne as he began the feast. Theseus was standing on his other side, and Ari was relieved that he was not locked in the dungeon anymore.

"...to celebrate this *brave* hero," Minos was saying, gesturing to Theseus, voice laden with sarcasm. "Perhaps this young hero will finally conquer the beast in the labyrinth," he said, pausing for the court to titter among themselves. "But more likely, he will simply be the next Athenian sacrifice to keep the minotaur appeased for another year!" At that, the court broke out in ruckus laughter. "Whatever the outcome," Minos shouted, enjoying this reception immensely, "We applaud Theseus for his bravery with this farewell!" He gave Theseus a great clap on the back, and Theseus side-eyed him disdainfully but said nothing.

"Enjoy your feast!" said Minos, and immediately, the crowd followed his instructions, eating, drinking and all around enjoying themselves.

Ari saw Theseus pick his way through the crowd deliberately, making his way toward the back of the courtyard, away from everyone else. She also noticed that among the servants offering trays and pitchers to the partygoers was Icarus. She did not see Solae anywhere, though. She decided to round up the boys so they could all try to look for her.

First, she walked up to Icarus, who was pouring drinks for a group of men who all leered at Ari as she approached. It made her uncomfortable, especially because she stood out in her silky purple gown that had gold embroidery all over. She was also wearing lots of gold jewelry, which further indicated her status and jangled when she walked, much to her embarrassment. She had a feeling though that all these men *could* do was look with King Minos watching, which provided a slim bit of comfort.

"Icarus," she began, quietly enough so that only he could hear. "What's the plan to find Solae?"

Icarus looked around before replying, "I don't think we can," he whispered, "Everyone would notice if we left, and I don't even think I'm supposed to be talking to you right now."

Ari glanced around, and sure enough, everyone in their immediate surroundings was giving them weird looks. Why was the princess talking to a servant?

"Do you think it would be okay if I talked to Theseus?"

Icarus shrugged, "Probably. I mean, the party is for him."

"Right. Um, bye, then," said Ari, and she left Icarus to join Theseus in a far corner.

"Hi," she said when she approached.

"Hey," Theseus replied, taking in her fancier dress, all her jewelry, her hair, which had been curled and put in a half-up style with a gold headband. She was stunning in the candlelight. He himself was wearing a newer-looking chiton than last time, black, with a blue sash.

"Icarus thinks we can't leave to find Solae."

"I figured as much."

Ari studied him, his black eye was gone, it must be part of the illusion. She wondered if the things Minos said had gotten to him, but she knew he'd never admit it if they had.

"You're going to kill the minotaur," she said, "I know you will."

He shrugged, "Whatever happens, happens. I don't want to talk about it right now."

Maybe it was the soft candlelight. Maybe it was the fact that they wouldn't be going anywhere for who knows how long. Maybe, like it had been for Icarus, the impossibility of this situation was like a shot of courage to Ari. For whatever reason, she found herself opening her mouth to say, "Theseus, are you ever going to ask me out?"

Theseus looked at her sharply. He stared for a moment, and Ari was beginning to regret everything, when suddenly they heard a roar of anger, and both turned to the source–

A large man had pinned Icarus to a wall, gripping the front of his tunic. His pitcher of water lay broken and spilled on the floor.

"For the record," said Theseus quickly, "I'm not doing this for you."

Ari watched as Theseus swiftly approached Icarus and his attacker. Many of the other guests also turned to watch, excitement working its way through the crowd. Icarus was trying to talk the man down, but it did not appear to be working. The man seemed to be drunk and angered by something, perhaps he simply did not like the look of Icarus.

Theseus forced himself in between him and Icarus, shoving Icarus out of the man's grip. "Leave him alone," he said in an even, yet warning tone.

The man's fist clenched, he raised it, but Theseus grabbed his wrist before he even threw a punch.

"Don't try it," Theseus warned.

Another man came up behind the first one, "Better not, that's the champion. Hurt him and you might just end up being the sacrifice."

There was a tense moment, but then the man who attacked Icarus backed off, reluctantly turning away.

Theseus turned to face Icarus, "Are you good?"

Icarus nodded, "Thanks," he said. All the anger between them was gone. He didn't have time to say more since he had to get back to work, but Theseus seemed to understand.

Theseus made his way back to where Ari was standing. She was not sure if she was relieved or just more embarrassed when he didn't bring up what she had asked him just minutes before.

✳✳✳

Solae found herself in a forest clearing, not in the sky, as she expected. She looked around, she was still glowing, but it was much dimmer than the first time. She was not alone, though. She was standing next to Apollo, who was talking to a group of nine women who were all sitting on stones in a large circle formation.

There was something different about Apollo this time. Solae had to stare at him for a moment before she realized that the difference was that he looked more human. Less ethereal, with regular skin and hair that didn't float. Solae wondered why the change and felt a little annoyed because she had plenty of questions for Apollo that she had saved up over the months, but hadn't anticipated there being more people there. It was at that moment that Apollo finally took notice of her.

"Ah, Solae," he said, turning towards her. She noticed that his eyes were no longer glowing, although still very bright blue.

Solae glanced around the circle apprehensively, "Hello," she said politely.

The nine women, who all looked much more normal than Apollo, smiled at Solae welcomingly.

"This is my council," Apollo said as a way of introduction, "The nine Muses."

Solae raised her eyebrows, she had been rusty on her mythology when they had taken the first trip, but they had all brushed up on their knowledge since then. Solae had especially, though secretly, paid special attention to myths relating to Apollo. She now knew that the Muses were the supernatural sources of different kinds of inspiration and knowledge. She had to admit that she was excited to meet them; perhaps they could help her find the inspiration and passion she was still searching for.

"We come together every year," Apollo went on, "To discuss how we would like to influence the creative spirit of humanity."

"It will be especially interesting to have you in our midst," one of the Muses commented, "Apollo has told us about your circumstances."

Solae was a little annoyed at this, she did not like the idea of being talked about when she wasn't around, but she wasn't particularly surprised.

"But we want to hear more," another of the Muses piped up eagerly, "Tell us about yourself, young Solae, particularly your desires and passions. I can sense that there are a multitude of stories within you."

Solae looked to Apollo, but he only nodded. Resignedly, she stepped into the middle of the circle. She had the slightly bashful sensation one gets when asked to play an icebreaker with absolutely no heads-up.

"Where should I start?" she asked.

"Are you in love?" one of the Muses asked.

Solae did not expect to be hit with such a personal question right off the bat. "Um, maybe," she said, feeling flustered, "I'm going out with a boy, but we haven't really talked about 'love' or anything like that yet."

"But you have the look of love," the same Muse said gleefully, "You have such potential for a great love story."

"Or tragedy," piped up another, "I can already smell some tragic event on you, what was it?"

Solae frowned, becoming increasingly uncomfortable under this scrutiny. This was not at all what she would have imagined meeting the Muses to be like. But at the same time, she saw no reason to not be honest with them. What did it matter? She would probably not ever see these women again.

"My mother left when I was little," said Solae, "I guess I've carried that with me ever since."

The Muses all murmured at this, the one who had asked the question nodded understandingly, "Of course you have. And now, you fear that tragedy runs in your blood."

"Yeah... I guess," said Solae, resisting the urge to fidget. She had the uncomfortable feeling she was being psychoanalyzed, which seemed absurd given the people, the *beings* she was talking to. "I mean, I don't want to be like her."

They continued to sling their questions at her, while Apollo stood by, simply watching and not saying a word. Some of the questions were less invasive than the first two, while others got progressively deeper.

Finally, they seemed satisfied. "You have the potential for a great love story, great tragedy, or simply... *greatness*." they concluded.

"Just one?" Solae asked, "Why can't I have more than one?" she was thinking of her daydreams from earlier, about taking Icarus with her to embark on a quest in search of more magic. She had just started to believe she could have everything she wanted, but their words planted doubt in her mind.

One of the Muses shrugged, "You might, but it all depends on the choices you make."

"Like what?"

All nine of the Muses laughed, even Apollo cracked a small smile.

"Solae," said one of the Muses, the one who had asked her about love, "*We* cannot predict the future."

"Wait!" said Solae desperately, because everything was beginning to fade away again, but she hadn't been able to ask any of her own questions, "Wait, what do you mean?" But it was too late, and they were all gone once again.

CHAPTER 16

Ordinary World – Duran Duran

This time when they returned to the lighthouse, Solae felt that she could tell the others where she had been without giving too much away.

"You met the Muses?" Icarus asked incredulously, "*The* Muses? Actual goddesses?"

"That's just what some people call them," Solae said automatically, recalling what Apollo had told her the first time. "They're just incarnate forces of nature."

Icarus looked at her curiously.

"That's just what they told me," Solae said quickly.

"So, if you were with the Muses," Ari said, "What does that make you in this story?" She seemed eager to talk about Solae, Solae had noticed that Ari was specifically not looking at Theseus ever since they got back.

Solae hesitated, then said very carefully, "They just called me by my name. But I don't think there are any 'Solaes' in Greek mythology."

"No kidding," said Theseus.

"What about you guys?" Solae said quickly.

"They threw me a party," Theseus said dryly, "Before they send me off to my doom."

Now Ari looked at him, a quick, furtive glance full of concern.

"Things really seem to be speeding up, huh," Icarus said quietly.

They gathered a load of books for Icarus' truck mostly in silence, everything feeling way more somber than their last venture into mythology. After they dropped the books off at The Book Loft, they split ways. Icarus took Solae home, while Theseus and Ari went to pick up Ari's car.

"I still can't believe you met the Muses," said Icarus as they drove.

"Yeah," said Solae absentmindedly. She was turning what the Muses had said to her over and over in her mind. *Great love, great tragedy, or simply greatness.* They said 'or.' Why did it have to be 'or?' Why couldn't she have love, *and* greatness? Maybe they were wrong. After all, did anything from that world matter in this one?

"Icarus?" she said tentatively.

Icarus smiled at the sound of her voice saying his name. "Yeah?" He reached over and held her hand as she spoke.

"Where do you think you'll end up?"

"What do you mean?"

"After college and everything. Do you ever think about getting out of Asphodel? Doing something bigger?"

"I mean, I'm going to go to an Ivy League school," said Icarus, "That's pretty big, I think."

"Yes, but I mean after college," said Solae.

Icarus contemplated this for a moment. Solae studied the little line that appeared between his brows when he took on a thoughtful expression.

"I've never really thought of living outside of Asphodel, if I'm being honest," Icarus said finally.

"Really?" asked Solae, half surprised, but at the same time, half expecting this answer. "You want to go to a big school like that just to come back *here*?"

"Yeah, I mean I grew up here, my parents too. And, after all this, who knows what else we could find here?"

"Maybe," said Solae, and it was at this moment that the difference between them became apparent to her. Solae needed to go out and find something, while Icarus was content to find wonder wherever he was already.

✳✳✳

The whole ride to the garage, Ari didn't know what to say to Theseus. They had been cut off before he could respond to Ari's bold question while they were in the world of mythology.

When Theseus spoke for the first time, Ari's heart leapt, but he only said, "Something's off about Solae in *Reflections of Mythology*."

"Oh," said Ari, surprised, a little disappointed, but also relieved that he hadn't brought up the obvious yet. "Why do you think so?"

Theseus shrugged, "It just doesn't make any sense. It's weird that her story doesn't line up with the rest of ours. I think she's not telling us something."

Ari frowned, "You think she's lying to us?"

"I mean, I wouldn't necessarily call it that. More like she's just leaving something out."

Ari still didn't like that idea. Solae was her best friend, and the implication that she was keeping something from Ari, something that they were all involved in, something so important as saving their home, rubbed her the wrong way.

"I don't think Solae would do that," she said firmly.

Theseus exhaled in a way that might have been a sigh, and Ari couldn't help but think he must be laughing at her in his mind. She must seem so naive in his eyes, and maybe it was more than just about Solae. Maybe she had been reading him wrong this whole time when she thought there must have been some chemistry between the two of them. What must he think of her? He hadn't even acknowledged her question and now was the perfect opportunity. Maybe he was just willing her to ignore it too, so that they could pretend it never happened, and save her from embarrassment. If that were the case, Ari supposed she should be grateful he wasn't teasing her about it, but instead, she felt a prickle of annoyance. Anger, even. Why wouldn't he dignify her with a response? Didn't she at least deserve to have him turn her down directly, instead of acting like she never said anything at all?

They made it to the garage, Theseus parked next to Ari's car, turned off the Mustang, then went inside to retrieve Ari's key. Ari waited for him next to her car with its newly repaired tire, silently simmering in her indignation. When he returned from inside the shop, Ari didn't even wait for him to offer her the key.

She marched right up to Theseus and said, "Look, I'm sorry if I assumed too much, or embarrassed you or whatever. I thought there was something there- clearly, I was wrong. You could have at least *said* you weren't interested, though."

Theseus stared at her dumbly, eyes wide with surprise at this outburst. His hand was open, her keys lying in his palm, frozen just before he offered them to her.

Ari snatched her purple sparkly keychain out of his hand, "Thanks for the help with the car," she said, trying not to sound too begrudging about that part at least, and turned on her heel to her own car, getting in and starting it up as tears began to sting her eyes.

There was a knock on her window, and Ari looked up to see Theseus, bent down at her level and gesturing for her to roll down her window. Ari wiped her eyes quickly, face burning, and rolled down the window, not sure what to expect.

"Look, I'm not so good with saying stuff like this, I thought you knew that," he said, and it was the first time Ari had ever seen him looking awkward, the cool facade gone momentarily.

"Oh," she said, taken aback, suddenly ashamed for accusing him when he simply hadn't known how to let her down. "I–I'm sorry," she said but trailed off at the sight of the intensity in his eyes.

They stared at each other for a moment, and Ari felt like something was about to happen, but she didn't quite feel real. Then Theseus leaned in, and Ari forced herself to stay still as he gave her a quick, gentle kiss. It was nothing like what she had imagined, but at the same time, *exactly* like she imagined.

Theseus pulled away, "I thought maybe that... would say it better than I can."

Ari nodded, feeling blissfully dazed. "I think you made your point," she said quietly.

Theseus grinned, all cavalier once again. "So, how does Friday sound?"

"Friday?" Ari repeated, confused.

He cocked his head to one side, "You asked if I was ever going to ask you out. Are you free Friday?"

"Oh!" Ari exclaimed, once again hoping he didn't think she was completely clueless. "Sorry, yes. That sounds… perfect."

"Good," said Theseus. He stood up straight and tapped on the edge of her car window before he walked away. "See you later, Ariadne."

"Bye," said Ari, and fumbled to roll up her window and back out of the driveway while still appearing somewhat collected.

Theseus watched her drive away before getting back in his own car. He was not quite sure what had made him respond to Ari the way he did, with a *kiss*. He had definitely thought about it before, more times than he cared to admit, but her question at Minos' party had caught him off guard. In all honesty, he wasn't sure if he ever would have made a move if Ari hadn't first. She deserved better than him, and he knew it. She deserved a prince or a knight. White horse, shining armor, and all. The whole ride here he had been trying to come up with a way to respond, torn between saying that he wouldn't be able to give her what she deserved, and the fact that she was sitting in his passenger seat, looking like she always did- *angelic*. Maybe he had planned the kiss, subconsciously. And then she had been telling him off, burning like a bright flame right in front of him, and it was then that all his inhibitions left him because she was glorious and good, and he just had to have her.

And now... he'd done it. Maybe it was a bad idea, or maybe, he could just keep pretending to be good enough and it would eventually come true. He allowed himself a smirk as he arrived home and saw Erik taking the trash down to the curb. One thing was for sure, this would drive him *crazy*.

CHAPTER 17

Head Over Heels - Tears For Fears

No matter how uncomfortable Icarus was with the idea of discussing dating with his parents at first, he had to tell them pretty quickly that he and Solae were going out. Then, of course, his parents insisted that they had to have Solae over for dinner. Icarus had managed to put it off longer than he had expected with excuses about how the school year had just started, they had a lot of homework, or already had plans. Icarus wasn't even totally sure why he *was* avoiding it. It wasn't that he was embarrassed by his parents, exactly. They had met Solae before, although after picking Solae up from her house, he wondered if she would feel uncomfortable seeing his house full of sunshine and care when hers spoke of neglect.

The thought occurred to him that maybe he was worried about what his parents might think of Solae. But that couldn't be right either. Aside from the fact that thought had never crossed his mind in the first place, he couldn't think of a single reason why anyone would object to Solae anyway. Sure, she had that alternative, whimsical style about her that didn't exactly jive with his parent's *Better Homes and Gardens* lifestyle, but his parents weren't the type to have prejudices based on someone's looks. They cared more about what a person was 'made of' and where they planned on going or what they planned on doing. But Solae had applied to Ivy League schools, just like Icarus, plus she was going to be named valedictorian.

Whatever it was, eventually Icarus couldn't put off dinner any longer. One Friday night, Solae accompanied Icarus home from school. She had accepted the invitation gracefully, eagerly even, which made Icarus feel a bit better about the whole thing.

In truth, Solae herself *was* excited about having dinner with Icarus' family. She had met them a handful of times when the whole group of them had hung out at Icarus' house, but she didn't really *know* them. If she was brutally honest with herself, she was a bit jealous of Icarus. His family was whole and unbroken, something she only barely remembered having.

Icarus' mother, Tyra, greeted them with a plate of cookies when they arrived at the house. "Just don't eat too many," she said, "Eli is grilling hamburgers for dinner."

"Thank you," Solae said as she and Icarus sat down at the bar to enjoy their cookies.

"So, Solae," Tyra began as she busied herself with prepping potatoes for homemade french fries. "Icarus tells me you're an excellent student, do you have any hobbies?"

"Um," Solae said, unused to small-talking with adults. *Hobbies?* Solae racked her brain. Ever since the start of their mystic quest, Solae had been spending all her free time researching Greek Mythology and all things strange and unusual in general, except for when she was on dates with Icarus. And even then, more than half of their dates consisted of the same thing.

"I like reading," she said finally, which was true, even though she wasn't as passionate as Icarus. Before becoming consumed with this more serious research, Solae often lost herself in the pages of some literary fiction book.

Tyra smiled, "Just like Icarus. is that what got the two of you together?"

"Mom," Icarus protested.

"What?" Tyra said, "You haven't told us much about it, I've got a right to be curious." She turned back to Solae, who laughed in spite of herself. "You should see his book collection. I swear, every time I go up there to dust, it seems like he's added more. It's his own personal library."

"Oh, really?" Solae said, turning to Icarus, whose ears had flushed with the embarrassment of being talked about. "You've been holding out on me."

He grinned, "Do you want to see them?"

"Sure."

Icarus glanced at his mother for approval, and Tyra nodded. "Just keep the door open," she said.

"*Mom!*"

Tyra waved her hand in dismissal, "Shoo, when your father gets home, he'll start on the burgers, we're eating on the patio tonight."

Solae followed Icarus up the narrow staircase to his bedroom. He opened the door and gestured inside with a flourish.

"Ta-da," he said.

Solae smiled as she stepped into the room, because it was exactly like Icarus. Wooden bookshelves covered every wall except for a space for his bed, with a wooden desk right next to it. A large corkboard hung over the desk, covered in photos, newspaper clippings, and sticky notes, with red string connecting some of the items in a charming way. The little bit of wall that was visible in between all the bookshelves was painted a warm, mottled beige. His bed was simple and covered in a warm, rustic-looking quilt, probably handmade, maybe even by his mother.

Icarus crossed the room to his desk and turned on the lamp, adding to the light streaming in from the window above the bed and bathing the room in a cozy glow.

"Nice room," said Solae as she began running her finger over the many titles on Icarus' shelves. "You really *have* been holding out on me."

"My apologies," said Icarus, sidling up next to her, "You are welcome to check out a book from my library anytime."

As Solae selected a volume from the shelf to peruse, Icarus reached out and caught a strand of her hair, twirling it around his finger. Solae felt a shiver course down her spine.

"I'm glad you're here," Icarus said softly.

Solae swallowed, her pulse thumping hard. "Me too." She turned from the shelf to face Icarus, keeping the book she had selected clutched to her chest, a barrier between the two of them.

Icarus let go of her hair and instead ran a thumb softly against Solae's cheek. "You're so beautiful, Sol."

Heat rushed to Solae's cheeks and she smiled weakly. "Thank you," she said, unsure how else to react.

Then, Icarus began to lean in closer, and Solae realized he was trying to kiss her. Without really thinking about what she was doing, Solae thrust the book into Icarus' chest, keeping him at bay.

Her mouth was dry, her heart pounding, her palms sweating. "Icarus," she whispered, it was all she could say, but she hoped she could communicate what she was feeling in her tone, even when she didn't fully know herself what she was feeling.

Icarus blinked, and Solae expected him to look hurt and storm out of the room, maybe even ask her to leave, forget dinner. She lowered the book, opened her mouth to apologize, but Icarus spoke instead.

"I'm sorry," he said, "I didn't mean to... I shouldn't have done that."

"It's okay, I'm sorry I'm so weird about it."

"You're not," Icarus said, "It's perfectly sensible."

Solae laughed, "You sound so old-fashioned."

"What can I say?" Icarus said, "I try to be chivalrous."

They heard the sound of a door downstairs, "That's probably my dad," Icarus said. "Hey, thanks for putting up with them. I know they can be a little intimidating."

"What? Your parents?" Solae said, "Who told you that?"

Icarus shrugged, "Theseus."

Solae nodded in understanding; Theseus wasn't really a 'meet the parents' type. They headed back downstairs, the sound and smell of potatoes frying in oil greeted them, and Solae's stomach began to growl.

Icarus' dad, Eli, was setting his bag down in his office and then returned to the kitchen to greet his wife with a peck on the lips. Solae vaguely wondered if she would be more comfortable with the idea of showing affection if she had grown up in a house seeing her parents be affectionate with each other.

It didn't take long for the food to be ready, and soon they were all four sitting out on the patio assembling their hamburgers.

"So, Solae," Eli began, "Icarus mentioned that you have also applied for the Ivy Leagues, which schools in particular?"

"Harvard, Brown, and uh, Princeton," Solae replied, counting them off her fingers.

"All great schools," said Eli, nodding approvingly, "I myself went to MIT. Did either of your parents attend any of those schools?"

"Well," Solae said, and Icarus saw her begin to fidget nervously. "My mom went to Princeton, actually."

"Oh! I've never met your mom, what does she do?" asked Tyra.

"Um," Solae said, scrambling for a response, and now Icarus knew why. His own mind began searching for a way to change the subject without seeming too obvious.

"She was a historian," said Solae.

"Was...?" Tyra said, covering her mouth, "Oh Solae, I'm so sorry-"

"No, no," Solae said quickly, "She didn't die, she's just... not around." Her face was bright red, and she was staring fixedly at the table.

"Oh dear," said Tyra softly.

Eli cleared his throat, perhaps feeling guilty for bringing up this sore subject. "Which college are you hoping to get into?" Icarus was grateful he had caught on quickly.

"Princeton, I think," said Solae, finally looking up again.

"Same one as me," said Icarus, grinning at her.

Tyra made a sound of approval, "Your father and I went to the same college, that's where we met actually, we took our engagement photos at the same time as graduation photos."

Solae looked surprised, "You got married while you were still in college?"

"Right after," said Eli, "Although if Tyra had her way..."

"Wow," said Solae with a laugh.

"Yes, we were young, but we knew we were ready."

"We figured, we know what we want, why wait to get the rest of our lives started?"

"Makes sense," Solae muttered. She couldn't help but glance at Icarus, but looked away as soon as she caught his eye. She wasn't exactly sure why, but she was beginning to get a sick, constricting feeling in her stomach, which only increased as the night went on.

At nine o'clock sharp, after Tyra had served them all slices of spice cake, Eli suggested that Icarus go ahead and take Solae home, 'so her father wouldn't worry.'

The whole drive, Solae was turning the evening over and over in her head trying to figure out *why* it felt off. Sure, when the subject of her mother had come up it had thrown her for a loop, but it had been more than that. Between Icarus' attempt to kiss her and getting a glimpse into his family, she felt as though she had a better idea of what Icarus expected out of life, and out of their relationship. And then after the last mythology trip... he'd said that he couldn't see himself ever leaving Asphodel. She thought of her first shining imagining of the future- untethered, moving from place to place, searching for magic. She'd thought that she would be able to take Icarus with her on that adventure, but she was quickly learning that life might not be possible with him. They clearly wanted very different things out of life, and she was beginning to see there was even a disparity between their feelings for each other. Perhaps the Muses had been right after all. Perhaps she did indeed have to choose between great love, great tragedy, or simply, greatness.

CHAPTER 18

Friday I'm In Love - The Cure

Persie was eager to help Ari prepare for her first date with Theseus, insisting on being a part of everything from helping her pick out an outfit to doing her hair and makeup.

"It's just a casual date," Ari protested as she was sat down at Persie's own vanity table in her room and Persie began to heat up a curling iron.

"Fine, fine," Persie said, "I promise it won't be too much, just trust the process. Getting ready is half the fun of a date."

"What?" Ari giggled.

"You need to sort out your priorities, Pers," came Cal's voice from the doorway to the bedroom.

Ari tried to look toward her oldest sister, but Persie wrapped a hand around her chin and turned her face back toward herself, brandishing a makeup brush in the other hand.

"And you're sure this guy is responsible? You don't think you should meet him in your own car?" Cal asked, trying for a light tone, but Ari could hear the underlying, big-sisterly concern.

"Come on, Cal, he's the one who helped me out when my car broke down, he drove me to school and everything."

"And is he responsible... otherwise?"

"Um, what?"

"He's not going to get you into any kind of trouble, is he?"

Ari thought back to Theseus' black eye and the way he had kissed her the last time she'd seen him. She had conveniently left the part about the black eye out when she had told her sisters about Theseus finally asking her out.

"He won't," she said, "I trust him." It was true. While Theseus may have been rough around the edges, especially when left to his own devices, Ari trusted that he had the best intentions. If nothing else, he would respect her if she asked him not to do something.

"Stop worrying Cal," Persie said as she applied a subtle, shimmery shadow to Ari's closed eyes. "Ari isn't a little kid anymore and she's known this guy for years now. If she thought he was no good, she wouldn't have wanted to go out with him in the first place."

Ari was touched, "I think that's the nicest thing you've ever said about me," she said.

"Yeah, yeah, shut up and pucker up," said Persie as she uncapped a rosy lipstick.

When Persie had finished with her, Ari gasped at the result in the mirror. The makeup wasn't overdone, but instead highlighted her features softly and her hair looked normal except for a slight curl at the ends. The chunky pink sweater and denim skirt she was wearing had come from her own closet, but Ari herself would have never thought to put them together like this. She spun around and gave Persie a hug.

"Thank you!"

"Alright, alright! Of course I was going to help, you clearly didn't know what you were doing." Persie managed to extricate herself from the embrace, "Okay, enough, you're going to mess up your hair."

The sound of a car horn carried from outside, and Ari dashed down the hallway to the front door, grabbing her purse on the way. Cal and Persie followed her and stood in the doorway as Ari walked, heart skipping, to Theseus' black Mustang.

"Hey," said Ari when she got in the car, but Theseus was staring at Cal and Persie, who were still watching from the front door. They waved when they saw that Theseus was looking at them.

"Should I be worried about them?" he asked warily.

"Only if you're intending to kidnap me or something nefarious like that," Ari said cheerfully as she buckled her seatbelt.

Theseus shot her a bewildered look and she inclined her head, as if it were obvious, "They're getting a good look at your car in case they need to track you down and make it so that nobody ever hears from you again, obviously."

Theseus smiled, "Ariadne, you never cease to surprise me." And with that, he put the car in reverse and, with a two-fingered salute at Ari's sisters, backed out of the driveway.

"So," Ari said, smoothing her skirt out to give her hands something to do. "Where are we going?"

"Did you know there's a drive-in movie theater just outside of town?" Theseus asked.

Ari shook her head, surprised, because it was rare, if not unheard of for Theseus to know something about Asphodel that she, Icarus, or Solae didn't know about. They had lived here their whole lives, and he had only been here a few years.

"They're showing *The Mummy* tonight," he said.

"I've never seen it," Ari confessed, then smiled when Theseus whipped his head around to look at her incredulously.

"You're kidding. You? The girl who has mandatory movie nights every Friday? That's why I picked this activity, you know."

"Sorry," Ari said, shrugging, "It's been on the list for years, just never at the top."

"Well, you're going to love it," Theseus said, "If you don't, this will have been a resounding failure."

"I'll hold you to that," Ari said.

The drive-in movie theater was about thirty minutes away, on the outskirts of town. There was an open field, probably farmland once upon a time, with a big, white screen set up to play the movie on, an operating booth, and even a little concession stand. Ari was surprised at how many people were there, unaware that there were still hidden gems to be found within Asphodel. Theseus got them popcorn and a soda to share, he acted so overwhelmingly chivalrous the entire time, Ari began to wonder if this really was Theseus she was on a date with.

At one point during the movie, through unspoken mutual agreement, they began holding hands. Ari found it slightly difficult to focus entirely on the movie, unable to stop herself from regularly glancing over at Theseus or down at their clasped hands, just to make sure this was all really happening. When the movie was over, Theseus started driving back into town.

"Where are we going?" Ari asked.

"You'll see," Theseus said cryptically.

They finally parked when they got downtown, Theseus got out of the car and went around to open Ari's door.

"I thought we could discuss the movie over ice cream," he said, gesturing toward the local ice cream shop, Clover Creamery, down the street.

Ari couldn't help but laugh as she got out of the car, "You really planned all this?"

Theseus raised an eyebrow, "What, you didn't think I was capable?"

"No, of course not, it's just... really nice."

He shrugged, "This is nothing, really. If we were in New York, I'd really show you a good time. This is just the best I could do with such a podunk little town like Asphodel."

"Hey, it's *my* podunk little town, so watch it, mister," Ari said, poking him in the chest reprimandingly.

"Oh yeah?" Theseus said, catching her hand in his, "What are you gonna do about it?"

Ari saw that familiar intense look in his eyes, which made her want to look away. But she held her ground and held his gaze. "I don't know yet, but you'll regret crossing me."

His gaze flickered down to her lips for a brief moment before he met her eyes again. "Would I regret kissing you?"

"What?" Ari breathed, a flutter in her voice.

"I want to kiss you again."

"O-okay. I would like that."

Theseus drew her in by the hand he was still holding and kissed her. This time, it was *more* than that first kiss. She had no other words for it. When they pulled away, Theseus was grinning ear to ear they started walking toward the ice cream shop, and Ari couldn't stop herself from just staring at that smile, knowing she'd kiss him again just to see it.

The downtown was a nice area to walk around, all old-fashioned streetlights and red-brick roads made it feel like something right out of a romcom. They decided to eat inside the ice cream shop before continuing walking around downtown. Theseus got cookie dough ice cream, Ari got mint-chip.

Theseus felt like he had momentarily stepped into another life; one where he didn't necessarily have to always have his guard up. Here he was, *he* of all people, the unlucky kid from New York, on a date with possibly the nicest girl in this small town. It felt like a mistake, like he had cheated somehow to get this outcome, or that it was all too good to be true and the rug was bound to be pulled out from under him. Whatever it was, Theseus wasn't complaining. If this was a fluke, he intended to enjoy every second of however long it lasted.

Almost as if the universe heard his thoughts, they walked out of the ice cream shop and nearly crashed into someone walking in.

"Sorry!" Ari started to say, but when she saw who it was, she tensed up noticeably.

"Erik," said Theseus, "What are you doing here?"

"What, I'm not allowed to get ice cream?" Erik's gaze flitted down to Ari and Theseus' clasped hands, "I see you didn't take my advice."

"What are you talking about?" Theseus demanded.

"Ari knows what I'm talking about," Erik said breezily.

"You know what, Erik?" Ari said, and Theseus was taken aback by the chill in her voice. "If I wanted your opinion on who to date, I would have asked. Leave us alone."

A smile spread across Erik's face, but Theseus was well-acquainted with the look of loathing in his eyes. "Fine," he said, and allowed Theseus and Ari to step past him.

Theseus grinned at the incensed look on Ari's face as they walked away. He had only glimpsed this side of her once before, when she confronted him about asking her out. It didn't exactly conflict with the Ari he knew, but it was a change from her normally cheerful demeanor.

Ari looked at him, "Why are you smiling like that?"

"Because it's funny to see you like this. I don't think I've ever seen you angry before."

Ari's hard gaze softened, "I'm sorry, I didn't mean to get so worked up."

"It's not bad," Theseus said quickly, "Erik was being a jerk to you, it was... *righteous* anger."

Ari squinted at him, "You just like seeing someone else give him a hard time."

Theseus shrugged, "That *is* a perk."

They returned to Theseus' car and began to leisurely drive, having reluctantly decided that it was probably time for Ari to go home, when suddenly a silver Corolla pulled alongside them at a stoplight. Theseus recognized the car instantly as belonging to Erik.

Ari glanced out of her window at the car and gasped, "What is he doing?"

Theseus scoffed, "He thinks he can race me," he said. "In *that* car. It's not even a manual."

Ari quickly turned to face him, "Please don't race him," she said.

Theseus tightened his grip on the clutch. "It wouldn't even really be racing," he said. He was itching to further humiliate Erik. The idea of whatever 'advice' he might have given Ari was eating at him, and this would be so easy. Really, he didn't know what Erik was thinking. Theseus would win no matter what. Then it hit him, and he loosened his grip on the clutch. There had to be a cop nearby, and Erik was just trying to get him caught.

He sighed, "I won't race him," he said.

"Thank you," Ari said.

But when the light changed and they went through the intersection, Erik suddenly sped up and got directly in front of Theseus and Ari.

Ari found herself clutching her seatbelt, heartbeat beginning to speed up, though not in a good way like at the beginning of the date.

"Theseus..." she whispered warningly.

"He's trying to provoke me," Theseus muttered through grit teeth, "But it won't–"

Before Theseus could even finish his sentence, he cut himself off as he slammed on the brakes, causing them to screech horribly. It wasn't enough. Erik came to a sudden stop directly in front of them. Ari couldn't stop herself from screaming as the car was suddenly much too close, and then came the impact. The horrible crunching of metal, the force of it pitching Ari forward against her seat belt so hard that she thought it would cut into her skin, then she was flung right back against her seat, so hard that her head immediately began to ache. Then, as quickly as it happened, it was over.

Ari could barely breathe, she was convinced that something else was going to happen, that her name would be in the newspaper the next day, just like her parents' names had been four years ago. She was going to die. Right here, the same way they did. She clawed at the seatbelt, but it was no use. Her chest hurt, her head hurt, and she was becoming lightheaded. Then, out of the fog, Theseus was there. He was leaning across the center console, unbuckling her seatbelt, gently taking her by the hands.

"Ari? Ari, listen to me, are you okay?"

Ari managed to focus on him for a moment and gave her head the briefest of shakes. She was trembling all over, and while she may not have sustained any serious injuries, the looming sense of death still hovered over her.

Grim realization dawned on Theseus. "Okay, what about physically? Any broken bones?"

The sound of his voice was slowly helping to bring Ari back to her senses. "I-I don't think so," she managed.

Theseus nodded, "Alright, let's get out of here."

He got out of the car and walked around to the passenger side, giving the crunched bumpers the briefest of glances on his way. The damage didn't seem to be too severe, but that was not his main concern at the moment. Erik had also gotten out of his car and had a phone to his ear. He stared Theseus down as he made his way to Ari's door.

He helped Ari out of the car, trying to assess her for any injuries that might have gone unnoticed before. He didn't see anything, but Ari was pale and shaking; Theseus knew what kind of memories this must be stirring up. He took off his bomber jacket and held it out to her.

"Put this on," he instructed, and though she stared blankly at it for a moment, she put it on over her sweater.

Having something to do, even momentarily, seemed to further help in grounding Ari. She took a deep, shuddering breath once the jacket was on. "Thank you," she said, "Are you okay?"

"I'm fine," Theseus said. He knew that there would probably be some bruising from the seatbelt, and he would be sore tomorrow, but that was still fine. "What do *you* need?"

"Um," Ari said, looking lost and helpless. "I think... I should call Cal."

"Okay," Theseus nodded, "Go ahead."

"What about the police?"

"I think Erik is handling that," Theseus said bitterly, "But don't worry about it. Call your sister."

Ari pulled her cell phone from her pocket and dialed the number. After a moment, she said "Cal? Hey, um, we… there was a wreck." She flinched at the response, though Theseus couldn't hear what Cal was saying, then continued hurriedly, "No, everyone's fine, nobody got hurt. I'm *fine*. It was just a minor one, but… can you come pick me up?" Her voice had started to waiver, and Theseus looked at the ground as Ari gave Cal their location.

Erik hung up his phone and walked over to inspect the collision with interest. Theseus felt white-hot hatred boiling over inside of him, but he forced himself to wait. He could *not* act now, not with cops on the way. Besides, Ari needed him. As soon as Ari hung up, she burst into tears. Theseus didn't know what to do, but at the same time, he found himself automatically wrapping Ari against himself in a hug, letting her bury her face in his chest and shielding her from the world with his arms.

"I'm sorry," Ari sobbed.

"It's not your fault," Theseus said. "You just need to get home. *I'm* sorry." And he really was. Sorry Ari was being put through this, sorry for his part in causing it, sorry that he had brought her here, to this moment, sorry that he had ever had the misfortune to gain a stepbrother in Erik. *He* was to blame for this, Theseus thought to himself, as sirens sounded in the distance, getting closer. Finally, a police car pulled up behind the two cars.

Theseus grimaced, "I've got to go deal with this, okay?" he said to Ari, stepping back from her.

Ari just nodded, still too much in shock to speak. She wasn't crying anymore as she watched the officer talk to Theseus and Erik while she stood on the median, still wearing Theseus' jacket. She wondered what would happen now. Would any of them get in trouble for this? Evidently not, as it only took a few minutes before the officer took his leave of them and got back in his car. Just as he was driving away though, Cal pulled up alongside them in her car.

Both Cal and Persie leaped from the car and hurried over to her. Cal was white-faced and tense as she took Ari by the shoulders and studied her intently, "Are you okay? What happened?"

"I'm fine," Ari managed, "Probably just a little bruising from the seatbelt is all. The airbags didn't even go off."

"Where is *he*?" demanded Persie, looking around. She spotted Theseus, who was walking back towards them and pointed an accusing lime-green fingernail at him. "How did this happen? What did you do?"

"Persie, no–" Ari began, but Persie waved her off.

Theseus waited until he was standing next to Ari to speak.

"All I did," he said, more calmly than Ari expected, "Was brake. The car in front of us came to a sudden stop, there was nothing I could do."

"That's not good enough–" Began Persie.

"It's not his fault!" Ari burst in.

Cal held up a hand to quiet both of them. "Pers, calm down," she said, then turned to Theseus, "Regardless of *how* it happened, if you want to keep dating our sister, you will not be allowed to drive her. Clear?"

Theseus hesitated, but ultimately nodded, "That's completely fair."

Ari glanced over at Erik and momentarily, all her fear vanished, replaced by anger. He was barely concealing a smile. He really had done this on purpose, simply because he was jealous.

"Let's go home," Cal said.

"One second," Ari said, through grit teeth.

She marched right up to Erik. He raised his eyebrows at her approach and opened his mouth to say something. Before he could get a word out, Ari drew back her hand and slapped Erik in the face with a resounding SMACK.

She heard Persie gasp. Cal said "Ariadne!" but Ari ignored both of them.

"Stop being such a selfish jerk before you get someone killed," she said to Erik, and although there was a tremor in her voice, it was low and dangerous-sounding.

Erik glared at her with watery eyes and one hand against his cheek, but Ari saw a new emotion behind the glare- fear. With grim satisfaction, she realized that she was certain he would not bother her again.

She turned and walked back to Cal, Persie, and Theseus. "We can go," she said to Cal, then looked at Theseus. "Sorry," she mumbled again, suddenly too mortified by the whole situation to speak. This was *not* how first dates were supposed to go. She almost wondered if he would bolt after this, taking the wreck as a bad omen.

Theseus shook his head, "You have nothing to be sorry for."

Ari nodded jerkily, then started to take off his jacket, but Theseus put his hand over hers and stopped her. "You can hang onto it," he said, with the barest hint of a smile. "I'll see you later."

Even though they were not the same as parents, Ari would have felt awkward kissing him goodbye in front of her sisters, but it didn't really feel right to kiss him right now anyway. Theseus seemed to intuit this because he just gave her hand a brief squeeze before letting go and walking back to the Mustang.

"Bye," Ari said softly and followed Cal and Persie back to their car. On the drive home, she toyed with the jacket zipper, keeping her mind off the road and imagining it was actually Theseus's arms wrapped around her like he had in the immediate aftermath.

Theseus waited until Ari and her sisters had driven away before he went back to his car, his beautiful car, and allowed himself to fully take in the damage. He ran a hand through his hair. It wasn't *too* bad, he knew he could fix it himself at the shop. What angered him more was how hell-bent Erik was on ruining things for him with Ari, how he had hurt her to get to Theseus. But he knew that he himself had some guilt in this too. Erik was trying to provoke him, because he had always gotten a rise out of Theseus before. This had to stop.

He turned around and was slightly surprised to see Erik still standing there.

"Get out of here," Theseus said, though there was no heat in his voice. "And leave both of us alone."

"What, no fight from you?" Erik spat.

"No," Theseus said, "You're not worth it." And with that, he turned to get into his car.

"It won't last," Erik called after him, "She's too good for you."

Theseus paused as he opened the door to the Mustang, "I know."

CHAPTER 19

Winter Time - Steve Miller Band

Both Ari and Theseus were traveling with their families for the holidays. The Darnell sisters went to visit their grandparents in Colorado, while Theseus and his family went back to New York to see various friends and relatives. This left Icarus and Solae with extra time to themselves. They spent nearly every day together, split between researching Greek Mythology and taking excursions to investigate unusual activity in Asphodel. Sometimes, they were delighted to find that rumors of the paranormal were connected to actual magic, but other explorations were not so fruitful. It was a thrilling mixed bag of hoaxes and true magic. Either way, Solae thought it gave a new meaning to the most magical time of the year. It almost made her forget her worries about her and Icarus' possibly diverging futures entirely.

On Christmas Eve, Solae and Icarus found themselves treading carefully through a patch of woods off Asphodel's main park. They were chasing down rumors about fairy activity, and while they were not entirely sure what they were looking for, they had enough experience by this point that they were confident they'd know it when they saw it. A light blanket of snow had fallen the night before, adding to the magical atmosphere.

Icarus, however, was distracted from the search, as he often was on these occasions. He kept looking over at

Solae, thinking that *she* could be a fairy herself. She was wearing a mulberry-colored corduroy jacket that she had embroidered with little white starbursts on the pockets. She had a navy-blue beret jauntily perched on her head and her short hair was tucked behind her ears, showing off her constellation of dainty silver earrings. Whenever the sunlight hit her hair directly it caught natural highlights, warm amber among her dark tresses. There was a merry twinkle in her eyes that Icarus had become familiar with on these adventures of theirs. She could easily be taken for an impish yet beautiful winter guardian of the forest.

Solae caught him looking at her, "What?" she whispered, but he could hear her perfectly with the snow muffling the world around them.

"Nothing," Icarus said quickly, though he couldn't help but smile.

Solae smiled back and shook her head good-naturedly before turning her attention back to the search. Then, she stopped in her tracks, crouching behind a tree and motioning for Icarus to join her.

"This has to be it," she said excitedly once Icarus was sitting next to her.

Icarus peered around the tree, following Solae's gaze to a small clearing up ahead. There was one spot where there was no snow on the ground: a perfect circle of startlingly green grass with a perfect ring of stones around the perimeter. They had stumbled upon a textbook fairy ring.

'Now is the moment,' thought Icarus, reaching into his inside coat pocket. "Merry Christmas, Sol," he said, holding out a small square package in Christmas wrapping paper.

Solae turned to him in surprise, "Oh, but I left your gift in the car."

"That's okay," said Icarus, "Your gift is just, uh, particularly applicable at this moment."

"Alright then." Solae took the carefully wrapped package from him and unwrapped it just as carefully, glancing at the fairy ring intermittently to see if anything was happening.

"Oh, Icarus," she said when she unveiled the black Polaroid camera he had found in a vintage store.

"I already put in a roll of film," Icarus said, "All you have to do is start taking pictures."

"Thank you," said Solae, her smile so bright he wondered that the snow around them didn't melt. "I love it."

Out of the corner of his eye, Icarus saw something sparkling. He looked over at the fairy ring and felt a jolt of excitement. "Now's your chance," he told Solae, gently guiding her hands to point the camera at the colorful, twinkling lights hovering over the fairy ring that had been vacant only moments before.

Solae gasped in delight, fumbling to hold the viewfinder up to her eye.

"They're beautiful," she said, snapping a picture. "Can you see their wings?"

"No," said Icarus, "Just little lights."

"I wonder…" Solae murmured, looking down at the camera as the printer began to whirr. "I wonder what will show up in the photos."

"I guess we're about to find out," said Icarus.

The camera spit out a blank white photo, and Solae held it against her coat to shield it from the light as it developed. After a couple of minutes, she held it out for Icarus to see. To Icarus' amazement, the photo did not only depict the colorful lights he could see with his own eyes, but within each light was a tiny person. They all had iridescent wings and wore clothes made from leaves and winter flowers.

"This is what you see?" Icarus asked, and Solae nodded in confirmation. "Wow, that's incredible."

"I know," Solae said, "They're amazing."

"Can I try something?" Icarus asked, suddenly getting an idea.

"Sure," said Solae, handing him the camera.

Icarus looked at the fairies through the viewfinder, but he could still only see the dancing colorful lights. He snapped another photo as an experiment, but when it developed it did not show fairies in their human forms like he had hoped. It was just blurry, colored lights.

"That's what you see?" Solae asked.

"Yeah," said Icarus, "I thought the camera would be a neutral party."

"Weird."

"But this is perfect," Icarus continued, "Because any photo you take will turn out the way you see it." He gestured at the photo Solae had taken.

"Yeah," Solae said, and as she watched the fairies, her eyes drifted out of focus and into her signature daydream look. "I could go around looking for magic, and document it."

"You could write a book," Icarus suggested.

Solae's heart skipped a beat at that suggestion. "You think so?"

"I'd read it."

Solae laughed, "You read anything."

Icarus shrugged, "Seriously though, you should. You have an eye for this stuff, literally."

"Maybe," Solae said, but then she frowned. "But you introduced me to this world, I never would have found out about magic without you."

This felt very important to say, giving credit where credit was due. Solae had been daydreaming about chasing magic wherever it might lead her for a long time now. Ever since their first date, Solae felt like magic was intertwined with the excitement of her relationship with Icarus. He had been chasing it first, after all. Being with him was synonymous with the thrill that encountering magic always gave her. But the fact that she was able to see more magic than Icarus, the fact that writing a book was *his* suggestion… it almost felt like she was stealing the magic from him.

"Are you sure *you* don't want to write a book?" she asked tentatively.

"I don't know," Icarus said, "For me, this is just a hobby. Besides, the fact that you can see it more clearly means you'd have a better perspective."

That made Solae's sudden feeling of guilt dissipate and her mind began to go a mile a minute. Magic was so much more than a hobby to her; writing a book could be the way for her to turn it into a livelihood if she played her cards right. She realized that this camera, this revelation, was the best Christmas present she had ever received. In a sudden burst of excitement, she threw her arms around Icarus in a hug.

"Thank you, Icarus," she said earnestly.

"Um, you're welcome," said Icarus with a bewildered laugh, forgetting to be quiet.

The fairies spooked at the sound, flying around in a frenzy and then disappearing as suddenly as they had appeared.

"Ah, I'm sorry, that was stupid," said Icarus.

"It's okay," said Solae, holding up the two photos. "We have records now."

CHAPTER 20

Girls Just Want to Have Fun - Cyndi Lauper

When the Darnell sisters returned from their Christmas trip, preparations for their annual New Year's Eve party began immediately. These parties were known among the sisters' respective circles to be memorable and seemingly extravagant, even though they created all the decorations and themed elements themselves, crafty as they all were. This year, the theme was 'Stars'. Everyone was expected to dress up as Hollywood movie stars. Cal was dressed as Clara Bow with accurate-looking 1920s hair and makeup, Persie had cut her own bangs specially to be Nicole Kidman from *Practical Magic*, and Ari dress as Judy Garland in *The Wizard of Oz*, complete with ruby slippers she had crafted herself using thrifted heels and red sequins.

By the time Icarus, Solae, and Theseus arrived together, most of Cal and Persie's college and work friends were already there, bringing the party into full swing. And swinging it was.

Upon entering the house, Icarus' ears were met with the sounds of laughter and mirth. People sat around card tables playing games, gathered in the living room to reminisce, or stood around the punch bowl and snack trays in the kitchen. As always, Icarus was impressed by how over the top the sisters had gone with their decorations. Garlands of hand-made paper stars were strung from the ceiling, classic movie posters lined the walls, there was even a cardboard copy of the "HOLLYWOOD" sign mounted over the TV, which played iconic films quietly in the background of the party. All the guests only added to the ambiance in their movie costumes. Characters such as Marilyn Monroe, Charlie Chaplin, and even more modern figures such as Heath Ledger and Drew Barrymore were all in attendance.

Ari threw her arms around Solae in the entryway, "You look incredible!" she cried, and Icarus heartily agreed. Solae was dressed as Audrey Hepburn from *Breakfast At Tiffany's*, clad in a simple black dress and adorned in faux diamond jewelry, even a tiara. She was born for the role and pulled it off magnificently.

"Holly Golightly and Indiana Jones," mused Ari, turning to inspect Icarus' costume- all khaki, with the unmistakable iconic leather jacket and hat. "What an unlikely pair."

"No more than Dorothy and Maverick," said Icarus, gesturing at Theseus. His costume was simple compared to the others, just his normal jeans and t-shirt, but with a cheap replica of the distinct jacket worn by Tom Cruise in *Top Gun,* and aviator sunglasses tucked in the collar for good measure. Theseus was immediately recognizable, despite the costume's simplicity, due to his natural swagger.

Ari looked at Theseus appraisingly, "You're lucky you got this much of a costume," he said warningly.

"I wasn't going to say anything!" Ari protested, she gave him a kiss on the cheek, "I think you look great."

That comment, or maybe it was simply the kiss Ari gave him, got a smile out of Theseus and he draped an arm around her shoulders. "Come on, let's get some snacks."

Icarus took Solae's hand as they followed Ari and Theseus, weaving through the crowd to the kitchen.

Persie was manning the punch bowl and gave Theseus a sidelong glance when they approached. "Moved on to wrecking planes now, have we?"

"Be nice," Ari said, taking two glasses of punch for herself and Theseus.

"Fine," Persie said, and nodded approvingly at Icarus and Solae's costumes, "Classic," she said.

After getting their snacks, the four of them troupe upstairs to their *real* party, in Ari's bedroom, away from the noise so that they could actually talk. It was their custom to spend most of their time at these parties in this manner, all of them preferring their own small gathering to the crowd. They went out to the little outdoor balcony attached to the bedroom and sat in a circle, still close enough to hear the party chatter in the background and feel the cool wintery air. It was cold enough to warrant blankets, but not enough to be uncomfortable. They were like their own little Algonquin Round Table, sitting and talking about life, the universe, and everything.

When the subject inevitably came around to their mythical quest, Theseus nudged Ari. "You should have made this a toga party, then we'd all feel right at home."

"Technically, it would have to be a chiton party," said Icarus.

"Whatever, genius."

"It's been longer than last time, hasn't it?" Solae said, "In between trips, I mean."

"Yeah," said Icarus, picking up on why Solae would bring this up; he knew that she was not ready to say goodbye to these magical excursions yet, even though they still had no idea where she fit into all of it. "Clio said that it would be longer in between every trip, though. I don't think it's anything to worry about."

"How will we know when we're done?" Ari asked.

"I mean, the stories have endings," Icarus said.

"Do you think there will be any noticeable effect on Asphodel?"

"Well," Icarus said with a glance at Solae. He had been thinking about this and knew she would not like it. "It's like Clio said- the tear in reality is the reason Asphodel is the way it is. If we're 'sewing it up', I assume all the paranormal activity will go away."

Solae did not say anything, but Icarus could detect a sadness radiating from her. Perhaps she had already thought about this too. It was a bittersweet thought, on the one hand, it would save the town. On the other, it felt like a tragedy that they had just discovered this unbelievable thing, their wonderful adventures finding magic in all the little corners of Asphodel, only to put the lid on it, tighter than before.

"I'll be glad when it's over," Theseus said, "We have enough to worry about without this whole 'saving the world' shtick."

"But glad it happened, too?" Ari said, but Theseus only shrugged.

They continued talking lazily and comfortably until they ran out of snacks and found they wanted more. They made the pilgrimage down the stairs, it was already 11:30, thirty minutes away from the start of a new year. Icarus's mind wandered as he brought up the rear of the group, wondering how many more occasions they would all spend like this, before graduation, before he and Solae went off to college far from here. He thought about returning here on holidays and after college, how someday they would all gather together again, maybe at their own house, maybe with children of their own who could be friends like they were. It was like looking back on childhood with nostalgia, but the longing for it was different. Looking back on the past, Icarus knew he could not ever have that again, but looking toward the future was a promise of possibilities. He and Solae, Ari and Theseus, if they were so lucky. This happiness could just extend and expand far beyond what it was now.

"Icarus?" Solae's voice disrupted him from his thoughts, and he looked at her, standing right in front of him. The light was catching her sparkly jewelry just right, and her dark doe-eyes glittered as if there were diamonds in them as well. He wanted to take a picture of her in this moment with his mind, this was quite possibly the most beautiful moment he'd ever seen her in.

He completely missed the next thing she said. "What?" he asked, shaking his head, "Sorry, I was distracted."

Solae gave him a funny look, and Icarus felt that she must have some idea of what he had been thinking. He suddenly felt uncomfortably warm. "Ari wants to get a group picture," she said.

"Oh, yeah," Icarus said, "Sure."

"Are you okay?"

"Yeah," Icarus said with a smile, "Just... thinking about how good things are, and how good the future will be."

Solae laughed unexpectedly, and Icarus thought it almost sounded like a nervous laugh, but he wasn't sure why that would be. He must be tired.

"Come on, enough with the sappy stuff!" Theseus called after them.

He and Ari were waiting for them in the photo backdrop that Persie had created to look like a red carpet with a backdrop of silver stars.

"Sorry!" Icarus said, taking Solae's hand as they joined their friends.

Cal was waiting with a camera as they got into position. Ari and Solae stood in the middle, with the boys on either side of them. On impulse, Icarus wrapped his arms around Solae and rested his chin on her shoulder in a playful pose.

She responded by holding onto his hands with one of hers and using the other to link arms with Ari. In turn, Ari wrapped an arm around Theseus' neck and pulled him in close so that his face was next to hers. They all smiled, and in the moment of that camera flash, Icarus didn't think he'd ever smiled so genuinely for a picture before.

They stayed down in the middle of the party to wait for midnight, Cal turned on the TV so that they could all watch the ball drop.

"You'll be my first New Year's kiss," Ari told Theseus.

"I'll do my best to live up to the expectation," he said.

Icarus glanced at Solae, he had thought about the possibility of kissing her at midnight, but that one time up in his room remained the only time either of them had attempted a kiss. Icarus said he would follow Solae's lead, and he knew that meant he would wait, and if she wanted to kiss him, she would. He supposed he could ask her, but he figured that would only make her feel pressured. He wanted their first kiss to be because she *wanted* to. He did not want to risk moving too fast for her, he'd almost blown it once already. Solae did not meet Icarus' eye; she was deep in conversation with Ari now. Theseus made eye contact with him, however, and winked. Icarus waved him off.

Finally, the countdown started, and they all joined in.

"10!"

Icarus wondered if Solae knew he was okay with it if she didn't want to kiss.

"9!"

He should make sure she knew.

"8!"

He took both of her hands in his.

"7!"

She turned to look at him, a searching look in her eye.

"6... 5!"

He leaned in and whispered in her ear.

"4... 3!"

He pulled back, she looked confused for a moment.

"2!"

Then realization dawned and she gave him the biggest smile.

"1!"

She threw her arms around his neck and hugged him fiercely, just as everyone shouted, "HAPPY NEW YEAR!"

Out of the corner of his eye, Icarus saw Theseus and Ari engage in a kiss, but he did not care. He had made Solae happy, and that was more than enough for him.

CHAPTER 21

Carry on Wayward Son - Kansas

After the New Year, Theresa began marking the days off on a calendar in anticipation of her brother coming to visit. Theseus took a peek at the calendar once and found that the circled date on which his mysterious uncle would appear was February 15th. He still had a feeling that there must be some other purpose besides simply coming to catch up with them. He did not have to wonder what this might be for very long, though.

Ari's birthday was on February 14th, the irony of which was not lost on Theseus. He had asked Ari if she wanted to celebrate both Valentine's Day and her birthday, but she had said that she just always thought of her birthday as 'Valentine-themed' anyway. He was supposed to go over to her house that evening with Icarus and Solae for a small party. Theseus had just gotten home from picking up Ari's present when Theresa came into his bedroom.

"Do you have a minute?" she asked.

Theseus knew that tone; it was the one his mother always adopted for having a serious conversation. It was gentle but stern.

"Sure," said Theseus, setting the bag with Ari's gift down. He still had several hours until the party.

Theresa sat on Theseus' bed, and he was uncomfortably reminded of the night he'd fought Erik. Other than the car accident, there had been no other incidents between them. That couldn't be what she wanted to discuss.

"I wanted to talk to you about your Uncle Jack," said Theresa.

Theseus sat down in his desk chair across the room, intrigued. "What about him?"

"You know what he does?" she began, a little questioningly.

"Captain of a research ship?"

Theresa nodded, "Well, an opportunity has opened up. Every few years, Jack takes on an apprentice, to teach the trade to. Usually, a recent high school graduate. We were thinking since you aren't interested in college-"

"You want me to do the apprenticeship?" surmised Theseus.

"We think it would be a really good opportunity for you," Theresa said, smiling.

"Who's 'we'?" Theseus demanded, though he already knew.

"Well, Jack let me know about it before we made the final arrangements to visit, and Mark and I discussed it-"

"So, you all just decided this without ever asking me?"

Theresa was no longer smiling, she looked resigned. "Nothing is final yet," she said, "Obviously, you have to decide you want to do it. Nobody is forcing you. However, I don't see why you wouldn't."

"What's that supposed to mean?"

Theresa paused; she looked like she was contemplating how to put something. "Theseus, there's no other way to say it. You have shown absolutely no initiative for making any plans after you graduate. You're barely going to graduate in the first place You *need* this, what will you do otherwise?"

"I don't know," said Theseus, he was angry, without really knowing why. Hurt, too, that his mother was trying to send him away without telling him until the *day before* his uncle showed up. "Why didn't you ask me about this before? You said you knew about it before school even started."

"I wanted to wait and see if you had any plans of your own," said Theresa, "I have put this off until the last possible moment. I don't know exactly why, maybe because I knew this is how you would react to it."

Theseus made a derisive noise. He didn't know what else to say, because deep down he knew she was right. He *hadn't* made any plans.

"You *need* this, Theseus," said Theresa again firmly, "I won't make you, but you don't have any other options."

"Except to end up like Dad," Theseus burst out. "That's why you want me to do this, isn't it? You think I'm going to be like him."

Theresa's face was like stone. He didn't know why he'd expected it to soften at the mention of Silas Gray. They had never spoken of him directly before, the man who had made their lives a living hell for twelve years, the man who Theseus resembled so closely. They had danced around the subject, made veiled references, but never brought him up like this in the years since.

Theresa stood up and walked across the room to Theseus. He remained seated, staring at the floor, but she cupped his face in her hand, turning it upwards to face her.

"I don't think you *are* like him," she said, "I have done my best to raise you so that you are nothing like your father. I want to give you every opportunity to be better than him, and better than me. That is why I want you to do this. Right now, you are not going down a path that will help you get there, but this- going with Jack- I *know* it will."

She dropped her hand from Theseus' face, but he didn't say anything. He didn't know how he felt.

"You can think about it, and then talk to Jack about it when he gets here. I think you might actually enjoy it if you give it a chance."

"Okay," Theseus said quietly, "I'll think about it."

Theresa smiled again, hopeful. "I have to go now, I'm meeting Mark for dinner. Have fun at the party, I love you." she ruffled his hair affectionately before walking out of the room.

"Love you too," Theseus mumbled.

As soon as she was gone, Theseus was hit with the overwhelming feeling of being alone. *'You can think about it'* she said, *'Nobody is forcing you.'* It wasn't true, though. He already knew that as much as he hated the fact that she was effectively sending him away, he would end up saying yes. Because his mother was right; Theseus had no other plans, other than to get out of Asphodel. The idea of being *sent* away with a practical stranger, though, grated at him, especially when he still couldn't make sense of his faint, tangled memories associated with this man.

He went out to his car, almost without thinking about what he was doing. His movements were mechanical as he retrieved the contraband bottle of vodka from under his seat in the car. There was still plenty of time before Ari's birthday party, he just had to take the edge off his emotions that were threatening to boil over. He could not go and be around his friends and his girlfriend in this condition. All he needed was one swig. He unscrewed the cap off the bottle and tipped it back.

CHAPTER 22

Heart Of Glass - Blondie

Birthdays were always a special occasion in the Darnell house, but ever since their parents' passing, the three sisters had put in extra effort for each other. However, unlike the New Year's Eve party, Ari's party was to be an intimate affair, with only her sisters and her three best friends in attendance.

Theseus did not show up with Icarus and Solae at Ari's house at 6:00 that evening. Of course, he was usually late, but Ari couldn't help but be a little disappointed when he wasn't standing there with the others when she opened the door. It struck her as odd, not because Theseus had a long history of showing up on time, but because ever since they had started going out, he always showed up on time for *her*. But she quickly dismissed this; it wasn't unreasonable for him to be a few minutes late.

6:30 came and went. 7:00 came and went. Ari tried not to show just how disappointed she was. Maybe it was too much to ask that he be on time for her birthday. Maybe she had told him the wrong time by mistake. She had Cal hold off on the cake, wanting, hoping that he would show up and explain that circumstances beyond his control were to blame.

Icarus, who had known Ari well enough to see past her fronts, could tell that Theseus' absence was really starting to bother her. He leaned over and whispered to Solae, "I'm going to go call him."

Solae nodded, looking a bit grim.

Icarus went out to the front porch, took out his cell phone, and dialed Theseus' number.

Theseus picked up after three rings. "Heyyy, Icarus!" His voice was uncharacteristically enthusiastic.

Icarus pinched the bridge of his nose, dread and exasperation mingling in his tone. "Theseus, *please* tell me you're not drunk."

"Oh no, I've just had a little bit. Had to clear my head, y'know, after what happened."

"What happened? Are... are you okay?"

"M'fine," Theseus said, and Icarus could practically smell the alcohol through the phone. "My mom just finally told me the *real* reason my uncle is coming." He paused, "Aren't you gonna ask-"

"Why is he coming, Theseus?" Icarus sighed.

"My mom wants to send me away with him," Theseus said, almost in a triumphant tone.

"What?"

"Yeah, she doesn't want me around anymore. I think I remind her too much of m'dad, so she wants good ol' Uncle Jack to knock some sense into me."

Icarus felt a sickening feeling in the pit of his stomach. "She can't force you-"

"Nah, nah, she's not," Theseus said. "She just said it would be 'a good opportunity' for me, but I can tell she really wants me to go. Be his apprentice, get my life together or whatever."

"I mean, that doesn't sound too bad," Icarus said. *Except that you'll be gone, you won't be here anymore,* he thought to himself, but he pushed that down. Theseus didn't need that right now.

"She's just so good," Theseus said, "It used to just be us, and I was supposed to turn out like her. But everyone's right... I'm just Silas Gray, 2.0."

"Oh, c'mon Theseus," Icarus said, dismayed. He doubted Theseus would ever be this vulnerable when sober.

"Ah! Look at the time," Theseus said suddenly, "I'm late for Ari's party, I didn't realize... I thought I had more time. I'll just head over now."

"No," Icarus said quickly, "You can't see her when you're wasted like this. You can't drive, anyway."

"But she's gonna be so upset!"

"It's a little too late for that, buddy." Icarus almost laughed in spite of himself. "You can apologize later. I'll tell her you can't make it, go sleep it off."

"Icarus wait," Theseus said, sounding more serious than he had for the entire call. "I-I didn't mean to get... please don't tell Ari what happened."

Icarus was quiet for a second. His love for each of his friends weighed on either side of his internal balance. Ari deserved to know the truth, but maybe Theseus deserved to tell her himself.

"That's your responsibility," he said finally, "She should hear it from you."

"Thanks, Icarus, I owe you."

"Just get some rest. And… Theseus?"

"Yeah?"

"Don't do this to her again."

"You got it, chief," Theseus said, and hung up.

Icarus took a deep breath and let it out slowly. He was certain that Theseus wouldn't normally share everything he had, and he wasn't sure what would happen when he sobered up. Right now, though, Icarus knew he needed to be there for Ari. He couldn't do anything for Theseus right now.

He went back inside and saw Ari sitting in his spot next to Solae on the couch, both of them whispering. Solae looked up when Icarus walked in.

"Everything okay?"

Icarus shrugged.

"Is Theseus alright?" Ari asked, turning to face him.

"Um, well, he's not going to make it tonight… a family thing came up."

Ari seemed to dim a little, "Oh."

"He feels really bad about it. I'm sure he'll make it up to you."

"That's okay," Ari said, always absorbing the impact, acting like everything was fine.

It was then that Cal and Persie entered the room, bearing a cake with lavender frosting and covered in silver stars, with eighteen lit candles on top. Persie carried a small box wrapped with a bow. They set the cake down on the coffee table in front of Ari, and everyone started singing 'Happy Birthday.' Ari smiled through the song, but Icarus knew his childhood friend too well to be fooled. No matter what she might say, he knew Theseus' absence was hurting her. Her smile had a fragility to it, in the way a still pond is like glass; only a small disturbance would cause the whole surface to ripple and shatter.

When the song was over, Cal looked around. "Where's Theseus? I thought I heard the door."

"He couldn't make it," Ari said quickly, "Something came up, but it's okay."

Cal and Persie exchanged a quick glance but said nothing about it.

The gift from Ari's sisters turned out to be a gold necklace, from which hung a pendant of amethyst in the shape of a dainty flower. Ari gasped when she opened it.

"We figured you should have your first piece of grown-up jewelry now that you're eighteen," Persie said.

"Like yours," said Ari, sounding slightly choked up, "From Mom and Dad."

Solae and Icarus exchanged confused glances, unsure if they were intruding on an intimate family moment.

Cal, however, noticed their discomfort, and slipped a ring with a ruby setting off her finger and showed it to them. "When I turned eighteen, our parents gave me this ring set with my birthstone. It kind of started a tradition."

Persie tucked her hair behind her ears to show off earrings set with emeralds. "Of course, we had to continue the tradition with Ari."

"That's really special," Solae said, knowing how much this must mean to Ari.

"It is," said Ari softly, eyes shining. "I love it, thank you." She stood up and reached out, embracing both of her sisters at the same time.

Unconsciously, Solae and Icarus scooted closer to each other, lowering their gazes. Not so much from awkwardness, but because they wanted to step back from this special moment. Neither of them had siblings, but they understood that Cal and Persie were more than sisters to her. They were her whole family.

After the cake, the party of five played games until Icarus went home for the night. Solae had planned to spend the night. They turned on Ari's favorite movie, *Ever After*. At one point, Solae looked over at Ari and saw silent tears running down her cheeks. But by the end of the movie, Ari had fallen asleep on Solae's shoulder.

In the morning, Solae and Ari ate French toast made by Cal before Ari was supposed to take Solae home. When they opened the front door to go out to the bug, however, Solae paused.

"You have a visitor," she said, a slightly distasteful look on her face.

Ari came up behind Solae and peered over her shoulder. Theseus was standing on the porch, looking like he had just been about to knock on the door. He held a bouquet of multicolored daisies and a pink gift bag in one hand.

"Should I give you a minute?" asked Solae, "Or do you want me to get rid of him?"

Ari grinned as Theseus looked slightly alarmed at the last statement. "I'll talk to him," she said, "Do you mind waiting inside?"

Solae nodded, and retreated into the house, Ari stepped out onto the porch, closing the door behind her.

Theseus looked awful; his eyes were bloodshot, and his skin had an unhealthy gray tinge. He had a particularly clammy look about him as well.

"I guess it's obvious I came here to apologize," he said, not looking her in the eye.

"Icarus said you had a family emergency," said Ari, folding her arms. She had a feeling that wasn't the whole story, that Icarus had oversimplified whatever had really kept Theseus from showing up last night so that his friend could explain himself. It was a very Icarus thing to do.

Theseus let out a breath slowly, "In a manner of speaking," he said. "There was some family stuff, and I didn't handle it particularly well. *That's* why I couldn't come last night. I'm sorry."

Ari stared at him, searching. Why wouldn't he just come out and say it? She could see it written all over his face, that there was something else that he wasn't telling her. She wanted to know; didn't she have a right to know?

"Family stuff?" she repeated, questioning.

Theseus sighed, "Yeah, my uncle's coming to town, there's just a lot going on with that. I really don't want to talk about it."

"O-okay," Ari said, somewhat reluctantly, but unwilling to push him in case it would push him away completely. Though she didn't have all the pieces, she knew that there was something in Theseus' life, something in his past, that hurt him. She had tried to forget it for Theseus' sake, but the comment Erik had made to her that one time resurfaced in her mind. *'I don't know what he's told you… he has a bad past.'* Theseus had not told her anything about his past. She wanted to know, she wanted to understand him, but knew better than to ask. Maybe she could be the one he opened up to, the one who could help him, if she let him come to her with it in his own time.

She smiled, extending forgiveness without saying a word. He smiled back at her tentatively.

"Happy Birthday, Ariadne," he said, holding out the flowers and the gift bag.

Ari accepted the offering and opened the gift. Inside was a slim wooden box about the size of her hand, and when she lifted the lid, she found a set of ten shimmering watercolor pans in beautiful jewel tones.

"I got it from a stand at the artisan market," Theseus said quickly, referring to the monthly gathering of local artists in the downtown square of Asphodel to sell their wares. "I don't know anything about paint. If you don't like it-"

Ari pressed her lips to his before he could finish his sentence. When she stepped back again, she said "They're perfect. I love them, thank you, Theseus."

He sighed in relief, "Good."

She reached out, taking his hand in hers, "Listen, I'm about to take Solae home, maybe you could come over later?"

Theseus gave her hand a tight squeeze, "I'm sorry, I have to work tonight."

Ari fought off the sensation of disappointment she felt in her stomach. It wasn't fair of her to be disappointed *now*. Of course, he had to work. He had to pick up a lot more extra shifts since the car accident.

"Okay," she said, "I guess I'll see you at school Monday, then."

"Yeah," said Theseus, "Happy Valen-birthday."

She laughed, he kissed her once more, then went back to the Mustang.

Ari went back inside, to find not only Solae waiting for her, but Persie and Cal, too. They all stood there in a line, with the distinct appearance of people trying to act natural.

Ari put her hands on her hips, "You were listening at the door, weren't you?" she demanded.

"Oh, come on, like you weren't going to tell us everything anyway," said Persie.

She couldn't really argue with that. "Well?" she said, knowing they'd all have an opinion on the interaction.

"He's still got some making up to do," Persie said.

"I don't think I've ever seen Theseus sincerely apologize like that," Solae said.

"I think he's hiding something," Cal said, sounding nonplussed.

"What do you mean?" Ari said. She knew he had been holding back, but she thought that was more just not wanting to open up all the way, not actively hiding something.

Cal shrugged, "I don't know. I just think he's not telling you something."

Ari exchanged a look with Solae, who shrugged. "Theseus isn't very open," said Ari carefully, "I think whatever happened yesterday must have affected him more than he wanted to let on."

Now Cal and Persie exchanged a look, it was a look Ari had seen before, something she privately dubbed the 'older sister look.' They never acknowledged it, but Ari had a pretty good idea what it meant- that the two of them thought they knew better than Ari on some matter. It was one of the few scenarios in which Ari felt truly annoyed at both of them. Because of their strange dynamic, it didn't feel like it had once upon a time when the sisters got upset with each other. They would have their spats like any other family, but usually it had neither the weightiness of parent and child nor the cattiness of sisters. In these rare moments, though, when Cal and Persie seemed like they were *actually* trying to parent her, Ari felt a spiteful annoyance towards both of them. It made her want to be ornery just for the sake of it.

"I trust Theseus," said Ari stubbornly, "He wouldn't lie to me."

Cal looked like she wanted to say something, but Persie beat her to the punch.

"I've been there," she snorted disdainfully.

Something about the way she said it made Ari's frustration burst out of her. She felt that it was one thing for *her* to be disappointed about Theseus, but having others question him just brought out a desire to defend him, despite what he'd done.

"Yeah, I bet you have," she said hotly, "With the number of guys you've dated, you'd have to have a couple bad apples in there."

Persie looked stricken, and Ari immediately regretted taking such a cheap shot.

"Ari!" Cal said in a sharp but soft voice.

Ari didn't know where to look, but then her eyes fell on Solae, who was looking like she'd very much like to disappear.

"Come on, Sol," she said, feeling guilty and frustrated at the same time.

Solae looked immensely grateful to escape the situation as she followed Ari out the door once more, to the baby blue beetle.

As they started to drive, Solae said timidly, "Are you okay?"

Ari huffed, "I'm fine, I guess. I'm sorry you were caught in the middle of all that. It just... seems like everyone expects the worst from Theseus, and I'm sick of it. Everyone screws up sometimes."

"Yeah," said Solae noncommittally.

"What do you think?" Ari asked.

Solae paused before she answered. She had meant it when she said that she thought Theseus' apology was sincere, but she also knew from Icarus' reaction yesterday that whatever had caused Theseus missing Ari's birthday hadn't just been a family emergency, it had ultimately been Theseus' fault. As someone who kept secrets herself, Solae knew the signs and knew it didn't bode well. However, also as someone who kept secrets, she knew how awful it would be to have someone else unveil them.

"I think he was really sorry," she said, "Theseus is careless. I think he's still learning how to be in a relationship."

"Aren't we all?" Ari asked with a wry laugh.

"You're telling me," Solae muttered, more to herself than to Ari.

CHAPTER 23

Let It Be - The Beatles

Icarus checked the mail religiously once college acceptance letter season began. He was awaiting a big envelope- three big envelopes if he was lucky. But as time went on, an uneasy feeling began to creep over him. He recalled how Mrs. Calloway had told him that just passing test scores and GPA wouldn't necessarily be enough. But he couldn't believe that. He had poured his very best writing into those application essays, and while writing wasn't his strongest subject, he knew that his intelligence would shine through. He had grown up hearing adults tell him how smart he was, and while he knew that compliments from parents should be taken with a grain of salt, he also had the grades and test scores to prove it. He *had* to get into an Ivy League school. How else was he supposed to successfully pursue a future in academia?

But the day after Ari's birthday party, Icarus went to check the mail and pulled out three regular-sized envelopes. One from Princeton, one from Harvard, and one from Brown. He just stood at the mailbox for a moment, staring in disbelief, his hands shaking slightly.

It couldn't be true. He couldn't have been rejected from *all three.* Maybe he was mistaken, maybe they didn't really send acceptance letters in big envelopes, or maybe this was something else entirely. It was this feeble hope that took him inside with the envelopes, to sit down at the dining table across from his father, who was reading the paper, and begin to tear open each letter.

His father lowered the newspaper at the sound. "College letters?" he said, "Already?"

But Icarus didn't respond as he began to read the first letter.

"Dear Mr. Icarus Easton,

We are sorry to inform you…"

He didn't have to read any further. He opened the other two letters, even though he knew what they would contain. Two more apologies. Three apologies in all, three apologies for dashing all his hopes and dreams of the future.

Icarus' mother came up behind him, "What's this?" she said, picking up one of the discarded letters. "Oh no," she gasped after reading, laying a comforting hand on his shoulder. "I'm sorry, Icarus. But this is just one, surely the others-"

"They all rejected me," Icarus said heavily. "Every single one I applied to."

His father set down the newspaper altogether. "All of them? Even your backups?"

Icarus' mouth felt dry, "I didn't apply to any backups," he said quietly.

"Well, that was foolish," said his father, "Why in the world not?"

"I don't know," Icarus said. He *felt* foolish, thinking back to his conversation with Mrs. Calloway at the beginning of the school year, thinking he could best the system on pure merit. "I mean, I figured if I put all my energy into applying at the schools I wanted, I'd be more likely to get in."

"Nothing is guaranteed," said his mother, still rubbing his back soothingly. "You can't stake everything on the best-case scenario."

"Well, luckily you still have time to apply *somewhere*," said his father, "Even if it's just community college for now. You can always finish your degree at a four-year school afterwards if you don't have time to make it in now."

"What's the point?" Icarus said, louder than he meant to. He was already defeated, having shot for the moon only to be told that he wasn't good enough. Community college felt like surrender. If that's all he was good enough for, why had he heard his whole academic life that he was "gifted", that he was "going places"? To not be extraordinary immediately felt like discovering it had all been a lie. Like he had lost whatever luster had graced him as a child and was now doomed to mediocrity as a man.

"The point is that you can still get a higher education. Ivy League or not, it's still beneficial."

"There's no way I'll be taken seriously in the academic world if I go to a community college," Icarus said, and as he felt his whole world falling to pieces, he had the strangest realization. Could this be the manifestation of his story in

Reflections of Mythology? Could this rejection be representative of flying too close to the sun?

Then, his father did something he did not expect- he laughed. "You think that just because someone goes to an Ivy League school, they should be taken seriously? You think *that's* the only worthwhile measure of success?"

Icarus felt his face grow hot with embarrassment, "I… I don't know," he said. It did sound silly when phrased that way.

"You should know by now that success is not tied to something like that."

"No matter where you go to school, if you apply yourself, you can achieve great things," put in his mother. "That's what we raised you to do."

"But that's what I did," Icarus protested, "I worked hard to get into those schools, and it didn't matter."

His father waved a hand, "Those schools aren't the real world. If it matters to you that much, apply to them again for grad school, but getting in straight after high school? That's a long shot, even with good connections."

Icarus was stunned into silence. He did not know what he had expected, but not this. Even though his father was lecturing him, he somehow felt better. It seemed the only person he had let down by not getting into a top school was himself, and even that felt less devastating now. But he had to be sure.

"So, you're not disappointed?" he asked.

"That you didn't get into those frivolous schools? No," his father said, "I'm a little disappointed in how you went about it, but I think you've learned your lesson."

"Yeah," said Icarus, feeling relieved in spite of himself. He had indeed learned his lesson; he still felt foolish, along with some sense of injustice, but he could at least see a way forward now. He had fallen, but he could recover.

✸✸✸

Solae took a deep breath as she entered Amos' office. She never broached this subject with her father, not since she was very small and had witnessed him break down in tears whenever she asked him about her mother. Eventually, she stopped asking. Now though, she felt like she had to brave the topic once more.

She had just returned from getting the mail, and inside the mailbox was a large envelope from Princeton College. Solae had opened the letter immediately, heart pounding. She had been accepted. A wave of mixed emotions had rushed over her; she felt excitement, because she knew she would go, but also a familiar sick feeling in the pit of her stomach because she knew what going would mean.

"Dad?" said Solae tentatively, quietly knocking on the open office door.

Amos' eyes flitted up from his book, which he put down upon seeing Solae looking so anxious. "Is something wrong, Solae?"

Solae hesitated for a moment, then jumped right into it. "Why did mom leave?"

Her father's face seemed to tighten. "Solae, that was so long ago-"

"Dad, no," Solae cut across him firmly. "I need to know."

He shook his head, "She's gone either way, it doesn't matter why."

"Yes, it does, it matters to me."

"But why?"

The full truth screamed in Solae's mind: *Because I don't want to make the same mistakes.* But she didn't want to say that, so she said something else that was true.

"Because I've been trying to figure it out my whole life." She swallowed hard, there were tears in her father's eyes, it was hard to keep looking at him, but she forced herself to. "Please, Dad, I need closure."

Amos just looked at her for a moment, and Solae almost held her breath in anticipation, then he pinched the bridge of his nose. "You're right," he said with a sigh. "It's not fair of me."

He stood up from his chair and walked to his desk, then pulled his keychain out of his pocket and unlocked the top drawer of the desk using the tiniest key on the chain. He opened the drawer, pulled out an old envelope, and handed it to Solae.

"This was the letter she left behind. You should have it."

"Thank you," Solae whispered, taking it.

Amos put his hands in his pockets. "I'm... I'm sorry I never talked to you about it. It was always so painful. Still is."

Solae nodded, tears beginning to sting her eyes and blur her vision. "I can never decide if I'm sad or angry."

"Try not to be angry," Amos said softly. "It's not good for the soul to hold onto anger. It changes you."

"So does holding onto sadness."

There was a brief pause, and Solae knew that he had understood her soft reproach.

"I'm sorry," he said again.

Solae just nodded, but before she turned to leave the room, she said, "I got my letter from Princeton. I… I was accepted."

For the first time in the conversation, Amos smiled. "That's wonderful, Solae."

"Yeah," said Solae, "I really wanted to get in." It was the first time she had ever said it, even in her mind, but she knew it was true.

"I'm so proud of you," said Amos, "You have your mother's brain- Ah- I mean..." He looked sheepish. It seemed for the first time he was realizing the effect comparing Solae to her mother might have.

But Solae smiled, "Am I really that much like her?"

Amos seemed to be fighting back tears again. "You remind me more of her every day."

Solae stepped forward and gave him a hug.

After she left her father's office, she retreated to her room, feeling better than she thought she would. Usually, the thought of her mother left Solae feeling empty. After talking to her father, though, having the most meaningful conversation they'd had in ages, her heart seemed fuller.

Once back in her room, Solae sat on her bed. With a flutter of mingled excitement and dread, she opened the letter from her mother.

Amos-

I don't know how to begin. There is no possible way to justify what I am doing, but I at least wanted to explain why I have to leave.

Please know that it's nothing to do with you or anything you've done, all the blame lies with me. I was never meant for this life, and yet I've tried to force myself into it. It's all so selfish, but I'm afraid of what might happen if I stay any longer. I'm afraid of the person I might become, and the hurt I might cause for you and Sol. I realize this is still going to hurt you, but I must believe that it is the lesser of two evils.

I know it doesn't mean much for me to apologize now, but I AM sorry. Whatever you may think, I do still love you and Sol. If I didn't, this would be much easier. Goodbye.

Love,

Morgan

Solae finished reading and let herself fall backward onto her pillow. She gazed at the ceiling as she held the letter to her chest. She honestly did not know if this made her feelings toward her mother better or worse. She said she had been afraid of becoming a horrible person, but the glimpses in Solae's memory showed gentleness and warmth. She remembered Morgan's voice reading stories to her when she was little while she colored in a coloring book. She remembered going to the farmer's market with her. She had never detected any hint of resentment from her mother. Could it be that distance, grief, and youth had put rose-colored lenses over her childhood? Had Morgan, like Solae, simply been adept at hiding her true feelings?

Solae continued to comb through her memories, then recalled a time when, not wanting to sleep, she had crept out of her room, intending to bargain with her parents for more time to stay up. She had gone halfway down the hall when she suddenly stopped at the sound coming from the living room. Solae's mother had been crying. She also heard the low, comforting murmur of her father's voice, though she couldn't hear what he was saying. It had frightened Solae, who at the time had still been under the illusion of young children that parents were unshakeable, too strong to cry. Solae had run back to her room and hidden under the covers until sleep had overcome her. Now, she wondered if the thoughts behind this letter were the reason her mother had been crying that night.

Solae's mind wandered even more, to the Muses, to her conversation with Icarus about wanting *more* than what Asphodel could offer. Had Morgan ever had a conversation like that with Amos? Would Solae be going down the same inevitable path as Morgan if she stayed with Icarus, who loved Asphodel too much to leave it? She needed to resolve this, sooner rather than later.

✳✳✳

Ari was painting in her bedroom with the new set of watercolors that Theseus had given her. She had not spoken to either of her sisters when she returned home from dropping off Solae, she wasn't *really* upset with them anymore, but another similarity between the three of them was that none of them wanted to be the one to call a truce first. Their father had once called it 'redheaded stubbornness', but it was affectionate, as he mostly used it to refer to their mother.

A knock came at the door and Ari turned to see Cal opening the door a crack to poke her head in.

"Hey," she said, "Can we talk?"

Ari shrugged, "Yeah. What about?" she said, before turning right back to her painting.

"Ouch," said Cal, slipping inside and sitting down on Ari's bed, which was right next to her desk. "Why the cold shoulder?"

Ari sighed, "It's nothing."

"Come on, I know you."

"I'm sorry I snapped at Persie," Ari said, "I'm tired of being babied by you two, I guess. I mean, I just turned eighteen."

"We're not trying to baby you," Cal said, "But don't you think we've got a right to be concerned about Theseus?"

"It's not just that," Ari said.

"Then what?"

Ari set down her paintbrush. "I don't know. Everything is going to be changing soon… It kind of scares me. You and Persie have always known what you want to do, but I'm still waiting for that to kick in."

Cal cocked her head to one side, "But you want to be an artist," she said, confused.

Ari threw her hands up, "I have no idea how to actually do that," she said. "I know I can study art in college, but beyond that? I have no idea how to make a living off this." She gestured at the painting she was working on, an impressionistic piece depicting the lighthouse as Ari saw it in her mind's eye. It had been on her mind more lately; she wondered what would happen to it once she and her friends finished their task and Clio left town.

Cal shrugged, "I didn't know what I wanted to do for a long time either."

"So?"

"So, it's okay that you don't know exactly what you want to do you. You still have plenty of time to figure it out."

"But I've always had a solid goal to work towards," Ari protested, "Until now, it was to get to college. Now, it's just the unknown."

"The unknown can be exciting."

"More like terrifying."

"Same thing sometimes," Cal said with a grin.

Ari gave a half-hearted laugh, then after a pause asked, "When did you decide you wanted to teach college chemistry?"

"Not until I was applying to grad school."

"What about Persie?"

"Oh, Persie's has pretty much known she wanted to work in cosmetology since she could talk, but it took her a long time to come up with a plan to open her own salon, and she's not even there yet now. I'm still in school. Neither of us have reached our end-goal yet."

Ari had never thought of her older sisters as not having everything figured out until now. Even before the passing of their parents, when they'd had to step up as guardians for Ari. She had always looked up to them as older, cooler versions of the person she wanted to be. The vast age difference between her and Cal especially lent itself to this rose-tinted version of her oldest sister. But hearing all this from Cal herself did help to lessen Ari's fears, at least a little bit.

"I still don't like the unknown," she said.

"Well luckily you have a safe home base," said Cal, "You're not facing it alone."

"Yeah," Ari said, "That makes it a little less scary."

"Good. Now, speaking of Persie," Cal said as she stood and came to lean over Ari's shoulder, affectionately laying her head against Ari's. "I think you still owe her an apology."

Ari sighed, "I know, I'll go do it."

"Thank you," Cal stood upright, giving Ari a peck on the cheek before leaving the room.

Ari leaned back in her chair and stared at the ceiling for a moment. Making up with Persie, especially when Ari was the one in the wrong, always felt a little humbling. She did genuinely feel bad though, so she gathered her nerve and went to knock on Persie's bedroom door.

"Enter," came Persie's slightly chilly-sounding voice.

Ari did so and found Persie sitting in the middle of her floor, bare feet out in front of her, bottle of nail polish in hand. The sharp scent of the polish hit Ari immediately.

"You should really open a window, so you don't die from the fumes," she said, crossing to the bedroom window and opening it herself.

"Didn't ask," Persie said, "What do you want?"

"To apologize," Ari said, trying not to sound strained.

"Go on."

"I'm… sorry for what I said this morning," Ari said, "It was mean. I was just frustrated with how harsh you were being toward Theseus."

Persie finally looked up from her toenails. "The only reason I'm so harsh is because what you said is true. I have dated a lot, enough to know what guys like Theseus are like."

"But you don't *really* know him," said Ari, "You've seen his mistakes, and those weren't even totally his fault. He's… he's been through a lot."

"That doesn't give him the right to treat you like dirt."

Part of Ari was genuinely touched by this statement, finally seeing that Persie was coming from a place of love, rather than just being annoying, but she did not back down.

"He doesn't treat me like dirt," she said firmly, though not angrily. "Trust me."

"You have to admit that getting you in a wreck and missing your birthday are pretty big offenses."

"The wreck *really* wasn't his fault," Ari said.

"Okay, fine, but what about last night? What excuse did he give anyway?"

"It was a family thing," Ari said, "Believe me, Persie, I wouldn't have let it slide so easily if I didn't think it was really serious. He has a lot of issues with his family, I think, but he doesn't like to talk about it much."

Persie waved the bottle of nail polish at her threateningly, "You know, a guy with a lot of emotional baggage is a whole problem on its own."

"Please, Persie. I really, *really* like him."

"*Like?*"

Ari fidgeted, "Love, maybe," she said quietly.

Persie studied her for a moment, then a resigned smile appeared on her face. She gestured at Ari's feet. "Toes," she said, unscrewing the just-closed top to the nail polish once again.

Ari just smiled as she sat down in front of Persie, allowing her to paint her toenails the same shade of red as hers, knowing that all was now mended between them.

✳✳✳

Captain Jack Bryant arrived at his sister's house that afternoon. When Theseus got home from work, he found the entire family sitting at the dining table, all enjoying a slice of cake that Theresa made herself.

"Theseus!" said Jack with a smile, "Look at you, almost a man already."

Theseus stared at his uncle whom he did not remember but recognized all the same. He knew Jack was his mother's older brother, but he looked older than he had expected, probably an effect of being at sea so much. His close-cropped hair was salt-and-pepper gray, his skin tan and weathered, but he had the exact same green eyes as his sister; a feature that Theseus himself did not inherit.

"Hi," said Theseus shortly, not too keen on exchanging pleasantries with the man who conspired with his mother and stepfather to make plans for Theseus' future without his knowledge.

"Theseus, come have some cake," Theresa said, patting the empty seat on her other side. She looked slightly uncertain, probably because of their last interaction. Theseus wanted to apologize to her for their argument, but not in front of the others.

"No thanks," he said, "I'm not hungry." He looked around as if looking for a tangible reason to escape the room. "I think I left something in my car," he said after a moment and turned on his heel to go back out the door.

Theseus did *not* leave something in his car, so he just sat inside the driver's seat, trying to decide how long he could get away with staying out there before someone came after him.

Apparently not very long at all, as someone came out after only a couple minutes. Theseus expected it to be his mother who was knocking on the passenger window but was surprised to see his uncle instead. He gestured in silent question, Theseus nodded in response. Jack opened the car door and slid into the passenger seat.

"Well," he said heavily, "I take it you're not too happy to see me."

"I don't even know you," said Theseus, in neither denial nor confirmation.

"True, but I know Theresa told you part of the reason I came here is to offer you an apprenticeship."

Theseus raised an eyebrow, not sure what he was trying to accomplish, "Yeah," he said.

"Do you want to tell me why you're so opposed to the idea of someone handing you a future career on a silver platter?"

Theseus' jaw tightened. "I don't really like having my own future planned by someone else. I don't even know you," he said again.

Jack looked him in the eyes and Theseus knew that his previous statement was not entirely true. He had his sister's eyes, Theseus' mother's eyes, proof that they were related.

"Theresa and I write to each other a lot," Jack said, "We always have. She tells me a lot about you, Theseus, and do you know what I think?"

Theseus shook his head.

"That you're a lot less like Silas Gray than you think you are, and more like me than you realize."

A jolt went through Theseus at the sound of his father's name; his mother must have told Jack about their conversation the day before. He hadn't spelled it all out exactly, but he guessed it didn't take much to infer.

"That's what Mom said," Theseus finally offered, "That I'm like you. But I don't know..." he trailed off, not quite sure how to phrase it, "I don't know what that means."

"You don't know whether you should take it as a compliment or not?" Jack said, and he laughed heartily.

Theseus smiled briefly, "Well, yeah." He sighed, "When my mom said you were coming, she said I'd met you before. But I don't really remember it, not exactly. It's... jumbled up with other stuff."

"Ah," said Jack. "That makes sense." He put a hand over his mouth, looking thoughtful. "The last time I visited you," he said, "Silas was still in the picture. Theresa had not told me what was going on, I still don't understand why, but when I showed up..." he shook his head at the memory, "I could just tell. I was so angry, Silas and I got in a fight, I don't remember how, and your mother was upset and trying to pull us apart. Somewhere in there, it hit me that I was making it worse for her, so I backed off, but I had scared him. He ran off, and that's when it came out that he was seeing that other woman. He came back to get his things and that was the last we all saw of him."

Theseus was stunned into silence. His father had left only seven years ago. How did he not remember all of this? As Jack had spoken, hazy traces of it all returned to him, but he could not recall the whole picture. He must have repressed everything around that time. It had gotten its very worst right before his father had left, after all. His uncle had *saved* them, driven off their tormentor, and he had absolutely no memory of it. Perhaps in an attempt to block out all the worst memories, his mind had gotten rid of this too. But the way he had described it, the anger, the fight... Theseus knew how all of that must have felt, because he had felt it before.

"You... really think I'm like you?" he asked.

"I can see it in your face," said Jack, "I used to be just as obstinate and reckless as you are." He smiled, and it was a mischievous smile that made him look years younger, but what surprised Theseus was that he recognized the smile. It was *his* smile. "I still am, sometimes," his uncle finished.

"And that's why you think I should do the apprenticeship?"

"What is it you want to do with your life, Theseus?"

He shrugged, "I don't know. To get out of here, mainly."

"Do you want to see places? Not be stuck behind a desk your whole life?"

Theseus nodded.

"This apprenticeship can give you all of that," Jack said, "And more."

When he phrased it that way, the whole thing didn't sound so bad. But something, maybe pride, maybe just the fact that it was still a monumental life decision, gave Theseus pause.

Jack seemed to sense his hesitation. "You don't have to answer now," he said, "Just give me an answer before your graduation. I'm leaving the next day."

"Okay," said Theseus.

"Now, let's go have some of that cake," said Jack, with an affectionate smack of Theseus' shoulder.

"Alright, Uncle Jack."

CHAPTER 24

The Boys of Summer – Don Henley

The next time they felt themselves being called back to the world of mythology it was even more jarring than the first time.

Theseus found himself filled with dread as he drove to the plant nursery to see Ari, rather than the usual excitement he felt about seeing her. Ever since Uncle Jack had come to town, Theseus had found himself hanging around him more than he expected, liking him more and more. His mother had been right; Theseus saw so much of himself in his uncle, and the idea of going with him for the apprenticeship was feeling less like being sent away and more like an exciting adventure with perhaps the first person to truly understand him. He felt safe with Uncle Jack, similar to how he felt at first going out with Ari. The difference was that Ari thought Theseus was better than he was, ignoring all his flaws, but Uncle Jack saw him for who he truly was and accepted him in spite of his flaws.

He had not told Ari about the apprenticeship yet. He knew he had to, and he had always known that the good thing they had going couldn't last forever, but he was enjoying playing pretend so much that he kept putting it off. He kept hoping that it would fizzle out naturally or that Ari would come to her senses and break it off. That way, he wouldn't have her broken heart on his conscience when he left. He had stopped putting so much effort into their relationship, stopped spending so much time with Ari, but so far, she had kept up her angelic patience and excused it all. Even though Theseus was sure that her sisters still resented him.

He had just given his final answer to Uncle Jack. Theseus *would* be taking the apprenticeship. This meant he *had* to tell Ari now. He'd leave the ball in her court, in hopes that it would speed things along. Thus, the feeling of dread in the pit of his stomach as he parked in front of the plant nursery.

Ari was helping a customer when Theseus walked in, but he caught her eye, and she gave him a wink. He waited at the counter and once she was done, she floated over to him and leaned over the counter for a kiss. Theseus obliged, feeling his resolve waiver. Why did she have look like that?

"I'm almost ready to go," Ari said, "Just have fifteen minutes left in my shift.

Theseus nodded. They were supposed to meet up with Icarus and Solae at The Haunt when Ari was done with work.

Ari noticed his silence immediately. "Is something wrong?" she asked gently.

"No," he said, "Just got a lot on my mind."

Ari smiled, though she clearly wasn't satisfied with this response.

Say something about it, Theseus thought.

"I feel like I haven't seen you in a while," she said casually.

"Yeah, I've been hanging out with my uncle a lot," he said. More hints, the perfect lead in. He sighed, gathering his willpower.

Ari sensed it. "Theseus, please be honest with me. What's wrong?"

Theseus finally met her gaze. Her halo eyes shone, and he hated to think of how they would look filled with tears.

"There's something I need to tell you," he began, but at that moment, the entire shop began to shake.

They both looked around, bewildered, and Ari gasped. Cracks began to appear in the floor, like a cartoonish earthquake. Was this an earthquake? Theseus wasn't sure, he didn't think earthquakes happened here. Then that awful fading sensation he'd felt once before. He turned back to Ari. He could see right through her.

"Theseus," she whispered fearfully.

It was so much worse this time, but in a rush of memory, Theseus acted. He lunged, going right through the counter with no resistance, and wrapped his arms around Ari, holding her close. Just like that, he could feel her in his arms, the ground under his feet, he was solid again. The shaking stopped.

"The book," Ari said.

Theseus nodded, "Let's go." He found he was almost relieved for this excuse to put off his distasteful task once again.

Ari hugged him tight, then held his hand as she stepped back. "Just don't let go."

"I won't."

They walked out of the plant nursery and found Icarus and Solae pulling up in Icarus' truck. Judging by the grim looks on their faces, they had just experienced the same thing Theseus and Ari had. Icarus signaled to them, and they climbed into the back seat of the truck and drove straight to the lighthouse.

When they pulled up to the lighthouse, they were met with a large red "FOR SALE" sign in front of the building. It had an imposing energy about it and made Ari in particular feel uncomfortable. Something about the idea of total strangers invading this space that was so sacred to her, possibly buying it and living in it, repurposing it, tearing it down even, brought a lump into her throat. Ari had known something had to happen to the lighthouse once Clio moved away, but she had always pushed it out of her mind until now. The sign was a glaring reminder that *something* would happen to it. The possibility of a remodel was sickening, the possibility that it would cease to exist altogether was unthinkable. Ari realized that the best-case scenario in her mind would be for someone to come along, see how special the lighthouse was, and live in it. But even then, they would be living *Ari's* dream. She had no real claim to the place, but the mark it had left on her soul over the years felt like it should mean something.

The lighthouse going away was just one more thing added on top of the pile of things that were changing. It was all moving too fast, and she couldn't catch her breath. She took Theseus' hand as they all walked up to the lighthouse, but he didn't even glance at her. She felt even closer to tears; even he was changing, ever since her birthday, and she didn't understand why.

The inside of the lighthouse was noticeably emptier than when they first began this endeavor. Ari guessed they had moved half the books now. She wondered if there was a way they could stall, because Clio couldn't sell the place if they weren't finished with their quest, could she?

It was almost routine now to gather around the table as Icarus picked up *Reflections of Mythology*, and began to read aloud from it, transporting them by some mysterious force to another time and place.

✳✳✳

Theseus found himself back in a cell in the palace dungeon. He hated it here; it was dark aside from torches in the corridors, it smelled bad, and he didn't think there was really a safe place to sit down. Maybe the reason the others enjoyed these mythological trips was because they never found themselves in a place like this.

He heard the sound of footsteps coming toward his cell. It was a familiar pattering of feet, one he recognized almost immediately. Ari appeared in all her princess-y splendor, wearing a soft pink dress this time, but the expression on her face was near panic.

228

"Theseus," she whispered, approaching his cell and taking hold of the bars.

"Hey," he said, "What's wrong?"

Ari bit her lip, "I thought they had already taken you to the Labyrinth, I thought I was too late to help you."

"You're not," said Theseus, "I'm okay."

"But I don't know how much longer we have," Ari said, "And I don't even know where I'm supposed to get the magic twine or whatever it is that's supposed to guide you."

"Where's Icarus?" Theseus said, "He knows this story backwards and forwards, surely he can help you."

"He's probably in Daedalus' workshop."

"Maybe that's where you're supposed to go this time," said Theseus.

"Maybe..." Ari said, "But I don't want to leave you here."

"Look, I'll be fine," Theseus said, "The Minotaur isn't in here. But I have a feeling I'm really going to need that twine or whatever it is once they take me to the Labyrinth." He wrapped his hands around Ari's, which were still holding onto the cell bars. "Please, princess," he whispered soothingly.

Ari looked like she wanted to cry. "What were you going to tell me before we went to the lighthouse?" she blurted out suddenly.

Theseus paused, "Odd time to bring that up, don't you think?"

Ari shook her head, "Something has been off with you lately, and everything is changing so much with graduation coming up, the lighthouse, this place-"

"Okay, okay," Theseus said, taking a deep breath. "Look, I just wanted to tell you that the reason things have been weird lately is because my uncle is in town."

Ari looked skeptical but waited for him to continue.

"He just gets it, y'know? He gets me. He's… helping me figure out what I want to do with my life, but it's also bringing up a lot of bad memories from a long time ago. It's just been a lot to process, and I've just been under a lot of stress lately. I'm sorry I've been distant." It was a half-truth. Nothing he said was a lie, but he was leaving out one crucial piece of information. He just couldn't deal with this right now, and she clearly couldn't either. He waited for Ari's response, hoping she would accept this.

For a moment, she kept that skeptical look on her face, and Theseus thought he had failed, but then she took a deep breath, and suddenly seemed much more at peace.

"That makes sense, I guess," she said, "Sorry I freaked out. Listen, I'll go find Icarus and get the twine, and if I don't see you here again, I'll meet you at the Labyrinth."

Theseus nodded, feeling relieved. "Good. Now, c'mere." He leaned in and they kissed between the bars.

Ari gave him a small smile "Bye," she said, and, looking reluctant, let go of the bars left him alone in the dungeon.

✳✳✳

Icarus was helping Daedalus put the finishing touches on the wings in the workshop when the door burst open. Ari stood in the doorway, and Daedalus hadn't even had time to cover up the wings. The old man stared at Ari for a moment, and then before Icarus could do anything, he grabbed Ari by her hair, pulled her into the workshop, slamming the door behind her.

Ari cried out, but Daedalus clapped a hand over her mouth. "I'm terribly sorry, Your Highness, but I can't have you telling your father about our little project," he said in a low voice, grabbing a knife from the desk as he spoke.

Ari made eye contact with Icarus, wide-eyed and terrified. He stepped forward, grabbing onto the old man's arm as he brought the knife towards Ari. "Stop!" he said, "Don't hurt her!"

"We can't risk this getting out," Daedalus said, "Let go, son."

"No," Icarus said firmly, "Ariadne won't tell anyone, I can promise you."

Ari made a muffled sound from behind Daedalus' hand, eyes tearful.

"Please," Icarus said, "Let her go."

Daedalus paused, then released Ari, "I hope for your sake my son is right," he said warningly.

"He is, I won't tell," Ari gasped, tears streaming down her face, "Please, I just need something to help Theseus get through the Labyrinth."

"The boy who volunteered?" asked Daedalus, "He's a lost cause, why would you want to help him?"

"Because I'm in love with him," Ari burst out, and Icarus stared at her, certain that statement was pure honesty.

Daedalus just looked at her for a moment, eyebrows raised skeptically. Icarus reached out and put a comforting arm around his friend. Daedalus trying to kill her had obviously upset her, but Icarus sensed that something else was amiss. It wasn't like her to burst into tears like this, even under duress.

"There is something that would help," Daedalus said finally, with a sigh. He turned and began rifling through a box in the corner. "Love," Icarus heard him murmur, "Makes people do the most foolish things."

He pulled out a ball of faintly glowing gold twine and handed it to Ari. "This is a magical thread," he said, "If you roll it out before you, it will show you the right path."

Ari took the thread from him, "Thank you," she whispered.

Daedalus waved a hand, "Get out of here now," he said, "We have work to do. We will not see you again."

Ari nodded, then with a look at Icarus, threw her arms around him. "Good luck," she said, and then she was gone.

"Come on son," Daedalus said, gesturing to the wings that still lay spread out on the desk, "We must finish these before the morning."

✸✸✸

Solae found herself sitting in the field of clouds once again, but this time they were a lilac purple, and the sky was dark. She looked around and saw Apollo walking over to her, he was back to his true form, inhuman and magnificent, but Solae herself was still glowing very dimly, it must be nighttime again.

"Back again, Solae," Apollo said, sitting down next to her. "You'll be pleased to know your efforts are working. I can sense that the fabric between our two realities is almost fully closed up."

"Oh," Solae said, feeling secretly disheartened, "How can you tell?"

"You would be able to see it in your world too, I'm sure," Apollo said, "If only you knew what to look for."

"What should I look for?" Solae asked.

"Have you noticed any strange things that are not normal in your world?" Apollo asked.

"Yes," Solae said, thinking back to all the photos she had taken with Icarus, on their dates that doubled as opportunities to search for more unusual phenomena in Asphodel.

"I believe you would begin to see less of that, as you finish your quest," Apollo said. "Fewer signs of this other reality leaking through."

Solae suspected as much; she had indeed been finding less and less since their last trip. She knew that this was for the best, that if they didn't keep going it would ruin Asphodel, but a selfish part of her wanted to keep the rift open so that she could continue seeing magic.

"Do not be sorrowful," Apollo said, apparently sensing Solae's thoughts. "I can see that this will not be your last encounter of this kind."

His words sent the wheels in her mind turning. Solae turned to Apollo, "You're the god of prophecy, right?"

The shining Olympian did not face her, but said, "What do you want me to show you, Solae?"

The Muses' words from last time played in Solae's head again, *Great love, great tragedy, or simply, greatness.*

"I was wondering if you were able to see... hypotheticals," she said.

"That is all my prophecies are," said Apollo, "I reveal what happens if certain paths are taken. That is why they call it a 'self-fulfilling' prophecy."

"Well then," said Solae, "Can you show me what would happen if I stayed with Icarus?"

Apollo turned to face her, his glowing eyes pierced hers, and suddenly it was like Solae was watching a film play out in her head.

She and Icarus, graduating together, going to college together. Solae saw herself, that feeling of ambition for something different shriveling up inside of her as she remained trapped in Asphodel. She saw herself staying in school after receiving her Bachelor's degree, her Master's degree, desperately trying to reawaken that ambition through empty accomplishments. She saw herself and Icarus standing alone, and then he was kneeling, putting a diamond on her hand. She couldn't say no, because he was so happy. She forced herself to be happy with him.

She saw a daughter. A miniature of Solae.

She saw herself suffocating. She saw herself become her own mother, leaving it all behind because she couldn't handle being tethered. It wasn't fair. She left behind a broken-beyond-repair Icarus and a watery-eyed child who didn't understand. She would continue the cycle. She saw herself steeped in regret and self-hatred for the rest of her life, but never going back because she was a coward. Then, it all came to an end. Solae was sitting in the clouds next to Apollo again.

Her heart was pounding, her face was wet with tears that she didn't remember shedding. "I can't do that," she gasped, "I can't do that to him, or myself."

"It all depends on your choices," said Apollo.

"I knew it," said Solae, barely hearing him. "I'm just like her. I didn't want to be, but I am, *I am.*"

Apollo reached out and placed his hands on Solae's shoulders. His touch was white-hot, but nothing compared to the heat of the sun.

"Do not make the mistake of heroes," he said, "What you saw is not your future. You are the only one who determines your future. What you saw was the answer to a specific question."

Solae shakily took a deep breath. She willed herself to feel the heat of Apollo's hands, imagining what it would feel like on her human skin. She could still avoid this. "So, if I leave him now, that won't happen?"

"Only you can decide," said Apollo.

"Then it won't happen," said Solae firmly. It would be far better for Icarus to fall now than it would be for him to fall after flying even higher, when recovery would be impossible.

CHAPTER 25

I Know It's Over – The Smiths

When they returned to the real world, Icarus jumped at the sight of Clio standing in the lighthouse with them.

"You-!" Theseus shouted, also surprised, "Were you just standing there watching us?"

Clio laughed, "No dear, I only just arrived."

"Is... something wrong?" Solae asked, and Icarus noted that she looked distressed, with a quiver in her voice.

"Quite the opposite," Clio said, "If I'm not mistaken, you are all coming to the end of your stories."

They all nodded hesitantly.

"I believe," Clio said, looking around at the remaining few boxes of books, "You have one trip remaining before your task is complete."

"What, are we basing this on the number of books we have left to move?" Theseus said, and Ari nudged him into silence.

"Not entirely, but it helps to tie the task to something physical to mark progress."

Icarus began to wonder if Clio knew more about magic than she was letting on.

"What do we do when it's finished?" he asked.

Clio shrugged, "That will be entirely up to you. There will be nothing tying you to the other reality any longer, so you will be free to move on with your lives however you wish."

"Good," Theseus said, "I'm ready to forget any of this ever happened."

"Forget?" Ari said, "I'm not sure how you could forget that magic exists. I think it will stay with me forever."

Icarus nodded, since his rejection from the Ivy Leagues and his enlightening conversation with his parents about his future, he had begun to feel like a chapter of his life was ending. The chapter where he fantasized about finding the source of strange happenings in Asphodel, fantasized about spending his college days studying in romantic, hallowed halls of some revered Ivy League school, fantasized endlessly about getting together with Solae... It had all come to a close. He had found what he was looking for in Asphodel and was content with the knowledge that he lived in a world where magic existed. His dreams of Ivy Leagues had been dashed, but if he were really honest with himself, he had always known that was just a pipe dream, he could still have the future he wanted without the pomp of those schools. And as for Solae... they were together now. He had thought that the rejection letters had been his mirrored version of flying too close to the sun, and maybe they were, but perhaps he needed to burn away the fluff to get at the heart of what he truly wanted out of life.

"I'm glad we found this," Icarus said, "I'm satisfied with knowing magic is real, I'm ready to move on."

Solae said nothing, and Icarus recalled what she said about not being ready to give it up. He wondered if those same thoughts were still running through her head, he thought about her declaration to write a book about all the things they'd seen together this year. Perhaps that would give her a sense of catharsis when it was all over. He reached out and took her hand, which she acknowledged with a furtive glance and a gentle squeeze of his hand. If she wasn't okay with this ending, Icarus would do his best to find a way to help her be okay with it.

Ari piped up again, "Ms. Clio, do you have anyone who's interested in the lighthouse yet?"

"No dear," Clio said, "I've only just put it on the market.

"Do… Do you think that whoever buys it is going to tear it down?" Ari looked almost afraid to ask this question, and Icarus wondered if this was related to what he had sensed in Daedalus' workshop.

Clio smiled understandingly, "Not if I can help it. I didn't save this place all these years just for someone else to come along after I'm gone and get rid of it. I plan on making sure whoever buys the lighthouse will do something worthwhile with it."

"Okay," Ari said, "That's a relief," although she did not feel very relieved. Whoever got the lighthouse, it would still never be the same. Just like none of them would be the same after this experience.

CHAPTER 26

I'll Be Your Mirror – The Velvet Underground & Nico

Just like the lighthouse parties, the Asphodel Spring Carnival was an important ritual for Solae, Ari, Icarus, and Theseus. This year, they elected to go on opening night. Ari and Solae had a sleepover at Solae's house the day before, a Friday, and then spent the day leading up to the carnival out and about town together, leisurely window shopping and existing in each other's space. They had been doing this more often than usual lately; late-night studying sessions turned into movie-watching and talking before inevitably going to sleep far too late on any weekend they weren't having date nights with the boys. It was as if they were trying to savor as much of their remaining girlhood as possible before the next phase of life began.

They always had so much more to talk about, but inevitably, the conversation turned to relationships as they perused the racks of a particular thrift store that was most definitely a hidden gem in Asphodel.

"So how are things going with you and Icarus?" asked Ari.

"We're fine," said Solae, skimming through her side of the rack of clothes. She pulled out a green cardigan that had whimsical beading along the edges. "This one is cute."

"Yeah," said Ari, side-eyeing her friend, a little taken aback by how quickly she had moved on. "Have you been hanging out much lately?"

"We go out at least once a week," Solae said briskly.

"Um, cool," said Ari, "So he's treating you right?" she said jokingly, but also from genuine concern. She could sense that something was not quite right.

Solae nodded, still intently focusing on the clothing rack. "Icarus is wonderful," she said, "He's so sweet, he remembers all my favorite things, he's beautiful… he does everything right!" As she spoke, she began to flip through the rack faster and faster, until Ari was startled into reaching over and putting her hand over Solae's, stopping her from tearing the clothing rack apart altogether.

"Sol, what's wrong?"

Solae stopped and looked into her best friend's eyes. Her best friend, who she would have to leave, just like she would have to leave Icarus.

"Can we go somewhere else to talk about this?" she asked.

At The Haunt, Ari got a latte, while Solae got a cup of Earl Grey tea and was stirring an ungodly amount of sugar into it.

"So, is there something wrong with you and Icarus?" asked Ari.

Solae took a swig of tea before replying. "That's just it, there's *nothing* wrong. Everything is going really well with us."

"I'm afraid I'm missing your point," said Ari, "Unless there's another factor here that you're not telling me."

Solae looked up at Ari without moving her head. *She really knows me*, she thought, regretting not telling her about Princeton as soon as she had gotten her acceptance letter. She hadn't told *anyone* except her father.

"I have a confession to make," she said, folding her hands on the table, almost as if in prayer.

"Okay," said Ari, her tone reflecting only curiosity, which helped to somewhat put Solae at ease.

"I got my acceptance letter from Princeton," Solae said calmly, "And I'm going. Originally when I applied, I wasn't even sure I'd get in, and I know I should have told you about this sooner, but-"

"Hang on," Interrupted Ari, "Are we just going to gloss over the fact that you got accepted into *Princeton College?*"

Solae shrugged modestly.

"Solae! That's amazing, congratulations! But… I still don't see how this is a problem."

"I don't know how to tell Icarus," Solae said, "He didn't get in, and now he's planning to go to college around here… Princeton's awfully far away from here."

"Ahh," said Ari, "I see now." She looked thoughtful, "You said everything else is going well?"

Too well, thought Solae, thinking about the vision Apollo had shown her. "Yeah," was all she said, though.

"You know Icarus, and I've known him a lot longer than you have. He would want you to do what's best for you. I'm sure he'd be willing to go long-distance."

"I don't want to be in a long-distance relationship," Solae said quickly. The idea of having a tether while she had the illusion of freedom was just as bad as being fully tied down to this small town.

"I don't think anyone *wants* to be," said Ari, "But I guess the two of you will have to discuss what you're willing to do for your relationship."

"Right," said Solae, the wheels in her head turning.

"I don't know if that helps at all, just my two cents," Ari said.

"It helps a lot," Solae said, "I feel a lot better now." This was true, though her reason for feeling better was probably not what Ari had in mind. The conversation had given Solae an idea. Solae could use Princeton as a way to let Icarus down easily. She could chalk it all up to her moving away but not wanting to do a long-distance relationship, which was true enough. It would still hurt, but at least it would be better than just saying, *'Hey, guess what? I don't love you as much as you love me.'*

"Hey," said Ari suddenly, reaching out and placing her hands over Solae's. "I'm gonna miss you when you go."

Solae smiled bittersweetly. "I'm going to miss you too."

"Will you come back to visit on breaks?"

"I'll try," said Solae. Though privately, she had no idea if she would ever return. She had to keep chasing the magic, or else she would suffocate. *Great love, great tragedy, or simply greatness.* But she didn't want to explain that to Ari, not today; she already had such a hard time with change. "Let's talk about something else," she said, "How are things with Theseus?"

Ari shrugged with a long-suffering smile. "It's good. Theseus has been kind of distant, but he's under a lot of stress right now. Something to do with his uncle being in town, I think. He won't tell me what exactly, but I think maybe it brings up bad memories from his childhood."

Solae frowned; she was pretty sure she knew exactly what was causing Theseus' stress. Icarus had told her afterward about his phone call with Theseus on Ari's birthday, how Theseus had been drunk and rambling about his mother wanting to send him away to apprentice with his uncle. Icarus had said that Theseus was planning on telling Ari on his own, but now Solae wasn't sure he had. Maybe he had decided not to go after all. But if that was the case, why would Theseus be distant with Ari? Had he simply not told her anything? Grimly, Solae decided she would get to the bottom of this.

They finished the rest of their outing and went back to Solae's house to get ready for their night at the Spring

Carnival with the boys. Ari was practically giddy with excitement, while Solae was carefully calculating in her mind when the best time to talk to Icarus would be. There was no doubt in her mind that this needed to be the last date, but she figured she should let them all enjoy the evening first. She decided she would bring it up afterward when she and Icarus were alone.

CHAPTER 27

Little Lies - Fleetwood Mac

The boys both showed up in Icarus' truck. Ari must have noticed Solae tense up a little at the sight of Icarus getting out and walking up to the door through her window.

She put a hand on Solae's shoulder, "Are you going to be okay? We can call this off if you need to."

Solae looked at her friend, this cinnamon-sugar girl, and lied through her teeth. "I'll be fine. You're right, Icarus and I will be able to work out going long-distance or something. We'll work it out later, I just want to enjoy tonight." At least that last part was true.

The doorbell rang, and Solae went to answer it, Ari following right behind her.

Icarus was smiling wide when Solae opened the door. It was as if she really were the sun, the way he lit up at the sight of her. "You look amazing, Sol."

It's just puppy love, thought Solae, because that's what she had to think. She couldn't stand the thought that she might be about to break Icarus' heart, for real.

Theseus did not meet them at the door with Icarus. He was sitting in the back seat of the truck, facing the other direction as Ari got into the truck and sat next to him. He turned his head in her direction when Ari kissed him on the cheek, "Hey," he said, but nothing else.

Ari, who Solae knew had been hoping that Theseus would notice her outfit, seemed to wilt slightly. She perked back up immediately though, as she began chatting happily to Theseus about their day. This interaction further engrained Solae's resolve to question Theseus about what he was hiding from Ari, but she was distracted as Icarus got in the driver's seat.

He reached over and gave Solae's hand a gentle squeeze, "Are you okay?"

Solae blinked, then smiled. "Yeah, just a little tired." She reached for the radio, "Got anything good in here?" Anything to distract, anything to distract, fill the silence, because she knew she wouldn't be able to.

"I think Juicebox is in there," said Icarus, "Go ahead and turn it on."

Solae did so and turned the volume *up*. A Fleetwood Mac song came on, and they all started singing along as they drove to the fairgrounds. Even Theseus seemed to come out of his sulking to join in.

When they pulled out of the neighborhood and onto the main road, Icarus cranked the volume even higher and rolled down the windows. Solae momentarily forgot everything else. She liked this song, and she loved the feel of the evening wind blowing on her face as she leaned out the truck window. She could feel Icarus' gaze on her at every red light, but she didn't mind. She had made up her mind to have fun tonight.

Since it was the opening weekend at the Asphodel Spring Carnival, it was crowded to say the least. It was not a particularly grand affair, not even as big as the fair which took place in the fall. But there were games, carnival food, and even rides, some of which were probably not the most structurally sound.

Solae, not wanting to get separated in the crowd, took hold of both Icarus' hand and Ari's hand. The four of them were now linked together in one long chain, weaving in between everyone around them until they found a space on the sidelines.

"What's on our list?" Icarus said, scanning the festive lights and colors around them.

"Carousel," Ari said.

"I want to play some games," put in Theseus.

"Hall of mirrors," Solae offered. It was her favorite attraction by far, whimsical and bewildering.

Icarus nodded, "Carousel might be best for last after some of the little kids have gone. Maybe we can do games, rides, hall of mirrors, and then the carousel as the grand finale?" It was very like him to create a plan. He always had a plan.

"Sounds good to me," Ari said.

They began going around to all the classic games, Theseus beating them all at most of them. Solae was keeping an eye on him, becoming increasingly more worried as he was not being particularly attentive to Ari, trying to find an opportunity to get him alone and interrogate him.

When they got in line for the Ferris wheel, Solae saw her chance. They were all four standing in line together in no particular order, but when they got to the front of the line, Solae broke through the gate taking Theseus with her, making it look as though she had tripped.

As the carnival worker directed Theseus and Solae to sit in the small cart, big enough only for two, Solae looked back at Icarus and Ari with a shrug. "We can do it again and swap," she said.

Theseus, to Solae's relief, did not say anything, though he no doubt knew she had orchestrated this.

They sat down and the attendant lowered the bar over their laps. After a few minutes, they began to slowly ascend the Ferris wheel.

"So, what's this about?" Theseus said.

"What are you doing with Ari?" Solae said, not mincing words. She may be a coward when it came to sorting things out in her own relationship, but she would not sit by while someone played with her best friend's heart, even if it was one of her other best friends.

"I don't know what you're talking about," said Theseus evasively.

"You've been practically ignoring Ari all evening. In fact, you've been acting off ever since her birthday, but Ari is too forgiving to admit it."

Theseus side-eyed her, "And you're not, apparently."

"No," Solae said, "I think you're leading her on."

"Takes one to know one."

Solae was struck dumb by this statement. She hadn't wanted to think of it that way, since she was planning on breaking up with Icarus, but she couldn't deny it, since she had been putting the decision off.

"Have you told Ari about the apprenticeship with your uncle?" Solae demanded, ignoring the accusation altogether.

Theseus looked bewildered, "How do you know-" understanding dawned on him, "Icarus told you about that, huh?"

"Yes," Solae said, "Are you going?"

Theseus sighed, "Yes. I am."

"Why haven't you told Ari about it? She has no idea you're leaving," Solae said, aware that they were in the same boat, charting the same exact course. Maybe that's why it bothered her so much.

"I just haven't gotten around to it."

"You're stringing her along."

"Hey," Theseus said a little angrily, "I don't exactly look forward to breaking her heart, okay? She really fell for me."

"But you didn't fall for her."

"I like how she makes me feel," he said, "Plenty of people date for less of a reason than that."

"Not if they're friends first," insisted Solae.

"What about Icarus?" Theseus shot back at her, seeming keen to steer the conversation away from himself.

Solae forced back against a sudden lump in her throat, "I didn't mean to lead him on," she said with a shake of her head, "I think I loved him at first… maybe I still do, in some way, but we're just not meant to be. We want different things out of life, so I have to break it off."

"Alright," Theseus said. They were both quiet for a moment, then, as they crested the top of the Ferris wheel, he spoke again. "I'll make a deal with you. I'll break up with Ari, you break up with Icarus. We'll do it by the end of school. I'm leaving the day after graduation, anyway."

"You're leaving?"

"Yeah," Theseus said, "I'm doing this apprenticeship with my uncle on his research vessel."

"Wow," Solae said, a little impressed. She was not entirely surprised though. She had always known in the back of her mind that Theseus, like her, didn't really belong in Asphodel. "I'm leaving too, actually. I'm going to Princeton."

"Impressive," Theseus said disinterestedly, then he captured her gaze. "So do we have a deal?"

Solae did not flinch away under his skeptical stare. As much as she knew this would hurt their friends, she knew it would be better for them all in the long run. It was sort of fitting, with graduation coming up and the end of their foray into mythology.

"Deal," said Solae, holding out her hand.

They shook on it, sealing their pact as if sealing something of far more consequence than this. At the same time, though, there was nothing *more* consequential at this moment in their lives, aside from *Reflections of Mythology*, but that would soon come to an end as well. They were tying up everything rather nicely.

As much as Solae resolved to have fun that night, she felt her newly formed deal with Theseus looming over her the whole time. Ari and Icarus, the bright sides in their dynamic, were blissfully oblivious as they continued enjoying the carnival. Solae was barely able to enjoy even the hall of mirrors; if she caught Icarus' or Ari's eye, she was stung by guilt, but if she caught Theseus' eye, she felt like she was being judged with no room to escape because as he'd said- *it takes one to know one.* The only safe thing was to catch her own eye in the mirror, and even then, she saw her mother looking back at her, getting ready to abandon those she loved.

It was a relief when they finally made their way to the carousel, the final stop before leaving. It was an old-fashioned-looking carousel, all bright colors trimmed in gold that looked dreamy from the lights.

They each chose their own imaginative steed. Ari chose a snow-white unicorn with a colorful pastel saddle and ribbons woven through the mane and tail, and a wreath of flowers adorning its neck. Theseus mounted a fearsome-looking black horse, covered in armor and frozen in the act of tossing its head defiantly. Icarus selected a sky-blue pegasus horse with outstretched wings as a private joke between the four of them, getting a laugh out of Ari and Theseus, but not Solae. She swung herself into the saddle of a leaping horse whose trimmings, mane, and even hooves were all shining gold.

As the carousel spun them merrily around, Solae did not look back at her friends once. She simply held on and kept her eyes straight ahead.

CHAPTER 28

As The World Falls Down - David Bowie

As soon as they left the carnival, Solae began mentally preparing herself for the impending conversations she knew she must have with Icarus. He dropped off Ari and Theseus first, just as Solae knew he would. She was simultaneously impatient and dreading to be alone with him. Before Icarus started driving to Solae's house, though, he switched the tape in the cassette player for one that he kept carefully hidden from Solae.

Curiosity got the best of her, "What's this?"

"Just something I finished putting together recently," said Icarus, with noticeable excitement in his voice.

The first few magical-sounding notes of 'As The World Falls Down' began playing out of the speakers.

Solae gasped, "I love this song!"

"I know," said Icarus, "You mentioned it a few months ago, so I tracked it down. That's when I started making this mixtape."

"*This* mixtape?"

Icarus grinned, "Just listen."

He took the long way to Solae's house, letting more of the songs play. It was a mixture of songs that were intimate favorites of Solae's, and songs that she had never heard before but fell in love with instantly. All she could think about the whole drive was how much Icarus must care to have taken the time to know her taste so completely and track down each one of these songs to put together. Some girls got flowers; Solae got music.

They listened in silence, though it wasn't awkward or tense. They were soaking in the music together like they had on that bus ride almost four years ago. By the time they reached Solae's house, she was holding back tears. How could she possibly break up with him, when he was so wonderful? When she knew she would never, *ever* find someone like him anywhere else?

Icarus parked and got out of the truck, walked around to Solae's side, and opened her door. When she slid down from her seat, Icarus could immediately tell something was wrong. He took her hand as they stood together in the glow of the headlights. "What's wrong, Sol?"

Solae sighed, she had to tell him. She had already promised herself, but now Theseus would hold her accountable. *Theseus*, of all people.

"Icarus, there's something I haven't told you."

He did not waver. "What's that?"

"I got into Princeton."

Icarus blinked, then before Solae knew what was happening, he was hugging her, spinning her around, even lifting her off her feet.

He was laughing, "That's amazing!" He let go of her, "Solae, I'm so proud of you, why didn't you tell me?"

The lump in Solae's throat was getting harder to swallow. This would be easier if he were upset, bitter and jealous that she had succeeded where he had not. "I was afraid you'd be upset," she said hesitantly, waiting for the full meaning to sink in, waiting for his smile to crumble.

Icarus sighed, shaking his head, but his smile didn't go away. "I always knew you could do it. I was arrogant to think I could get in so easily. I think… I think that was my version of flying too close to the sun in this life. I'm not upset that you got in." He tentatively reached out, gently brushing Solae's hair aside and cupping her face with one hand. "I'm happy for you."

Solae did not want to move on from this moment, from his gentle touch, but she *had* to. "But… it means I have to go away," she said, "To New Jersey."

"Is that what you're worried about? Sol, I don't mind going long-distance, we can work it out."

Solae bit her lip, "What if I don't *want* to go long-distance?"

Now Icarus paused, his smile finally faltering. *Now he's getting it,* thought Solae.

But Icarus took both of Solae's hands in his. "Y'know, I would do anything for you. I would do long-distance, but if you can't do that, I will find a way to go with you. I can find another college near Princeton, or even do one of those online programs."

Solae stared at him in disbelief, "*What?*" she croaked, tears finally overcoming her.

This wasn't supposed to happen. This was supposed to be letting him down easy. Icarus' smile was warm, his hair was slightly windblown in the night air, and the headlights made him look like a dream. It was as if every force in the universe were conspiring against Solae.

"But *why?*" she asked, voice laden with a mixture of emotions.

Icarus reached into his pocket and pulled out something small and yellow. It was an MP3 player, just like Solae's pink one from her mother. He handed it to her, gently wrapping her fingers around it, and Solae knew that when she listened to the contents, they would be the same as the mixtape they had just listened to on the way here. A special collection of songs, just for her, gathered by Icarus.

"Because I love you, Solae," said Icarus, voice earnest.

Solae did not know what to do at that moment. She wasn't sure of the last time she had felt this; the feeling of being actively *loved*. She wanted to forget everything for a moment and accept this declaration. She couldn't tell him she loved him back though, could she? Maybe she did love him, in a broader sense. In the sense that she wanted him to be happy because he was one of her dearest friends and he deserved it. But she did not love him the same way he loved her, not enough to hold onto him, to sacrifice her dreams, because even though he claimed he would go with her to New Jersey, she knew he would eventually need to return to this place. But even still, she did not want to let go, not just yet. She knew it was incredibly selfish, but there would be time to feel guilty later.

Solae did not tell Icarus she loved him. She leaned in, standing on tiptoes, and kissed him on the lips.

Icarus seemed momentarily surprised, but then he wrapped Solae in his arms gently, as if she were a delicate and breakable thing, but he was also so solid and warm. Solae felt safe in his embrace.

When the kiss ended, Icarus only hugged her tighter. Solae let herself melt into his arms as much as she dared. She buried her face in his shirt, and he leaned his head gently against her shoulder. It felt like they were both too afraid to move, too scared to pop this bubble they found themselves in.

But that logical side of Solae's mind told her that she needed to stop, to retreat, before she lost all her resolve forever.

Gently, she pushed herself away from Icarus. "I should go," she said. She held up the yellow MP3 player. "Thank you, you don't know how much this means to me."

Icarus looked breathless, starstruck, even. "O–Okay," he said.

"Goodnight," said Solae, turning to go inside the house.

"Goodnight, Solae," said Icarus. He did not get back in his truck until Solae was at her front door, and then he waited until she was inside to drive away.

Solae went straight to her bedroom, connected her headphones to the yellow MP3 player, then sat in the middle of the floor and wept, holding this most precious gift to her chest.

CHAPTER 29

99 Luftballoons - Nena

Graduation crept up unnoticed and was upon them before they even realized it. Icarus didn't even know how he came to be sitting on that stage, wearing a cap and gown, his friends on either side of him. Surprisingly, the weather cooperated, and it was a pleasantly warm, sunny day, so the ceremony was held outdoors, on the football field.

Icarus looked up into the stands and saw his parents smiling down at him, his mother holding a camera at the ready. He hadn't realized how much pressure he had been feeling about the Ivy League schools until it was gone. He no longer felt like he was standing on the edge of a cliff, no longer felt like he was flying precariously between scorching burnout depth of failure. He had successfully avoided melting his wings or falling into the sea to drown in this life, which gave him confidence about the last chapter of his story in the myth. He could rewrite the tale. In his retelling, Icarus would not fall, but fly farther than ever before.

✳✳✳

Ari cried tears of grief the morning of graduation. She was mourning that this phase of her life was coming to an end, but there was something more. Every major life event brought up the stony fact that her parents would not be there to witness any more of her life. She sometimes felt it was very unfair that she was the youngest, and thus her sisters both had more time with her parents than she had. They had both finished growing up before they had to say goodbye, but Ari had to spend nearly her entire adolescence without them. And yet, on the other hand, she knew that line of thinking was unfair to Cal and Persie.

She had not shown her tears in front of her sisters, but as always, Persie had been able to see past the surface.

"Mom and Dad would be so proud," she had said before they left for the school that morning.

Ari, not for the first time, cursed her tendency to cry so easily as fresh tears began to well up at that.

She was fighting back tears once again when her name was called, and she walked across the stage to receive her diploma. Not tears of grief this time, but a mixture of nostalgia at what she was leaving behind, and excitement at whatever was to come after. She was *supposed* to be excited about this. It wasn't just an ending of an old chapter, but the beginning of a new one. She was learning to feel good about what was on the horizon, whatever it might be.

❋❋❋

Theseus did not feel any particular way about graduation itself. He was more concerned about the fact that he was leaving Asphodel with his uncle tomorrow, and he had yet to break up with Ari. He had hoped it would come up naturally in between the carnival when he and Solae made their pact, and now, but it had not.

He had run into Solae in the hall before the ceremony and grabbed her wrist to stop her. "Have you done it yet?" he asked.

"No," said Solae guiltily.

"Me neither."

"Time's up today," he said, "I'm leaving Asphodel tomorrow."

Solae frowned as if something had just dawned on her. "Theseus, what about *Reflections of Mythology*? You can't leave before we've finished."

Theseus felt a new wave of dread come over him. He hadn't even considered that fact. It had been much longer since their last trip than it had been between any of the others. How was he supposed to delay his uncle if they weren't called back today?

"Well," he said, "I guess we better hope that it happens today."

Solae closed her eyes and pinched the bridge of her nose, "I sure hope you know what you're doing, Theseus."

"Same to you, *sunshine*." With that, he turned on his heel and left Solae flabbergasted, wondering how he had guessed this secret she had never revealed to any of them. In truth, it was only a guess, but her face after he said it had been all the confirmation he needed.

Now, as he waited for his name to be called, Theseus tried to focus on something, anything else besides his two last daunting hurdles before he could kiss Asphodel goodbye forever.

His eye caught his mother in the crowd, with Uncle Jack sitting next to her. They were looking at him with clear pride on their faces, which caused a jolt to go through Theseus. He was unused to that look and thought it didn't matter to him, but he found that maybe it did after all. For a little while, he forgot everything else, because this *was* a day to be proud of.

✳✳✳

The entire graduation ceremony was a blur to Solae. Theseus' revelation that he had figured out her role in *Reflections of Mythology* had completely thrown her off. The actual ceremony wasn't that big of a deal to her, she was sure her dad wouldn't even be there. She went through the motions of clapping for her friends and other classmates, walking across the stage to get her diploma, even making her way off the stage at the end while everyone else around her ran to celebrate with their families.

It wasn't until Icarus took her hand and said her name that she snapped out of her stupor.

"What?" she said, finally focusing on him.

He was grinning ear to ear, "Come on, Sol, our parents are over here."

Solae frowned at the word 'our', confused, but then she looked over to where Icarus was leading her, and her mouth dropped open in surprise.

Amos McClaine was standing with Icarus' parents, beaming at Solae as they walked over.

"Dad," she said, "You're here!" And threw her arms around him, unable to contain herself.

"Of course," he said, "I wouldn't miss it." He reached into his pocket and pulled out a set of keys with a red bow tied around it. He handed it to Solae, "So you can get around at Princeton," he said.

Solae's eyes began to fill with tears. She hugged her father again, "Thank you," she said, her voice catching.

They all walked out to the parking lot to see Solae's new car, a little red convertible. It was a bright spot of scarlet in a sea of neutral-colored cars, and Solae fell in love with it immediately. For one shining moment, everything was normal. Solae was a normal girl, with her normal boyfriend, and they were celebrating their normal graduation with their parents.

But it ended as quickly as it began. Solae felt herself begin to fade away. Nothing was solid anymore, even the very ground seemed to vanish beneath her. The earthquakes started again, the sky darkened, and the wind began to blow in gusts, like it would *actually* tear the world apart. Without thinking, Solae whirled around and reached out for Icarus, who was ironically, the only thing she knew was solid at this moment. He apparently had the exact same thought and was also reaching out to her. They clasped hands, anchoring each other to this world. However, even though they were solid once again, everything else around them continued to fall apart. The scariest part of all was that nobody else but them seemed to notice that anything was wrong.

"We have to go," Soale gasped before she could think of a viable excuse.

"What?" Amos said, "Right now?" Somehow, he had not noticed his daughter flicker in and out of reality.

"Yes," said Icarus, "There's something we have to do before we can go home. Us and Ari and Theseus, for Ms. Clio, before she leaves." He was babbling wildly, trying to string the truth together into something believable.

"Okay…" said Icarus' mother. "Just be back for dinner, Icarus."

He nodded, and then he and Solae ran off to find the others.

Since they now all had cars, all four of them drove to the lighthouse, one last time.

Before they went inside, Icarus hesitated with his hand on the doorknob. "This is it," he said.

"Let's get it over with," Theseus said.

CHAPTER 30

Heat Of The Moment - Asia

Theseus found himself standing outside of the entrance to the labyrinth; stone steps leading down in between larger-than-life stone walls. There was no roof so that there would be light to see by when in the maze. Theseus took in his surroundings, there was nobody else around, nothing to stop him from just abandoning this endeavor, but he had a sneaking suspicion that would not be allowed in this game. He had a sword strapped to his side, and out of curiosity, he pulled it out of its scabbard. Immediately, Theseus found that he liked how the sword felt in his hands. It was natural, almost like an extension of his arm. It gave him a new sense of confidence, like maybe he could actually do this.

He heard a noise coming from behind him and whirled around, sword automatically poised. It was only Ari, though, and she flinched at his sword. Theseus felt a pang at her flinch, forcibly reminded of his father. He quickly lowered the sword.

"Sorry," he said, "I didn't know it was you."

"It's okay," said Ari with a smile. "I got the twine." She held up a large ball of faintly glowing golden thread. Yep, that definitely looked magical.

"Thanks," said Theseus, holding out a hand. "I should probably get this over with."

But Ari didn't hand it over. "Actually, I was thinking I could go with you."

Theseus shook his head, "Are you crazy?"

"No, I just want to make sure my boyfriend is okay," she said pointedly.

Right. Her *boyfriend*. Theseus had to end it; he was almost out of time. He could do it now… but what if she got mad and wouldn't give him the twine? Besides, it might not be such a bad idea to have some company in the Labyrinth. Better to wait and do it afterward.

"Fine, come with me," he said, "But you'll need to stay hidden when I fight the thing. I don't want you to get hurt."

"So chivalrous," said Ari, standing on tiptoe and planting a kiss on Theseus' cheek. Her kiss burned, as did her touch when she intertwined her fingers in his. "Come on, then we'll be able to leave this place once and for all,"

"Right," said Theseus, and privately thought about how there was another place he would soon be leaving, once and for all.

They began their walk through the Labyrinth, a tedious process. The magic twine rolled ahead of them, but the way forward was long and winding. At one point, they came to a wall and found a human skeleton. It was propped up against the wall of the maze so perfectly, like in a movie or haunted house. Ari stifled a scream when they came upon it, covering her eyes, and Theseus instinctively wrapped his arm around her and hugged her to his chest.

"It's okay," he said quietly, "It can't hurt you."

Ari peeked up at him through her fingers, "I know, I'm sorry. It just startled me… I guess I should have expected to find stuff like that in here, but I wasn't thinking about it."

"I know," said Theseus.

The skeleton had been unexpected by Theseus, too, but for some reason, it didn't seem to affect him. In fact, the farther into the Labyrinth they went, the more his nerves seemed to numb and harden. He supposed that was a good thing since he would probably need nerves of steel to win his impending battle. Ari's reaction, on the other hand, reminded him of their first date- her scream when they had collided with Erik's car. It had been stupid, unnecessary, and traumatizing for her. He supposed it was just further evidence of the fact that he wasn't the guy for her. Solae was right, this really did need to end as soon as possible.

Eventually, the magical thread began to dwindle, and Theseus knew this meant they were getting close. They reached a wall that seemed to curve all the way around into a circle, save for a single opening. This had to be the center of the Labyrinth, home of the Minotaur.

"You should go back a little way to wait for me, just to be safe," whispered Theseus.

"I'm not leaving you," Ari whispered back firmly.

Theseus led her around the next wall back, so they could have more space between them and the Minotaur.

"Please just stay here, at least," Theseus said. "I don't want you getting hurt."

"I'll be fine," said Ari.

"But you'll distract me," said Theseus, "And then it'll kill me, then you." He wasn't quite sure if they *could* die here, in this dream world, but he didn't want to test it. "Please, Ari." He held her gaze as he said it.

Even if he didn't love her, Theseus had to admit that he would miss this view. Ari's golden-hazel eyes had a habit of awakening a kind of *wanting* in him. He felt it now; he was going to leave her, might as well take as much as he could, while he had her.

Theseus crashed into Ari like a wave, kissing her more fiercely than ever before. She gasped in surprise but did not hesitate to kiss him back. He had to get enough of this *now*. He had to fill up on it so that he wouldn't miss it when he left her behind.

After a moment, Ari reached up and pushed against his chest, breaking the kiss. "Hey," she said faintly, "What's that about?"

"Just in case," said Theseus. It wasn't a full lie, but it wasn't the full truth either.

"You're going to be fine." Ari took a deep breath, and Theseus thought she might kiss him again, but she just hugged him tightly. "You *have* to be fine," she said.

"I know," he said, then pulled away from her. "I guess I should get it over with."

"I'll be right here if you need me."

"No, you'll *stay* right here, and if I take too long, you'll go back."

"Okay."

Theseus didn't think that 'okay' sounded very convincing, but he decided not to push it. "Well then, see you soon," he said, turning back toward the center of the Labyrinth.

"See you soon," Ari echoed and even waved a little.

Then, without looking back, Theseus walked up to the stone enclosure. This time, he went all the way around until he found the opening. He took a deep breath, adjusted his grip on the sword, and turned the corner.

As soon as he was inside the enclosure, Theseus halted. The Minotaur lay sleeping in the middle of the circle, facing Theseus. There was a shackle around its ankle that connected to a very sturdy chain that looked as though it would allow the beast to move freely around the enclosure, but not leave it.

The sight of the Minotaur made Theseus' stomach roil. He had seen cartoonish illustrations in books before, but he hadn't expected the real thing to be so horrific. The beast's lower half was covered in fur, with bull's legs and hooves. Its torso was humanoid, though larger and more muscled than any man Theseus had ever seen. What really made him sick, though, was the head of a bull that sat upon the creature's shoulders. It didn't look like a true bull's head. It was more twisted and grotesque, like something out of a nightmare.

Theseus clenched his jaw and forced the sick feeling that was creeping up his throat to go away. He had a job to do if he was going to finally be able to leave this place.

He realized that he could just sneak up and kill the monster right now, while it was sleeping. He could get away without even having to fight. But the half-humanoid form of the Minotaur gave him pause. Would it be right to kill it without giving it a chance? How much of it was human? Would it be able to understand Theseus, or was it completely animalistic? The bones scattered around that were undoubtedly human suggested the latter.

Before he could make up his mind, though, the Minotaur's eyes snapped open, staring right at Theseus. He was so startled that he stumbled back, raising his sword higher.

The Minotaur let out a kind of roar and got to its feet so fast that Theseus' brain couldn't process how it was physically possible. Then, the monster spoke.

"Theseus," it growled, sounding almost pleased.

Theseus couldn't believe his ears, but he managed to collect himself enough to respond. "How do you know my name?" he demanded, as they began to slowly circle each other.

"I know you," the Minotaur said, "And I know what you fear."

"You don't know anything about me," snapped Theseus, "And I'm not afraid of you."

"No," conceded the Minotaur, "You're afraid of yourself, of what you might become. That is far more interesting."

"What are you talking about?"

"You are afraid that the things they say about you, how you are like your father, are true."

"SHUT UP," Theseus had no idea how the beast knew anything, and that fact was like a spark that lit the fuse of the mounting fear inside of him.

Without thinking about what he was doing, Theseus swung his sword at the Minotaur. It was ready for him though, and before Theseus' arm had even made a full swing, the sword was torn from his grip and flung across the enclosure.

The Minotaur took another swing at Theseus, and he had to leap out of the way to avoid being hit. "You are afraid of being useless," continued the Minotaur, carrying on talking as if it wasn't trying to kill Theseus.

Theseus tried to make a run for his sword, but the Minotaur's enormous hand caught him in the chest, slamming him to the ground and knocking the breath from his lungs.

"You are afraid of being *weak*."

The Minotaur lifted him roughly off the ground by his tunic and threw him against the wall of the enclosure.

Theseus cried out involuntarily, sure he had broken something in the impact. He had never been in this much pain before, but he had a feeling the adrenaline was keeping him from feeling everything. He rolled over and tried to drag himself along, but the Minotaur was already towering over him again.

"And most of all," it said as it reached down, grabbing Theseus by the throat and lifting him into the air. "You're afraid of becoming *just like* your father."

Theseus felt true panic, he couldn't breathe. His throat was being crushed, and he knew it was only a matter of seconds before the Minotaur crushed his windpipe completely. His vision was already getting blurry around the edges.

"But don't worry," the Minotaur chuckled, it was a bone-chilling sound. "You won't be alive long enough for that to come true."

This wasn't supposed to happen. He couldn't die here, now. It shouldn't be *possible* for him to die here, it wasn't real. Theseus wanted to yell, to fight back, but for once, he couldn't do anything. He was completely helpless. Useless. Weak.

The world began to fade to black.

Suddenly, there was a sickening, squelching sound, followed by an animalistic cry from the Minotaur. The massive hand released Theseus' throat and he hit the ground before he could process the sensation of falling. He curled up on his side, gasping as he massaged his throat with a shaky hand.

"Theseus!"

He opened his eyes; Ari was leaning over him. Her face was streaked with tears and blood. "Are you okay?" she asked, touching his face tentatively.

Theseus' voice came out hoarse and painful, "I think so," He cleared his throat, wincing a little. "What happened?"

Ari glanced over her shoulder, "I…" she bit her lip to stop from crying.

Theseus managed to sit up. The excruciating pain he felt all over his body only a moment before was mysteriously fading away as if he dreamed it. The Minotaur lay sprawled on the ground, Theseus' sword sticking out of its back and blood steadily leaked out of the surely mortal wound.

"Wow," Theseus said, looking from the felled monster to the slight, angelic girl kneeling beside him. "Thank you."

Ari gave a weak smile, "Of course."

"Let's get out of here," Theseus said, and Ari helped him to his feet.

They followed the path laid by the golden twine out of the Labyrinth, and Theseus found himself frustrated that it was a much shorter journey than it had seemed when they were trying to navigate the maze originally.

Once they made it out, Ari looked at Theseus, "What now?"

"I think," Theseus said slowly, as if it were just dawning on him, "We go to my ship and get out of here."

Ari grinned, "The *real* ship of Theseus."

Theseus rolled his eyes, "You hang out with Icarus too much."

They made their way to the docks, where a magnificent ship with black sails waited for him. Even though he had never sailed before, Theseus found himself able to command the crew, *his* crew, with ease. It made him think about his impending apprenticeship with Uncle Jack, it would not be like this, he knew, but the basic elements of being 'at sea' awakened inside of him a boyish excitement that he had not felt in a very long time.

"There's Icarus!" Ari gasped suddenly after a little while when Crete was still in sight, but they were closer to a smaller island.

Theseus looked around and saw the two tiny figures that could have been birds flying toward them but were much bigger. It seemed that all their stories were coming to an end. At that thought, an idea suddenly came to Theseus. He remembered a detail of this story that the rest of them had all forgotten; they had not even talked about it amid the worry about him and Icarus being in life-threatening situations. Maybe this was how the story *really* had to end.

"Drop anchor," he called out, "And prepare a rowboat." His men obliged, but Ari looked at him in confusion. "We should wait at this island," Theseus explained, "To make sure Icarus is alright."

Ari beamed at him, it was a look that made Theseus feel like a low-down, good-for-nothing snake for lying to her. For making her think he was being noble, better than he was, like always.

When the boat was ready, Theseus and Ari departed for the island alone. Ari kept her eyes skyward, tracking Icarus' progress, willing him to keep that perfect balance. They got out of the boat once they made it ashore and walked along the beach for a little while, then Theseus stopped in his tracks.

"Ari," he said slowly, "I think it's time to end this."

Ari, who had been walking in front, turned to face him. She just stared at him blankly for a moment. "I'm sorry, what?"

"I mean this–" he gestured between the two of them, "It's time to end it. It was never going to work out."

Ari's smile melted from her face, "Never… What are you talking about?"

Theseus sighed, looked up at the sky for a moment, and then back at Ari. Her face was so sweet, so open, so trusting. He had to tell her the truth, even if it hurt her. She deserved at least that much; it would be better in the long run.

"Ari, I asked you out because you're… well, beautiful, and you made me feel like I was… different than I am. Better than I am. I figured, why not give it a shot?" He took a deep breath, and didn't look at her when he said, "I never intended it to last, and I thought surely you didn't expect it to either."

Ari did not speak for a long time. She wasn't sure where this was coming from. She had thought their relationship was fine. And the way Theseus had kissed her before fighting the Minotaur… But now he was saying that none of it had meant anything to him the way it had to her. And he *knew* it. He never intended for them to last. What did 'last' mean, anyway? Maybe she hadn't thought about an *extended* future with Theseus, but she certainly hadn't been dating him with the intention of breaking up. The awful thought that everyone had been right about him occurred to her, making her feel sick.

"I… don't know what I thought," she said, hating that tears had already crept into her voice. She swallowed hard, "Are you saying you never… felt anything for me?"

"I don't know. I just… can't do this anymore."

"What do you mean you don't know?" The question burst out of Ari almost involuntarily. "You can't do *what* anymore?"

Theseus said nothing. He couldn't tell her that he had no idea what he was doing when he asked her out, that he'd hoped there was a chance things would work out in spite of everything, in spite of the fact that it never felt real. It would be too painful.

"I thought that what we have is more than that, I *love* you, Theseus."

"You love everyone, Ari," Theseus said, his tone gentler than before. "I'm nothing special."

Ari was speechless. She had no response, no idea what meaning she was supposed to take from that or how to process it. *'You love everyone, I'm nothing special.'*

"I'm sorry I had to end it this way," he continued, "I had hoped it would just die out naturally, but I've run out of time. I have to go."

"*Go?*"

"I'm leaving Asphodel to apprentice on my uncle's ship. I didn't know how to tell you before, but… we're leaving tomorrow."

The hits just kept coming. One right after another. All Ari could think to say was "Why?"

Theseus looked at her for a long time before answering. He went into this intending to pay her the courtesy of at least being honest with her now. He *could* tell her everything. She already knew vaguely about his real father; it would not take much to explain that he had to do this so he wouldn't *become* his father. It would probably make things easier for her, in fact. But that was a part of him that he had never shared with anyone. Theseus' fear of becoming like his father was a part of himself that he kept secret and sacred. The Minotaur had known. The one time that someone else had known his secret and Theseus hadn't been given a choice about it. Perhaps that was why, now that he *was* given the choice, he chose to keep his secret even closer to his chest. To make up for it being stolen.

"I just have to get out of here," he said firmly, "It's nothing personal, it's just something I have to do."

'Nothing personal.' Tears blurred Ari's vision. She wanted to reach out, take his hand, and make him realize that it *was* personal, that her love *was* special. She wanted to change his mind. But at the same time, he had hurt her. He *was* hurting her, so deeply that she wasn't even sure how bad the damage would be in the end. She wanted to pull him close and push him away at the same time. She had to look away. She looked up toward the sky while she collected her thoughts. She caught sight of Icarus, and all at once, everything else drained from her mind.

Icarus, who had been flying only a few minutes before, was plummeting toward the water, his wings going up in flames.

CHAPTER 31

(I Just) Died In Your Arms - Cutting Crew

Icarus felt nothing but excitement as Daedalus strapped his wings along his shoulders and arms, preparing him for flight. Everything else had gone so beautifully, wonderfully well, the nervous anticipation he'd felt before was all but gone. He had graduated high school. They were saving Asphodel. And he and Solae were doing better than ever. He still resolved to remain vigilant, not wanting to lull himself into a false sense of security, but it was hard not to.

He did his best to pay attention to Daedalus' 'preflight' talk, but all he said was, "Do not fly too close to the sun, lest your wings melt, and do not fly too close to the water lest the water dissolve them."

"Yes sir," Icarus said.

They made final preparations, then, just as Daedalus instructed Icarus to get into position on the tower windowsill, the door burst open, and there stood King Minos, surrounded by guards.

"Seize them!" he cried.

"Jump now!" Daedalus yelled, and Icarus, full of new fear, didn't hesitate to obey.

He threw himself out of the window, arms spread wide and panicked for a split second as he felt himself falling, hurtling toward the bottom of the cliffs that the castle sat on, but his large wings quickly caught hold of the wind and bore him aloft. Icarus laughed in spite of himself, taking it all in. He was *flying*.

✳✳✳

Solae found herself riding alongside Apollo in the sun chariot, the eerie silent galloping of the horses carrying them across the sky.

She looked over the edge of the chariot immediately, eyes scanning the sky below them desperately for a sign of Icarus.

"What is causing your distress, Solae?" Apollo asked.

"Icarus," she said, "I have to make sure he does not fly too close."

"The best thing you can do," Apollo said sagely, "Is nothing at all."

"What?" Solae demanded, "How is that supposed to help? I'm the only one who can save him."

"He doesn't know your role in this tale, correct?"

"Well, no," Solae said, cheeks burning in shame, even more than when Theseus had guessed it. "I never told him."

"If you were to reach out to him at this point, he would come straight to you, not understanding what he was doing."

Solae thought for a moment, trying to calm herself. "I'll try," she said, "But if he starts flying too high, I have to do something."

"Heroes never learn," Apollo muttered, but Solae didn't hear him.

***

Icarus had been flying for a while. It was getting a little tedious, and he was beginning to wonder when they would be able to stop, when the story would be complete. He had no idea how to tell since he did not know what the story would look like with a happy ending.

He looked down at the ocean from time to time, but it was unchanging as ever. But wait- he saw a ship, with black sails. His heart leaped in excitement and relief; this had to be Theseus and Ari. They had made it out of the Labyrinth. This had to mean that it was all coming to an end. The only regret that he had was that they had never found out where Solae was. The thought occurred to him that perhaps she would be at their destination, and they would finally see each other in this world before they left for the last time. This idea buoyed him even more, and before he even realized what had happened, he had flown much higher than he intended.

He should go back down, he knew, but something about the warm sunlight was familiar… something wonderfully familiar. It was warm not just on the outside, but on the inside too. It felt like when Solae had agreed to go out with him for the first time, it felt like their first date, it felt like the exhilaration of every touch, it felt like the first and only time they kissed, after the Spring Carnival.

"Icarus, no!"

Bewildered, Icarus looked up and nearly fell out of the sky in sheer surprise.

Solae was calling down to him from a golden chariot that was flying a few yards above him. It *was* Solae, her face and her voice, but she looked different. She was glowing with a light that could only be described as ethereal, almost too brightly for him to look at. She was… she was…

Beautiful.

"Solae!" He called out, beginning to fly up to meet her.

"Stop!" She said, "Icarus, you have to go back down!"

"What?" He didn't understand, something was wrong, clearly, by the terrified expression on her face. He had to save her from whatever was causing her distress. He flew higher, reaching out to her, he hoped his wings would carry them both.

Solae reached out too, but she was holding her hand out as if to push him away, "Icarus, stop! Your wings!"

He grasped her hand, not fully comprehending what she was trying to tell him until their skin made contact. And then, all at once, everything felt terribly, horrifyingly *wrong*.

Solae's hand was white hot to the touch, but more excruciating was the feel of molten wax dripping onto his skin. He looked back at his wings and felt the bottom of his stomach drop in horror.

The feathers of his wings had gone up in flames and were disintegrating before his very eyes, the wax was melting all over his back. The only thing keeping him in the air was Solae's painful grasp.

Icarus was in too much pain to speak, but he looked at Solae in bewildered horror.

Solae was in tears, "Icarus, I'm so sorry," she said, "I have to let you go."

"Solae," Icarus gasped, it was the only thing he could say, her name.

"I'll see you back at the lighthouse," Solae whispered, and let Icarus slip from her grasp.

And then he was falling. *Falling*. Despite how sure he was, how certain he would be able to avoid it, he was falling to his death. And he didn't even understand why. His last thought before losing consciousness as he plunged toward the sea, was that it had been Solae who did this to him.

✳✳✳

"ICARUS!" Ari screamed. Without stopping to think, she began running toward the shore. When she hit the water, she plunged in without hesitation and began swimming as fast as she could.

Icarus was not too far from the shore, but Ari's heart still lurched when he hit the water. She immediately dove under the water and began propelling herself toward Icarus. She did everything without having to decide to do it; it was like instinct. All Ari knew was that she could not let Icarus drown, and it seemed that her brain had simply given this objective, while her body did whatever was necessary to accomplish it. She managed to wrap her arms under Icarus' and pull him to the surface. He was unconscious, but Ari was practically unaware of his dead weight as she kicked for all she was worth to make it back to shore.

Once they were back on land, her burning muscles were only a whisper as she began giving Icarus chest compressions, skills from the first aid class she had once taken coming back without having to reach for them. All she was aware of was Icarus, the faint promise of his heartbeat, and the phrase that kept repeating in her head like a chant:

I'm going to save you. I'm going to save you. I'm going to save you.

She did not rest until, finally, Icarus gasped, rolled onto his side, and began coughing up water. When he turned, Ari saw the damage his burning wings had done. The fabric of his tunic had burned away around his shoulders, and his skin had angry red burns. The sight turned Ari's stomach.

When Icarus finished coughing, he apparently noticed the pain from the burns. He moaned, convulsing on the ground and curling up in the fetal position.

"It's okay, Icarus," said Ari, surprised at the calm, soothing tone of her voice. She gently brushed Icarus' wet hair off his forehead, "I'm here, it's Ari. You're going to be okay."

"A-Ari," he croaked, reaching out a trembling hand, his eyes still closed.

"I'm right here," she said again, taking his hand.

After a while, Icarus' breathing began to settle, and Ari let out a sigh of relief.

Suddenly, for the first time since seeing Icarus fall, she thought of Theseus. As the horrible memory of their conversation resurfaced in her mind, Ari blinked back tears as she looked around. Theseus was nowhere to be seen. She looked over her shoulder, to the shore where the rowboat had been, waiting to take them back to the ship, and her stomach sank.

Theseus' ship was no longer waiting near the shore. It was already much too far away to catch up with and was sailing farther away as Ari watched.

He had left her. He had left *them*. But how could he? How could Theseus have just left when Icarus was dying? Did he even know that Ari had managed to save him? Did he even care?

Their conversation from before would suggest otherwise. Ari hadn't wanted to believe any of it while Theseus had been saying it, but this was like a slap in the face of confirmation. She knew it was only an expression, but at that moment, Ariadne could have sworn that she felt her heart break into a million little pieces inside her chest.

CHAPTER 32

Who Wants to Live Forever - Queen

This time when they returned to the real world, it was different from all the others. Solae opened her eyes, still wet with tears, to the sound of Icarus gasping for breath. Both she and Ari immediately reached for him.

"Icarus!"

"I'm okay, I'm okay," he said quickly, clutching his hands to his body as if trying to confirm whether the burns he had felt only moments before were gone.

Ari's eyes were rimmed with red and her face blotchy as she threw her arms around Icarus in a fierce embrace. "I wasn't sure what was going to happen," she said, "What *did* happen? One minute you were flying fine, then the next…"

Icarus glanced at Solae as Ari let go of him. Solae's heart dropped. *So, he knew.* He had been able to tell it was her who had burned him.

"It just happened," Icarus said, "I barely even realized what was happening until it was too late. Thank you for saving me, Ari. I don't know what would have happened." He looked around, "Where's Theseus?"

To Solae's horror, Ari's face crumpled again at the question, and she hid her face in her hands.

Icarus' face drained of color, "Did he- did the Minotaur- did Theseus not make it?" he said in a choked voice.

Ari shook her head, "No, nothing like that," she said shakily. And then, through tears, she explained it all to them. How Theseus had fought the Minotaur, how he had nearly been killed but Ari had managed to sneak up behind the beast with Theseus' sword and save him. How they had gone out to Theseus' ship, how Theseus suggested they go out to the island to make sure Icarus made it. Then, how Theseus had callously informed Ari that he was leaving her because none of it had meant anything to him. How Ari had then seen Icarus fall, how she had saved him from drowning, but when she made it back to shore, Theseus had abandoned them both.

"I guess he woke up before us," Ari finished, "And he just left."

Solae was shocked, angered at Theseus for treating Ari this way, but also ashamed; she knew that she also had a part of this, she had been the one to tell Theseus that he needed to break it off and stop leading her on.

"I'm so sorry, Ari," Icarus said, but she shook her head.

"I'll be fine. I just wanted to make sure you're okay, I need to go now."

With that, Ari fled from the lighthouse to her car, leaving Solae and Icarus alone.

Solae didn't know how to meet Icarus' gaze, even though she knew he was staring at her. He had finally put the pieces together.

"Solae, you were the sun," Icarus finally said, and for the first time, Solae could finally hear that he was upset with her like he should be, though he tried to keep it muted.

She sighed, it was both a sigh of reluctance and relief. Now everything was out in the open, the worst was over, and she did not have to hide her reasons anymore. "Yes," she said simply, "And… you got too close to me."

Icarus shook his head in disbelief, "But why didn't you tell me before?"

"Because I was selfish," Solae said, remembering the night he gave her the yellow MP3 player, the night he said he loved her, and instead of breaking up with him, she kissed him. "I knew what being the sun meant, and I didn't want to admit it yet."

"But you *lied* to me, Solae. You lied to all of us, this whole time."

"I know. I'm really sorry, Icarus. I thought maybe if you didn't know, it wouldn't happen like this. But I guess no matter what I did, you would still end up getting burned if you got this close to me."

It was like glass shattered and every word Solae said was like another jagged shard lodging in Icarus' heart. But no, the pain was hotter, more intense. It *did* feel eerily the same as when he had felt his wings melting, the hot wax burning his skin as he fell, and fell, and fell. But this time, it was not his waxen wings melting, nor Icarus himself falling. It was all in his heart.

"So, you just thought of us as doomed from the start?" he asked, doing his best to hold back any bitterness from creeping into his voice.

Solae wiped a tear from her eyes, "No, not at all," she said. "For a while, I thought I had been wrong. I really did love you, I think, and I wish I could keep loving you…"

"But?" prompted Icarus, knowing that was not all.

"But I am more like my mother than I thought," said Solae with a sad little smile. "I realized that I am not ready to be attached to someone, to stay in one place. We just want different things in life, Icarus, and it's better for me to end it now rather than do what my mother did and pretend everything is fine until it's too late."

It was this moment, this sentiment, that made Icarus realize that as much as he wanted the two of them to work out, Solae was right. He could accept breaking up now because he could not be with someone who did not and had no desire to feel any sort of attachment to him. He did not *want* to be with someone who did not love him. The only problem he would have left was: how on earth was he supposed to stop loving *her*?"

"I have to go now," Solae said after a moment, "But I want you to have this." She produced from her pocket the small, pink MP3 player.

Icarus' eyes widened, "Solae, that's all your music."

Solae nodded, "I want to start over, with the one you gave me. I want you to have this one to remember me by, and all the good memories."

"But it means so much to you."

Solae smiled. He didn't know just how much it really meant to her. He didn't know who the MP3 player had belonged to before; it was the final secret she kept from him.

"Please take it," she said, holding it out to him.

Hesitantly, Icarus reached out and took the little device from Solae's outstretched hand.

They just looked at each other for a moment. There was nothing else left to say.

Finally, Icarus took a deep breath, and through one final stab of pain, said "Goodbye, Solae."

"Goodbye, Icarus," she whispered, and then walked out to her car, leaving Icarus alone in the lighthouse.

✻✻✻

He wasn't quite sure how it happened, but Icarus found himself driving to The Book Loft one last time with the final boxes of books. He felt them in the back of his truck like they posed a massive weight that he was struggling to pull, even though there were hardly any books left.

When he entered The Book Loft carrying the boxes, Clio smiled at him, but Icarus did not return her smile. For the first time since this whole affair began, he felt put upon by the old woman.

"Icarus, you did it," Clio said, "Asphodel is now firmly grounded in reality, as it should be."

"That's great," Icarus said flatly, because though the world around him might be grounded, he felt hopelessly adrift in a sea of warring emotions.

Clio's smile melted away instantly. "Are you alright, dear?"

"No," Icarus said after a beat. "I thought I would make it through the myth alright. I figured, since I knew the story, I wouldn't fly too close to the sun. If it hadn't been for Ari… I might be dead."

"Ari?" Clio asked, tilting her head to one side.

"She swam out and saved me from drowning after I fell," Icarus explained, "But I still fell. I still… got burned. I couldn't avoid the tragedy."

Clio looked sympathetic, "Icarus, I am sorry you experienced this pain. But if you think about it, you *did* avoid the tragedy, ultimately. The Icarus in mythology had no one to save him, but you had Ari."

Icarus had not considered it from this point of view. It did not make him feel much better at the moment, though. Not when he could still feel the phantom burns along his shoulder blades, and the pain from Solae's betrayal was still so fresh.

"I guess so," he said finally. "But…" he took a deep breath in preparation for what he had decided to say on his way over. "I think I've had enough of magic."

It felt odd to say. He had already sort of decided that he would be okay with this chapter of his life ending with the rest of his childhood, but the strangeness of Asphodel had been such a facet in Icarus' life for so long. It was a wrench to let it go, but he was learning to let go of a lot of things today.

Clio nodded wisely at his declaration. "I understand. It is probably for the best."

Icarus looked around, "I am going to miss this place," he said. "And I'll miss seeing you, Ms. Clio." He smiled sadly, the first smile since waking up in the lighthouse.

"I will miss you too, Icarus," said Clio, and she walked up to him with arms outstretched, giving him a firm hug. "You have a wonderful life ahead of you."

Icarus nodded but said nothing in response. He had no idea what life had in store for him now. All his best-laid plans had melted in the heat of a dazzling sun.

CHAPTER 33

Come As You Are - Nirvana

The sadness of being left by Solae seemed to heighten Icarus' anger, and in turn, the anger fueled his sadness. He was not angry at Solae, though. Hurt, confused, betrayed, but never angry.

All his anger was directed at Theseus, who had been so cruel to Ari, sweet, trusting Ariadne. His oldest friend had been hurt, and Icarus felt it keenly. He was headed for the old garage, where he knew Theseus would probably be. Sure enough, when Icarus parked at the curb in front of the rusty old shed, Theseus was there. He appeared to be changing the oil on the Mustang, only his legs were visible while his torso was underneath the car. Icarus got out of his truck, slammed the door, and began storming toward the garage.

"Theseus!" he said, almost not recognizing his own voice; it was shaky, gritty, and aggressive.

Theseus seemed to hesitate for a moment, then slid out from underneath the car and got to his feet, facing Icarus by the time he reached him.

"What do you want?" he asked, folding his arms.

"I want-" said Icarus, jabbing a finger at Theseus' chest, "To know who you think you are."

"I take it you talked to Ari," said Theseus in a tired voice.

"Yeah, I talked to Ari!" said Icarus incredulously, "You're a real jerk, you know that?"

"What, for breaking up with her?"

"You know what I mean," said Icarus, "You knew exactly what you were doing, you broke her heart. And to top it off, you just abandoned her on a random island."

Theseus scoffed, "Oh, come on, that wasn't real."

"It felt pretty real when I was falling to my death," said Icarus in a low voice.

"So that's what this is about," said Theseus, "You're mad because I didn't 'save' you. You don't care about Ari at all."

All Icarus processed was the last sentence. Suddenly, he was seeing red, and before he could think about what he was doing, his fist shot out and decked Theseus in the jaw.

Theseus didn't have time to block the punch. He stumbled back against his car, hand flying to his face. But then, he moved like lightning, rushing Icarus and pinning him against the wall.

"Don't try to fight me, Icarus," he warned, "You may have forgotten, but I took on the Minotaur today."

Icarus glared at him, "You only survived because Ari saved you," he spat. "She saved your life, and you turned around and hurt her. This is not about me. This is about you hurting someone I care about."

"If you care about her so much, maybe *you* should date her," said Theseus. "Listen, people get hurt in life. I don't expect you to understand that, but Solae and I do. It's part of why we're leaving."

Theseus saw the bewildered expression on Icarus' face after he spoke and deemed it safe to let him go.

Icarus did not lash out at Theseus again, but instead asked: "You knew about Solae?"

"Yeah," said Theseus, "She told me she was planning on leaving when she told me to stop stringing Ari along, that night at the carnival."

"*She* told you to…" Icarus whispered, trailing off.

"Pretty much," said Theseus. "She probably didn't like *how* I broke up with Ari either, but it's done now." He got in his car, leaving Icarus standing there. He rolled down the window. "Don't worry, you won't see me again. I'm leaving this place."

Icarus' expression turned stony again. "Are you going with Solae?"

Theseus rolled his eyes, "You are so stupid sometimes. No, I didn't steal her from you. I'm going with my uncle."

"Oh," Icarus said, a look of epiphany coming over him.

"Yeah," Theseus said.

"I just…" Icarus reached out and put a hand on the side of the mustang, as if imploring him to stay without words. "What happened, man?" His tone was desperate, and

Theseus felt a twinge of regret at leaving his last remaining friend in this place like this.

But regret would not change that this was always how it was going to be.

"I dunno," Theseus said truthfully, "But everything has to end, right?"

Icarus stared at him for a moment. Finally, he said, "Yeah. I guess so."

"Well, goodbye."

Icarus did not say anything, just nodded, and stepped back from the Mustang.

Theseus rolled up the window and started the car. He pulled out of the garage onto the street and sped away, never to look back. He was done with this place. When he was gone, Icarus walked back to his truck. He knew he would not tell Ari about this interaction, at least, not for a long time. He no longer felt angry, but the sadness was so heavy now, that he felt he might drown from it.

CHAPTER 34

Landslide - Fleetwood Mac

Solae blasted music through her new car radio as she drove farther and farther away from Asphodel to her new life. Her father was following behind her in his own car, they had decided to leave early for Princeton and make a road trip out of it. She was glad they were doing it this way; she needed to get out of here. She felt raw. *Raw.* That word. The way it tugged at her throat. It was the perfect word for how she felt at that moment.

She had done the one thing she had tried so desperately to avoid; she had hurt Icarus. Maybe if she had broken up with him sooner, or trusted her gut in the beginning and never went out with him in the first place, this could have been avoided. But no, he would have been broken-hearted anyway, and they wouldn't have made all those memories together this year. She did not regret a single one of those.

A new song came on: 'Landslide', by Fleetwood Mac. It had always been one of Solae's favorites because of how it sounded. She had never considered the lyrics very much, though. But now, as she drove away from everything in her life thus far, she thought she might understand it.

It was time for a change in the seasons of life. Solae would be fine on her own. Icarus would be fine on his own. Except he had Ari, so he wasn't really alone. Solae would be fine on her own. She *would* be fine on her own.

She wondered if this was how her mother had felt when she left.

Her phone began to ring, and she glanced at the caller ID before answering. It was not Icarus, but Ari. Solae took a deep breath before answering. She had not told her best friend that she was leaving early, she hadn't known *how* to tell her. More cowardice. She felt even more guilty for this than she felt about Icarus, if possible.

"Hello?"

"Hey Sol," Ari's voice had a fragile quiver to it, and Solae's stomach knotted into dread at the sound of it.

"Hey," she said, trying to press as much comfort into the word as she could.

Ari sniffed, "Could you come over?" she asked, "I just need someone to talk to, y'know?"

Oh, *no*. Solae closed her eyes. This was the worst possible time, but she had to tell her.

"Ari, love, I'm so sorry, I can't. I'm-" Solae's own voice caught in a soft, dry sob. "Ari, I'm leaving Asphodel."

There was a beat of silence.

"Leaving?" Ari asked in a smaller voice.

"Yeah, my- my dad and I are going on a road trip to get to New Jersey."

"New Jersey? For Princeton? But school doesn't start for... Why are you- what about Icarus?"

Solae could hear in Ari's tone how hard it was to put the pieces together in her emotional state. Why did she keep waiting until it was too late?

"Solae?"

She had to answer.

"Icarus and I… aren't together anymore," said Solae, "I broke up with him."

"What? Why? I thought you worked it out, I thought he was going to find another school near you, so you didn't have to be long distance."

"We weren't right for each other, Ari," said Solae gently. "I'm sorry I didn't explain it before, but I have to get away, I need to start fresh. *Completely.*"

Another beat of silence.

"Completely?"

"I'm sorry," said Solae, tears beginning to run down her face. Somehow, this was hurting more than leaving Icarus had hurt. "Really sorry. I'll- I'll still try to visit on breaks, if you ever want to see me again. But I know you might not."

"Yeah," said Ari noncommittally, and Solae could tell that she was trying to keep it together a little longer before inevitably completely breaking down. "I guess I should let you get back to your trip."

"I love you, Ari."

"I love you *too*, Solae," she said with a desperate sigh. "I just wish…"

"I know. Me too."

"I hope you find what you're looking for."

"Thank you."

"Goodbye, Sol."

"Goodbye, Ari."

✳✳✳

Weeks later, as Solae was unpacking in her dorm at Princeton, she recalled her final stop before leaving Asphodel. On her way out of town, Solae had gone to the Book Loft, where she found Clio sitting amongst a few remaining boxes of books.

"Hello dear," Clio said, "You're all alone."

Solae ignored the last part of the statement. "We finished the story," she informed the old woman.

"Yes, I know," said Clio. "I could tell as soon as you returned; balance returned to the air in Asphodel."

"I wanted to thank you," Solae continued, "For opening up this whole new world to me."

Clio smiled, "You're very welcome, dear. It's fascinating stuff, isn't it?" there was a knowing twinkle in her eye, like she knew what Solae had come to ask about.

"Yes," Solae said, "And I want to keep looking for magic in this world. Do you know how I can find more?"

Clio studied Solae for a moment. "You know," she said, "I always thought it would be Icarus who came to me with that question. He's always been so interested in these kinds of things."

"I think his curiosity is satisfied," Solae said mildly.

"You may be right," said Clio thoughtfully. "Wait right here." She turned away, walked into her storage closet, and returned a moment later with a small silver business card in hand. She held it out to Solae, "These people would be able to tell you more," she said.

The card read simply, "The Keeper Society", and had a phone number and email address listed below in a whimsical font.

"Are you one of them?" Solae asked.

Clio shook her head, "Not for a very long time. I'm too old for that sort of thing. But if you want to find more magic, more strange phenomena, and learn more about it, these are the people for you."

"Thank you," said Solae.

Solae still had not contacted the Keeper Society yet, having been too focused on moving to New Jersey and getting all her things in order for college. But now, as she thought about it again, she pulled the yellow MP3 player out of her pocket, hit pause, then went over to her purse and pulled out the silver business card, turning it over and over.

She thought back to all the impossible things that happened in the last year. The excitement she felt when she first learned that magic was real, the excitement she still felt every time she thought about it. She thought about all the strange phenomena she witnessed with Icarus by her side, the camera he gave her at Christmas, the idea of writing a book to document all the magic she found.

Well, if she was going to write a book, she would need a lot more information. Solae sat down at her desktop computer and began to type an email.

She would spend the rest of her life immersing herself in every possibility of magic that she could find, but she would never forget her first encounter, with her three closest friends, in the small town of Asphodel.

CHAPTER 35

Time After Time - Cyndi Lauper

Ariadne had been awake long before the sunrise. Now, as rays of light leaked in through her white linen curtains, she waved her fingers through the rays, fascinated by how the white-gold sunlight touched her pale skin and turned it rosy. She had always thought of light as a good thing, and she still believed it was. But Solae had been the sun in Icarus' story, and she had burned him. She had hurt Ari's oldest friend in both the story, and in real life, causing him to fall and drown in the sea in one world, and leaving him to drown in sorrow in the other.

Ari sat up too quickly, causing her to feel dizzy for a moment. She had been so distracted by Theseus… why hadn't she seen it before? Icarus had fallen into the sea in the story, but he *hadn't* drowned. She, Ari, had saved him. That meant it was she who must also save him from drowning in sorrow.

It was too early to call Icarus, he was a late sleeper. She took her time getting ready, dressing in a cardigan, black t-shirt, and jeans. Around 8:30, she left the house in her beetle.

When she turned on the car, the song 'Time After Time' started playing. Ari realized this must be the mixtape that all four of them had made together. The one Icarus had entitled 'Juicebox.' Unlike the others, Ari remembered the reason behind the name.

"Why Juicebox?" she had asked.

"It's kind of a play on 'jukebox,' but also because all of the songs are so nostalgic," Icarus had said.

"For our parents, maybe, but we weren't even alive when most of these songs came out."

"But do you remember the first time you heard them?"

Ari did not. She had always known these songs, whether it was her dad playing them in the car or hearing them on the radio or in a random store, ever since she was little.

She listened to Juicebox all the way to the donut shop. She went in and ordered an apple fritter for Icarus, a blueberry cake donut for herself, and a couple chocolate-iced donuts for the both of them.

As she was walking out of the donut shop, a flier posted on a telephone pole caught her eye. She got closer and saw that the flier had a picture of the lighthouse, *her* lighthouse. She stared at the flier, trying to make sense of it.

"LIGHTHOUSE ART STUDIO" it said in large letters. Then below that, "Seeking Instructors."

A giddy smile began to slowly spread across Ari's face. So, she had not lost the lighthouse after all. There it was, still serving its true purpose in her life, guiding her to shore. Part of her wanted to go put in her application right away, but she had something more important to do now. The future could wait a little longer.

When she got back to her car, she pulled out cell phone and dialed Icarus' number.

"Hello?" Icarus said groggily on the other end of the line.

"Sorry, did I wake you?" Ari asked.

"No. I didn't sleep much anyway."

"Meet me outside your house in ten minutes."

"Why?"

"You'll see."

Ten minutes later, Ari drove up to see Icarus standing in his front yard wearing a wrinkled hoodie and jeans. She motioned for him to get in the car. He did so, picking up the bag of donuts as he sat down.

"Aw, what's the occasion?" he asked, still tired sounding, but with a note of delighted surprise.

"The occasion is that we need to wake up and realize that our lives aren't over just because they're gone," said Ari matter-of-factly as she backed out of the driveway.

"I don't think-"

"Yes, you do," said Ari. "I know you do because I feel the same way." She sighed, "They left, but you know what?"

"What?" she could hear the sting in his voice from thinking about Solae and Theseus.

"We're both still here."

She saw Icarus smile weakly out of the corner of her eye, "Yeah, we are."

"And…" Ari glanced over at Icarus meaningfully, "I know we won't heal overnight, but we can do it together. We can start making new memories right now."

"What did you have in mind?" asked Icarus.

Ari looked excited that he finally asked. "What's something that I've wanted since we were little?" she asked.

Icarus had to think for a moment, but then it came to him. Of course, they hadn't talked about it in so long, Ari had always, for as long as Icarus had known her, wanted a puppy.

"You're getting a dog?" he guessed, the sad little smile spreading into a wide grin.

Ari nodded, "It's my graduation present from Cal and Persie. One of the girls Persie works with has a dog who just had puppies, and they asked her to hold onto one for me. We're going to pick her up now."

Icarus couldn't have thought of a better way to enact Ari's call to action. They drove out to the address Persie had given Ari, and Persie's coworker showed them inside where they found a small white and brown spotted puppy of no discernable breed, aside from her very fluffy coat. She was a friendly dog, though not overly hyper, and politely sat in Icarus' lap on the drive back to Ari's house, looking out the window the whole way.

"What are you going to name her?" Icarus asked.

"I'm going to call her Luna," said Ari, "She has that one spot on her head that kinda looks like a crescent moon."

"Oh yeah," said Icarus, petting the puppy's head where the spot was. "That's perfect."

That afternoon while they were in Ari's backyard with Luna, Icarus watched Ari play with her new puppy. Her hair fell into her face, and she ran a hand through it to brush it away. As the light caught her red waves, giving it a glint of gold, Icarus wondered how anyone could break this girl's heart when it wasn't just on her sleeve, but blooming forth from her every smile.

'If you care about her so much, maybe you should date her.'

Right now, Icarus' heart was still too hurt to think about dating anyone. He did have to admit though, he could see the possibility of a future where he and Ari were happy together. They had been through so much together and understood each other so well; now that he thought about it, he realized how natural it would feel.

Then a whirlwind of unbidden images flashed through his mind, one after another. Ari, smiling at him and standing so close he could count her freckles. Ari, glowing from within as she walked toward him wearing a white dress. Ari, sleeping peacefully beside him as morning light caught the glint in her hair just like it had a moment ago. Ari, leaning down to kiss a baby that Icarus himself held in his arms. Ari, no longer young, her golden-red hair turned white, sitting next to him as they watched the sunset.

"Icarus?"

He came back to the present and looked at Ari, holding Luna, that same joy in her eyes that he had seen in those flashes.

"Sorry," he faltered, "Zoned out for a second."

Icarus knew that both he and Ari had a lot of healing to do, as she'd said, and it would be a good while before either of them was ready to think about falling in love again. But that was okay, they had all the time in the world.

THE END